FOREVER,
INTERRUPTED

FOREVER, INTERRUPTED

~ *A Novel* ~

TAYLOR JENKINS REID

WASHINGTON SQUARE PRESS
New York   Toronto   London   Sydney   New Delhi

Washington Square Press
A Division of Simon & Schuster, Inc.
1230 Avenue of the Americas
New York, NY 10020

First Washington Square Press trade paperback edition July 2013

WASHINGTON SQUARE PRESS and colophon are registered trademarks of Simon & Schuster, Inc.

For information about special discounts for bulk purchases, please contact Simon & Schuster Special Sales at 1-866-506-1949 or business@simonandschuster.com.

The Simon & Schuster Speakers Bureau can bring authors to your live event. For more information or to book an event contact the Simon & Schuster Speakers Bureau at 1-866-248-3049 or visit our website at www.simonspeakers.com.

Designed by Jill Putorti

Manufactured in the United States of America

10 9 8 7 6 5 4 3 2 1

Library of Congress Cataloging-in-Publication Data

Reid, Taylor Jenkins.
    Forever, interrupted : a novel / Taylor Jenkins Reid.—1st Washington Square Press trade paperback ed.
      p. cm.
    1. Grief—Fiction. 2. Loss (Psychology)—Fiction. 3. Female friendship—Fiction. I. Title.
PS3618.E5478F67 2013
813'.6—dc23

2012035073

ISBN 978-1-4767-1282-6
ISBN 978-1-4767-1283-3 (ebook)

To Linda Morris
(for reading the murder mysteries of a twelve-year-old girl)

And to Alex Reid
(a man the whole world should fall in love with)

Every morning when I wake up I forget for a fraction of a second that you are gone and I reach for you. All I ever find is the cold side of the bed. My eyes settle on the picture of us in Paris, on the bedside table, and I am overjoyed that even though the time was brief I loved you and you loved me.

—CRAIGSLIST POSTING, CHICAGO, 2009

PART ONE

JUNE

"Have you decided if you're going to change your name?" Ben asks me. He is sitting on the opposite end of the couch, rubbing my feet. He looks so cute. How did I end up with someone so goddamn cute?

"I have an idea," I tease. But I have more than an idea. My face breaks into a smile. "I think I'm gonna do it."

"Really?" he asks, excitedly.

"Would you want that?" I ask him.

"Are you kidding?" he says. "I mean, you don't have to. If you feel like it's offensive or . . . I don't know, if it negates your own name. I want you to have the name you want," he says. "But if that name happens to be my name"—he blushes slightly—"that might be really cool."

He seems too sexy to be a husband. You think of husbands as fat, balding men who take out the trash. But my husband is sexy. He's young and he's tall and he's strong. He's so perfect. I sound like an idiot. But this is how it's supposed to be, right? As a newlywed, I'm supposed to see him through these rose-colored glasses. "I was thinking of going by Elsie Porter Ross," I say to him.

He stops rubbing my feet for a minute. "That's really hot," he says.

I laugh at him. "Why?"

"I don't know," he says, starting to rub my feet again. "It's probably some weird caveman thing. I just like the idea that we are the Rosses. We are Mr. and Mrs. Ross."

"I like that!" I say. "Mr. and Mrs. Ross. That is hot."

"I told you!"

"That settles it. As soon as the marriage certificate gets here, I'm sending it to the DMV or wherever you have to send it."

"Awesome," he says, taking his hands off of me. "Okay, Elsie Porter Ross. My turn."

I grab his feet. It's quiet for a while as I absentmindedly rub his toes through his socks. My mind wanders, and after some time, it lands on a startling realization: I am hungry.

"Are you hungry?" I ask.

"Now?"

"I really want to get Fruity Pebbles for some reason."

"We don't have cereal here?" Ben asks.

"No, we do. I just . . . I want Fruity Pebbles." We have adult cereals, boxes of brown shapes fortified with fiber.

"Well, should we go get some? I'm sure CVS is still open and I'm sure they sell Fruity Pebbles. Or, I could go get them for you."

"No! I can't let you do that. That would be so lazy of me."

"That is lazy of you, but you're my wife and I love you and I want you to have what you want." He starts to get up.

"No, really, you don't have to."

"I'm going." Ben leaves the room briefly and returns with his bike and shoes.

"Thank you!" I say, now lying across the sofa, taking up the space he just abandoned. Ben smiles at me as he opens the front door and walks his bike through it. I can hear him put the kickstand down and I know he will come back in to say good-bye.

"I love you, Elsie Porter Ross," he says, and he bends down

to the couch to kiss me. He is wearing a bike helmet and bike gloves. He grins at me. "I really love the sound of that."

I smile wide. "I love you!" I say to him. "Thank you."

"You're welcome. I love you! I'll be right back." He shuts the door behind him.

I lay my head back down and pick up a book, but I can't concentrate. I miss him. Twenty minutes pass and I start to expect him home, but the door doesn't open. I don't hear anyone on the steps.

Once thirty minutes have passed, I call his cell phone. No answer. My mind starts to race with possibilities. They are all far-fetched and absurd. He met someone else. He stopped off at a strip club. I call him again as my brain starts to think of more realistic reasons for him to be late, reasons that are reasonable and thus far more terrifying. When he does not answer again, I get off the couch and walk outside.

I'm not sure what I expect to find, but I look up and down the street for any sign of him. Is it crazy to think he's hurt? I can't decide. I try to stay calm and tell myself that he must just be stuck in some sort of traffic jam that he can't get out of, or maybe he's run into an old friend. The minutes start to slow. They feel like hours. Each second passing is an insufferable period of time.

Sirens.

I can hear sirens heading in my direction. I can see their flashing lights just above the rooftops on my street. Their whooping alarms sound like they are calling to me. I can hear my name in their repetitive wailing: *El-sie. El-sie.*

I start running. By the time I get to the end of my street, I can feel just how cold the concrete is on the balls of my feet. My light sweatpants are no match for the wind, but I keep going until I find the source.

I see two ambulances and a fire truck. There are a few police cars barricading the area. I run as far into the fray as I
can get before I stop myself. Someone is being lifted onto a
stretcher. There's a large moving truck flipped over on the side
of the road. Its windows are smashed, glass surrounding it. I
look closely at the truck, trying to figure out what happened.
That's when I see that it isn't all glass. The road is covered in
little specks of something else. I walk closer and I see one at
my feet. It's a Fruity Pebble. I scan the area for the one thing I
pray not to see and I see it. Right in front of me—how could
I have missed it?—halfway underneath the moving truck, is
Ben's bike. It's bent and torn.

The world goes silent. The sirens stop. The city comes to a
halt. My heart starts beating so quickly it hurts in my chest.
I can feel the blood pulsing through my brain. It's so hot out
here. When did it get so hot outside? I can't breathe. I don't
think I can breathe. I'm not breathing.

I don't even realize I am running until I reach the ambulance doors. I start to pound on them. I jump up and down as I
try to pound on the window that is too high above me to reach.
As I do, all I hear is the sound of the Fruity Pebbles crunching
beneath my feet. I grind them into the pavement each time I
jump. I break them into a million pieces.

The ambulance pulls away. Is he in it? Is Ben in there? Are
they keeping him alive? Is he okay? Is he bruised? Maybe he's
in the ambulance because protocol says they have to but he's
actually fine. Maybe he's around here somewhere. Maybe the
ambulance was holding the driver of the car. That guy has to
be dead, right? No way that person survived. So Ben must be
all right. That's the karma of an accident: The bad guy dies, the
good guy lives.

I turn and look around, but I don't see Ben anywhere. I start to scream his name. I know he's okay. I'm sure of it. I just need this to be over. I just want to see him with a small scrape and be told he's fine to go home. Let's go home, Ben. I've learned my lesson to never let you do such a stupid favor for me again. I've learned my lesson; let's go home.

"Ben!" I shout into the nighttime air. It's so cold. How did it get so cold? *"Ben!"* I shout again. I feel like I am running in circles until I am stopped in my place by a police officer.

"Ma'am," he says as he grabs my arms. I keep shouting. Ben needs to hear me. He needs to know that I am here. He needs to know that it's time to come home. "Ma'am," the officer calls again.

"What?" I yell into his face. I rip my arms out of his grasp and I spin myself around. I try to run through what is clearly a marked-off area. I know that whoever marked this off would want to let me through. They would understand that I just need to find my husband.

The officer catches up to me and grabs me again. "Ma'am!" he says, this time more severe. "You cannot be here right now." Doesn't he understand that this is exactly where I *must* be right now?

"I need to find my husband!" I say to him. "He could be hurt. That's his bike. I have to find him."

"Ma'am, they have taken your husband to Cedars-Sinai. Do you have a ride to get there?"

My eyes are staring at his face, but I do not understand what he is saying to me.

"Where is he?" I ask. I need him to tell me again. I don't understand.

"Ma'am, your husband is on his way to Cedars-Sinai Medical Center. He is being rushed to the emergency room. Would you like me to take you?"

He's not here? I think. He was in that ambulance?

"Is he okay?"

"Ma'am, I can't—"

"Is he okay?"

The officer looks at me. He pulls his hat off his head and places it on his chest. I know what this means. I've seen it done on the doorsteps of war widows in period pieces. As if on cue, I start violently heaving.

"I need to see him!" I scream through my tears. "I need to see him! I need to be with him!" I drop to my knees in the middle of the road, cereal crunching underneath me. "Is he all right? I should be with him. Just tell me if he is still alive."

The police officer looks at me with pity and guilt. I've never seen the two looks together before but it's easy to recognize. "Ma'am. I'm sorry. Your husband has . . ."

The police officer isn't rushed; he isn't running on adrenaline like me. He knows there is nothing to hurry for. He knows my husband's dead body can wait.

I don't let him finish his sentence. I know what he's going to say and I can't believe it. I won't believe it. I scream at him, pounding my fists into his chest. He is a huge man, probably six foot four at least, and he looms over me. I feel like a child. But that doesn't stop me. I just keep flailing and hitting him. I want to slap him. I want to kick him. I want to make him hurt like I do.

"He passed away on impact. I'm sorry."

That's when I fall to the ground. Everything starts spinning. I can hear my pulse, but I can't focus on what the policeman is saying. I really didn't think this was going to happen. I thought bad things only happened to people with hubris. They don't happen to people like me, people that know how fragile life is, people that respect the authority of a higher power. But it has. It has happened to me.

My body calms. My eyes dry. My face freezes, and my gaze falls onto a scaffolding and stays there. My arms feel numb. I'm not sure if I'm standing or sitting.

"What happened to the driver?" I ask the officer, calm and composed.

"I'm sorry?"

"What happened to the person driving the moving truck?"

"He passed away, ma'am."

"Good," I say to him. I say it like a sociopath. The police officer just nods his head at me, perhaps indicating some unspoken contract that he will pretend he didn't hear me say it, and I can pretend I don't wish another person to have died. But I don't want to take it back.

He grabs my hand and leads me into the front of his police car. He uses his siren to break through traffic and I see the streets of Los Angeles in fast-forward. They have never looked so ugly.

When we get to the hospital, the officer sits me down in the waiting room. I'm shaking so hard that the chair shakes with me.

"I need to go back there," I say to him. "I need to go back there!" I yell louder. I take notice of his name tag. Officer Hernandez.

"I understand. I'm going to find out all of the information that I can. I believe you will have a social worker assigned to you. I'll be right back."

I can hear him talking but I can't make myself react or acknowledge him. I just sit in the chair and stare at the far wall. I can feel my head sway from side to side. I feel myself stand and walk toward the nurses' station, but I am cut off by Officer Hernandez coming back. He is now with a short, middle-aged man. The man has on a blue shirt with a red tie. I bet this idiot calls it his power tie. I bet he thinks he has a good day when he wears this tie.

"Elsie," he says. I must have told Officer Hernandez my name. I don't even remember doing that. He puts out his hand as if I were going to shake it. I see no need for formality in the midst of tragedy. I let it hang there. Before all this, I would never have rejected someone's handshake. I am a nice person. Sometimes, I'm even a pushover. I'm not someone who is considered "difficult" or "unruly."

"You are the wife of Ben Ross? Do you have a driver's license on you?" the man asks me.

"No. I . . . ran right out of the house. I don't . . ." I look down at my feet. I don't even have on shoes and this man thinks I have my driver's license?

Officer Hernandez leaves. I can see him step away slowly, awkwardly. He feels like his job is done here, I'm sure. I wish I was him. I wish I could walk away from this and go home. I'd go home to my husband and a warm bed. My husband, a warm bed, and a fucking bowl of Fruity Pebbles.

"I'm afraid we cannot let you back there yet, Elsie," the man in the red tie says.

"Why not?"

"The doctors are working."

"He's *alive*?" I scream. How quickly hope can come flying back.

"No, I'm sorry." He shakes his head. "Your husband died earlier this evening. He was listed as an organ donor."

I feel like I'm in an elevator that is plummeting to the ground floor. They are taking pieces of him and giving them to other people. They are taking his parts.

I sit back down in the chair, dead inside. Part of me wants to scream at this man to let me back there. To let me see him. I want to run through the twin doors and find him, hold him. What are they doing to him? But I'm frozen. I am dead too.

The man in the red tie leaves briefly and comes back with hot chocolate and slippers. My eyes are dry and tired. I can barely see through them. All of my senses feel muted. I feel trapped in my own body, separated from everyone around me.

"Do you have someone we can call? Your parents?"

I shake my head. "Ana," I say. "I should call Ana."

He puts his hand on my shoulder. "Can you write down Ana's number? I'll call her."

I nod and he hands me a piece of paper and a pen. It takes me a minute to remember her number. I write it down wrong a few times before I write it down correctly, but I'm pretty sure, when I hand over the piece of paper, it's the correct number.

"What about Ben?" I ask. I don't know what exactly I mean. I just . . . I can't give up yet. I can't be at the call-someone-to-take-her-home-and-watch-her phase yet. We have to fight this, right? I have to find him and save him. How can I find him and save him?

"The nurses have called the next of kin."

"What? I'm his next of kin."

"Apparently his driver's license listed an address in Orange County. We had to legally notify his family."

"So who did you call? Who is coming?" But I already know who's coming.

"I will see if I can find out. I'm going to go phone Ana. I'll be back shortly, okay?"

I nod.

In this lobby, I can see and hear other families waiting. Some look somber but most look okay. There is a mother with her young daughter. They are reading a book. There is a young boy holding an ice pack to his face next to a father who seems annoyed. There is a teenage couple holding hands. I don't know why they are here, but judging from the smiles on their faces and the way they are flirting, I can only assume it's not dire and I . . . I want to scream at them. I want to say that emergency rooms are for emergencies and they shouldn't be here if they are going to look happy and carefree. I want to tell them to go home and be happy somewhere else because I don't need to see it. I don't remember what it feels like to be them. I don't even remember how it feels to be myself before this happened. All I have is this overwhelming sense of dread. That and my anger toward these two little shitheads who won't get their smiles out of my fucking face.

I hate them and I hate the goddamn nurses, who just go on with their day like it isn't the worst one of their lives. They make phone calls and they make photocopies and they drink coffee. I hate them for being able to drink coffee at a time like this. I hate everyone in this entire hospital for not being miserable.

The man in the red tie comes back and says that Ana is on her way. He offers to sit down and wait with me. I shrug. He can do whatever he wants. His presence brings me no solace, but it does prevent me from running up to someone and screaming at them for eating a candy bar at a time like this. My mind flashes back to the Fruity Pebbles all over the road, and I know they will be there when I get home. I know that no one will have cleaned them up because no one could possibly know how horrifying they would be to look at again. Then I think of what a stupid reason that is for Ben to die. He died over Fruity Pebbles. It would be funny if it wasn't so . . . It will never be funny. Nothing about this is funny. Even the fact that I lost my husband because I had a craving for a children's cereal based on the Flintstones cartoon. I hate myself for this. That's who I hate the most.

Ana shows up in a flurry of panic. I don't know what the man in the red tie has told her. He stands to greet her as she runs toward me. I can see them talking but I can't hear them. They speak only for a second before she runs to my side, puts her arms around me. I let her arms fall where she puts them, but I have no energy to hug back. This is the dead fish of hugs. She whispers, "I'm sorry," into my ear, and I crumble into her arms.

I have no will to hold myself up, no desire to hide my pain. I wail in the waiting room. I sob and heave into her breasts. Any other moment of my life, I'd move my head away from that part of her body. I'd feel uncomfortable with my eyes and lips being that close to a sexual body part, but right now, sex feels trivial and stupid. It feels like something idiots do out of boredom. Those happy teenagers probably do it for sport.

Her arms around me don't comfort me. The water springs from my eyes as if I'm forcing it out but I'm not. It's just falling on its own. I don't even feel sad. This level of devastation is so far beyond tears, that mine feel paltry and silly.

"Have you seen him, Elsie? I'm so sorry."

I don't answer. We sit on the floor of the waiting room for what seems like hours. Sometimes I wail, sometimes I feel nothing. Most of the time, I lie in Ana's arms, not because I need to but because I don't want to look at her. Eventually, Ana gets up and rests me against the wall, and then she walks up to the nurses' station and starts yelling.

"How much longer until we can see Ben Ross?" she screams at the young Latina nurse sitting at her computer.

"Ma'am," the nurse says, standing up, but Ana moves away from her.

"No. Don't ma'am me. Tell me where he is. Let us through." The man in the red tie makes his way over to her and tries to calm her down.

He and Ana speak for a few minutes. I can see him try to touch Ana, to console her, and she jerks her shoulder out of his reach. He is just doing his job. Everyone here is just doing their job. What a bunch of assholes.

I see an older woman fly through the front doors. She looks about sixty with long, reddish brown hair in waves around her face. She has mascara running down her cheeks, a brown purse over her shoulder, a blackish brown shawl across her chest. She has tissues in her hands. I wish my grief were composed enough to have tissues. I've been wiping snot on my sleeves and neckline. I've been letting tears fall into puddles on the floor.

She runs up to the front desk and then resigns herself to sit. When she turns to face me briefly, I know exactly who she is. I stare at her. I can't take my eyes off of her. She is my mother-in-law, a stranger by all accounts. I saw her picture a few times in a photo album, but she has never seen my face.

I remove myself and head into the bathroom. I do not know how to introduce myself to her. I do not know how to tell her that we are both here for the same man. That we are both grieving over the same loss. I stand in front of the mirror and I look at myself. My face is red and blotchy. My eyes are blood-shot. I look at my face and I think that I had someone who loved this face. And now he's gone. And now no one loves my face anymore.

I step back out of the bathroom and she is gone. I turn to find Ana grabbing my arm. "You can go in," she says and leads me to the man in the red tie, who leads me through the double doors.

The man in the red tie stops outside a room and asks me if I want him to go in with me. Why would I want him to go in with me? I just met this man. This man means nothing to me. The man inside this room means everything to me. *Nothing* isn't going to help losing *everything*. I open the door and there are other people in the room, but all I can see is Ben's body.

"Excuse me!" my mother-in-law says through her tears. It is meek but terrifying. I ignore it.

I grab his face in my hands and it's cold to the touch. His eyelids are shut. I'll never see his eyes again. It occurs to me they might be gone. I can't look. I don't want to figure it out. His face is bruised and I don't know what that means. Does that mean he was hurt before he died? Did he die there alone and lonely on the street? Oh my God, did he suffer? I feel faint. There's a sheet over his chest and legs. I'm scared to move the sheet. I'm scared that there is too much of Ben exposed, too much of him to see. Or that there is too much of him that is gone.

"Security!" she calls out into the air.

As I hold on to Ben's hand and a security guard shows up at the door, I look at my mother-in-law. She has no reason to know who I am. She has no reason to understand what I am doing here, but she has to know I love her son. That much has to be obvious by now.

"Please," I beg her. "Please, Susan, don't do this."

Susan looks at me curiously, confused. By the sheer fact that I know her name, she knows she must be missing something. She very subtly nods and looks at the security guard. "I'm sorry. Give us a moment?" He leaves the room, and Susan looks at the nurse. "You too. Thank you." The nurse leaves the room, shutting the door.

Susan looks tortured, terrified, and yet composed, as if she has only enough poise to get through the next five seconds and then she will fall apart.

"His hand has a wedding ring on it," she says to me. I stare at her and try to keep breathing. I meekly lift up my own left hand to match.

"We were married a week and a half ago," I say through tears. I can feel the corners of my lips pulling down. They feel so heavy.

"What is your name?" she asks me, now shaking.

"Elsie," I say. I am terrified of her. She looks angry and vulnerable, like a teenage runaway.

"Elsie what?" she chokes.

"Elsie Ross."

That's when she breaks. She breaks just like I have. Soon, she's on the floor. There are no more tissues in sight to save the linoleum from her tears.

A na is sitting next to me holding my hand. I am sitting next to Ben's side, sobbing. Susan excused herself some time ago. The man in the red tie comes in and says we need to clear some things up and Ben's body needs to be moved. I just stare ahead, I don't even focus on what's happening, until the man in the red tie hands me a bag of Ben's things. His cell phone is there, his wallet, his keys.

"What is this?" I ask, even though I know what it is.

Before the man in the red tie can answer me, Susan appears in the doorway. Her face is strained; her eyes are bloodshot. She looks older than she did when she left. She looks exhausted. Do I look like that? I bet I look like that.

"What are you doing?" Susan asks the man.

"I'm . . . We need to clear the room. Your son's body is going to be transferred."

"Why are you giving that to her?" Susan says, more directly. She says it like I'm not even here.

"I'm sorry?"

Susan steps further into the room and takes the bag of Ben's stuff from in front of me. "All decisions about Ben, all his belongings, should be directed to me," she says.

"Ma'am," the man in the red tie says.

"All of it," she says.

Ana stands up and grabs me to go with her. She intends to

remove me from this situation, and while I don't want to be here right now, I can't just be removed. I pull my arm out of Ana's hand and I look at Susan.

"Should we discuss what the next steps are?" I say to her.

"What is there to discuss?" Susan says. She is cold and controlled.

"I just mean . . ." I don't actually know what I mean.

"Mrs. Ross," the man in the red tie says.

"Yes?" Both Susan and I answer at the same time.

"I'm sorry," I say. "Which one did you mean?"

"The elder," he says, looking at Susan. I'm sure that he meant it as a sign of respect, but it's torn right through her. Susan doesn't want to be one of two Mrs. Rosses, that much is clear, but I bet she resents even more being the elder one.

"I'm not going to give this any more credence," she says to everyone in the room. "She has absolutely no proof that my son even knew her, let alone married her. I've never heard of her! My own son. I saw him last month. He never mentioned a damn thing. So no, I'm not having my son's possessions sent home with a stranger. I won't have it."

Ana reaches toward Susan. "Maybe it's time for us all to take a step back," she says.

Susan turns her head, as if noticing Ana for the first time. "Who are you?" she asks. She asks it like we are clowns coming out of a Volkswagen. She asks it as if she's exhausted by all the people that keep appearing.

"I'm a friend," Ana says. "And I don't think any of us are in a position to behave rationally, so maybe we can just breathe—"

Susan turns toward the man in the red tie, her body language interrupting Ana midsentence. "You and I need to discuss this in private," she barks at him.

"Ma'am, please calm down."

"Calm down? You're joking!"

"Susan—" I start to say. I don't know how I planned on finishing, but Susan doesn't give a shit.

"Stop," she says, putting her hand up in my face. It's aggressive and instinctual, as if she needs to protect her face from my words.

"Ma'am, Elsie was escorted in by the police. She was at the scene. I have no reason to doubt that she and your son were as she says . . ."

"Married?" Susan is incredulous.

"Yes," the man in the red tie says.

"Call the county! I want to see a record of it!"

"Elsie, do you have a copy of your marriage certificate that you can show Mrs. Ross?"

I can feel myself shrinking in front of them. I don't want to shrink. I want to stand tall. I want to be proud, confident. But this is all too much and I don't have anything to show for myself.

"No, but, Susan—" I say as tears fall down my face. I feel so ugly right now, so small and stupid.

"Stop calling me that!" she screams. "You don't even know me. Stop calling me by my name!"

"Fine," I say. My eyes are staring forward, focused on the body in the room. My husband's body. "Keep all of it," I say. "I don't care. We can sit here and scream all day but it doesn't change anything. So I really don't give a shit where his wallet goes."

I put one foot in front of the other and I walk out. I leave my husband's body there with her. And the minute my feet hit the hallway, the minute Ana has shut the door behind us, I regret walking out. I should have stayed with him until the nurse kicked me out.

na pushes me forward.

She puts me in the car. She buckles my seat belt. She drives slowly through town. She parks in my driveway. I don't remember any of it happening. Suddenly, I am at my front door.

Stepping into my apartment, I have no idea what time of day it is. I have no idea how long it has been since I sat on the couch like a cavalier bitch whining about cereal in my pajamas. This apartment, the one I have loved since I moved in, the one I considered "ours" when Ben moved in, now betrays me. It hasn't moved an inch since Ben died. It's like it doesn't care.

It didn't put away his shoes sitting in the middle of the floor. It didn't fold up the blanket he was using. It didn't even have the decency to hide his toothbrush from plain view. This apartment is acting like nothing has changed. Everything has changed. I tell the walls he's gone. "He's dead. He's not coming home." Ana rubs my back and says, "I know, baby. I know."

She doesn't know. She could never know. I walk carelessly into my bedroom, hit my shoulder on the door hinge and feel nothing. I get into my side of the bed and I can smell him still. He's still here in the sheets. I grab his pillow from his side of the bed and I smell it, choking on my own tears. I walk into the kitchen as Ana is getting me a glass of water. I walk right past her with the pillow in my hand and I grab a trash bag, shoving the pillow into it. I tie it tight, knotting the plastic over and over until it breaks off in my hand and falls onto the kitchen floor.

"What are you doing?" she asks me.

"It smells like Ben," I answer. "I don't want the smell to evaporate. I want to save it."

"I don't know if that's going to work," she says delicately.

"Fuck you," I say and go back to the bed.

I start crying the minute I hit my pillow. I hate what this has made me. I've never told anyone to fuck off before, least of all Ana.

Ana has been my best friend since I was seventeen years old. We met the first day of college in line at the dining hall. I didn't have anyone to sit with and she was already trying to avoid a boy. It was a telling moment for each of us. When she decided to move to Los Angeles to be an actress, I came with her. Not because I had any affinity for Los Angeles, I had never been here, but because I had such a strong affinity for her. Ana had said to me, "C'mon, you can be a librarian anywhere." And she was absolutely right.

Here we were, nine years after meeting, her watching me like I'm going to slit my wrists. If I had a better grip on my senses, I'd say this is the real meat of friendship, but I don't care about that right now. I don't care about anything.

Ana comes in with two pills and a glass of water. "I found these in your medicine cabinet," she says. I look in her hand and I recognize them. It's Vicodin from when Ben had a back spasm last month. He barely took any of them. I think he thought taking them made him a wimp.

I take them out of her hand without questioning and I swallow them. "Thank you," I say. She tucks the duvet around me and goes to sleep on the couch. I'm glad she doesn't try to sleep in bed with me. I don't want her to take away his smell. My eyes are parched from crying, my limbs weak, but my brain needs the Vicodin to pass out. I shuffle over to Ben's side of the bed as I get groggy and fall asleep. "I love you," I say, and for the first time, there's no one to hear it.

I wake up feeling hungover. I reach over to grab Ben's hand as I do every morning, and his side of the bed is empty. For a minute I think he must be in the bathroom or making breakfast and then I remember. My devastation returns, this time duller but thicker, coating my body like a blanket, sinking my heart like a stone.

I pull my hands to my face and try to wipe away the tears, but they are flowing out of me too fast to catch up. It's like a Whac-A-Mole of misery.

Ana comes in with a dish towel in her hands, drying them.

"You're up," she says, surprised.

"How observant." Why am I being so mean? I'm not a mean person. This isn't who I am.

"Susan called." She is ignoring my outbursts, and for that, I am thankful.

"What did she say?" I sit up and grab the glass of water on my bedside table from last night. "What could she possibly want from me?"

"She didn't say anything. Just to call her."

"Great."

"I left the number on the refrigerator. In case you did want to call her."

"Thanks." I sip the water and stand up.

"I have to go walk Bugsy and then I'll be right back," Ana

says. Bugsy is her English bulldog. He drools all over everything and I want to tell her that Bugsy doesn't need to be let out because Bugsy is a lazy sack of shit, but I don't say any of this because I really, really want to stop being so unkind.

"Okay."

"Do you want anything while I'm out?" she asks, and it reminds me that I asked Ben to get me Fruity Pebbles. I get right back into bed.

"No, nothing for me. Thank you."

"Okay, I'll be back shortly." She thinks for a minute. "Actually, do you want me to stick around in case you decide to call her now?"

"No, thanks. I can handle it."

"Okay, if you change your mind . . ."

"Thanks."

Ana leaves, and as I hear the door shut, it hits me how alone I am. I am alone in this room, I am alone in this apartment, but more to the point, I am alone in this life. I can't even wrap my brain around it. I just get up and pick up the phone. I get the number from the front of the refrigerator and I see a magnet for Georgie's Pizza. I fall to the floor, my cheek against the cold tile. I can't seem to make myself get up.

DECEMBER

It was New Year's Eve and Ana and I had this great plan. We were going to go to this party to see this guy she had been flirting with at the gym, and then we were going to leave at 11:30 p.m. We wanted to drive to the beach, open a bottle of champagne together, and ring in the new year tipsy and drenched in sea spray.

Instead, Ana got too drunk at the party, started making out with the guy from the gym, and disappeared for a few hours. This was fairly typical of Ana and something that I had come to love about her, namely that nothing ever went as planned. Something always happened. She was a nice reprieve from my own personality. A personality for whom everything went as planned and nothing ever happened. So when I was stranded at the party waiting for Ana to pop out of wherever she'd been hiding, I wasn't angry or surprised. I had assumed things might take this turn. I was only slightly annoyed as I rang in the new year with a group of strangers. I stood there awkwardly, as friends kissed each other, and I just stared into my champagne glass. I didn't let it ruin my evening. I talked to some cool people that night. I made the best of it.

I met a guy named Fabian, who was just finishing med school but said his real passion was "fine wine, fine food, and fine women." He winked at me as he said this, and as I gracefully removed myself from the conversation shortly thereafter, Fabian asked for my number. I gave it to him, and although he was cute, I knew that if he did call, I wouldn't answer. Fabian seemed like the kind of guy who would take me to an expensive bar on our first date; the kind of guy who would check out other girls while I was in the bathroom. That was the kind of guy who found victory in sleeping with you. It was a game to him and I . . . just never knew how to play it well.

Ana, on the other hand, knew how to have fun. She met people. She flirted with them. She had whatever that thing is that makes men fawn over women and lose their own self-respect in the process. Ana had all the power in her romances, and while I could see the point in living like that, from an outside view it never seemed very full of passion. It was calculated. I was waiting for someone that would sweep me off my feet and would be swept up by me in equal parts. I wanted someone who wouldn't want to play games because doing so meant less time being together. I wasn't sure if this person existed, but I was too young to give up on the idea.

I finally found Ana asleep in the master bathroom. I picked her up and cabbed her home. By the time I reached my own apartment, it was about 2:00 a.m. and I was tired. The bottle of champagne intended for our beach rendezvous went unopened and I got in bed.

As I fell asleep that night, eyeliner not fully cleaned off my face, black sequined dress on the floor, I thought about what this year could bring and my mind raced with all of the possibilities, however unlikely. But out of all the possibilities, I didn't think about being married by the end of May.

I woke up New Year's Day alone in my apartment, just like I woke up every other day, and there was nothing in particular that seemed special about it. I read in bed for two hours, I took a shower, I got dressed. I met Ana for breakfast.

I'd been up for about three and a half hours by the time I saw her. She looked like she hadn't been up for five minutes. Ana is tall and lanky with long brown hair that falls far beyond her shoulders and perfectly matches her golden brown eyes. She was born in Brazil and lived there until she was thirteen, and it's still noticeable every once in a while in some of her words, mostly her exclamations. Other than that, she's fully Americanized, assimilated, cleansed of all cultural identity. I'm pretty sure her name is supposed to be pronounced with a long *a* like "*ahn*-uh" but somewhere in middle school she gave up explaining the difference, and so now, she's Ana, any way anyone would like to pronounce it.

That particular morning, she was wearing big sweatpants that didn't make her look fat because she was so skinny, and she had her hair pulled up into a ponytail, a zip-up sweatshirt covering her torso. You could barely tell she wasn't wearing a shirt underneath her sweatshirt, and it occurred to me that this is how Ana does it. This is how she drives men crazy. She looks naked while being entirely covered. And you would have absolutely no indication she does this on purpose.

"Nice shirt," I said, as I pulled my sunglasses off and sat down across from her. Sometimes I worried that my own average body looked oversize compared to hers, that my own plain, all-American features only served to highlight how exotic she was. When I made jokes about it, she would remind me that I am a blond woman in the United States. She'd say blond trumps everything. I've always thought of my hair as dirty blond, almost mousy, but I saw her point.

Even with how gorgeous Ana is, I've never heard her express

satisfaction with her own looks. When I would say I didn't like my small boobs, she'd remind me that I have long legs and a butt she'd kill for. She'd always confess how much she hated her short eyelashes and knees, that her feet looked like "troll feet." So maybe we're all in the same boat. Maybe all women feel like "before" photos.

Ana had already made herself comfortable on the patio, having a muffin and an iced tea. She pretended like she was about to get up when I sat down, but just reached for a half hug.

"Are you ready to kill me for last night?"

"What?" I said as I pulled out the menu. I don't know why I even bothered to look at the menu. I ate eggs Benedict every Saturday morning.

"I don't even remember what happened, honestly. I just remember parts of the cab ride home and then you taking my shoes off before you pulled the covers over me."

I nodded. "That sounds about right. I lost you for about three hours and found you in the upstairs bathroom, so I can't speak to how far you and that guy from the gym got, but I would imagine . . ."

"No! I hooked up with Jim?"

I put the menu down. "What? No, the guy from the gym."

"Yeah, his name is Jim."

"You met a guy at the gym named Jim?" Technically, this wasn't his fault. People named Jim should be allowed to go to gyms, but I couldn't shake the feeling this somehow made him ridiculous. "Is that a bran muffin?"

She nodded, so I took some of it.

"You and I might be the only two people on the planet that like the taste of bran muffins," she said to me, and she might have been right. Ana and I often found striking similarities in each other in meaningless places, the clearest one being food. It doesn't matter if you and another person both like tzatziki. It has no bearing on your ability to get along, but somehow, in these overlaps of taste, there was a bond between Ana and me. I knew she was about to order the eggs Benedict too.

"Anyway, I saw you making out with Jim from the gym, but I don't know what happened after that."

"Oh, well I'm going to assume that it didn't get much further because he's already texted me this morning."

"It's eleven a.m."

"I know. I thought it was a bit quick. But it is flattering," she said.

"What can I get for you two?" The waitress who came up to us wasn't our usual waitress. She was older, had been through more.

"Oh, hi! I don't think we've met before. I'm Ana."

"Daphne." This waitress wasn't nearly as interested in being friends with us as Ana might have hoped.

"What happened to Kimberly?" Ana asked.

"Oh, not sure. Just filling in for the day."

"Ah. Okay, well, we'll make this easy on you. Two eggs Benedict and I'll have an iced tea like she has," I said.

"You got it."

Once she left, Ana and I resumed our earlier discussion.

"I've been thinking about resolutions," Ana said, offering me some of her iced tea while I waited for mine to get there. I declined because I knew if I had some of hers, she'd take that as license to drink some of mine when it arrived and she'd drink my whole damn glass. I'd known her long enough to know where to draw my boundaries and how to draw them so she wouldn't notice.

"Okay. And?"

"I'm thinking something radical."

"Radical? This should be good."

"Celibacy."

"Celibacy?"

"Celibacy. Not having sex."

"No, I know what it means. I'm just wondering why."

"Oh, well, I came up with it this morning. I'm twenty-six years old and last night I got drunk and can't be entirely sure if I slept with someone or not. That seems to be the closest to slut rock bottom that I want to get."

"You are not a slut." I wasn't exactly sure if this was true.

"No, you're right. I'm not a slut. Yet."

"You could just stop drinking." I had an interesting relationship with drinking in that I could take it or leave it. Drink, not drink, it did not matter to me. Most people, I'd found so far, fell strongly on one side or the other. Ana fell strongly on the "drinking" side.

"What are you talking about?"

"You know, stop getting drunk."

"At all?"

"Stop it. I'm not saying something preposterous here. There are plenty of people that just don't drink."

"Yeah, Elsie, they're called alcoholics."

I laughed. "Fair enough, drinking isn't the problem. It's the sleeping around."

"Right. So I'm just going to stop sleeping around."

"And what happens when you meet someone you really want to be with?"

"Well, I'll cross that bridge when I come to it. I didn't meet anyone last year worth my time. I can't say I expect that to change this year."

Daphne showed up with two eggs Benedicts and my iced tea. She put them down in front of us, and I didn't realize how hungry I'd been until the food was staring me in the face. I dug right in.

Ana nodded, chewing. When it started to look like she could speak without spitting food, she added, "I mean, if I meet someone and fall in love, sure. But until then, nobody's getting in here." She made an *x* in the air with her utensils.

"Fair enough." The best part about this place was they put spinach in the eggs Benedict, kind of an eggs Benedict Florentine. "This doesn't mean I can't sleep around though, right?" I said to her.

"No, you still can. You won't. But you still can."

Ana was soon on her way back to the other side of town. She was living in Santa Monica in a condo that overlooked the Pacific Ocean. I'd've been jealous enough to resent her if she hadn't offered on a regular basis for me to move in. I always declined, knowing that living with Ana might be the only thing that could teach me to dislike her. I never did understand how Ana could live the way she did on the salary of a part-time yoga teacher, but she always seemed to have enough money for the things she wanted and needed when she wanted and needed them.

After she left, I walked back to my apartment. I knew exactly how I'd be spending my afternoon. It was a new year and I always felt like a new year didn't feel new without rearranging the furniture. The problem was that I had rearranged my apartment so many times in the two years I'd lived there that I'd exhausted all rational possibilities. I loved my apartment and worked hard to afford it and decorate it. So as I moved the couch from wall to wall, ultimately realizing that it really looked best where it was originally, I was still satisfied. I moved the bookcase from one wall to another, switched my end tables, and decided this was enough of a change for me to commemorate the year. I sat down on the couch, turned on the television, and fell asleep.

It was 5:00 p.m. when I woke up, and while it was technically a Saturday night and single people on Saturday nights are supposed to go out to bars or clubs and find a date, I opted to watch television, read a book, and order a pizza. Maybe this year was going to be the year I did whatever the hell I wanted, regardless of social norms. Maybe.

When it started raining, I knew I'd been right to stay inside. Ana called a few hours later asking what I was doing.

"I wanted to make sure you're not sitting on the couch watching television."

"What? Why can't I watch television?"

"It's a Saturday night, Elsie. Get up! Go out! I'd say you should come out with me but I'm going on a date with Jim."

"So much for celibacy."

"What? I'm not sleeping with him. I'm eating dinner with him."

I laughed. "Okay, well, I'm spending the night on my couch. I'm tired and sleepy and . . ."

"Tired and sleepy are the same thing. Stop making excuses."

"Fine. I'm lazy and I like being alone sometimes."

"Good. At least you admitted it. I'll call you tomorrow. Wish me luck keeping it in my pants."

"You'll need it."

"Hey!"

"Hey!" I said back.

"Okay, I'll talk to you tomorrow."

"Bye."

With the phone in my hand, I ordered a pizza. When I called Georgie's Pizza to order it, the woman on the phone told me it would be an hour and a half before it was delivered. When I asked why, all she said was "Rain." I told her I'd be there in a half hour to pick it up.

Walking into Georgie's Pizza, I felt nothing. No part of my brain or my body knew what was about to happen. I felt no premonition. I was wearing bright yellow galoshes and what can only be described as fat jeans. The rain had matted my hair to my face and I'd given up pushing it away.

I didn't even notice Ben sitting there. I was far too involved with the minutiae of trying to buy a pizza. Once the cashier told me it would be another ten minutes, I retired to the small bench in the front of the store, and it was then that I noticed there was another person in the same predicament.

My heart didn't skip a beat. I had no idea he was "it"; it was "he." He was the man I'd dreamed about as a child, wondering what my husband would look like. I was seeing this face I had wondered about my whole life and it was right here in front of me and I didn't recognize it. All I thought was, He'll probably get his pizza before I get mine.

He looked handsome in a way that suggested he didn't realize just how handsome he was. There was no effort involved, no self-awareness. He was tall and lean with broad shoulders and strong arms. His jeans were just the right shade of blue; his shirt brought out the gray in his green eyes. They looked stark against his brown hair. I sat down next to him and swatted my hair away from my forehead again. I picked up my phone to check my e-mail and otherwise distract myself from the waiting.

"Hi," he said. It took me a second to confirm he was, in fact, speaking to me. That easily, my interest was piqued.

"Hi," I said back. I tried to let it hang there, but I was bad with silence. I had to fill it. "I should have just had it delivered."

"And miss all this?" he said, referencing the tacky faux-Italian decor with his hands. I laughed. "You have a nice laugh," he said.

"Oh, stop it," I said. I swear, my mother taught me how to take a compliment, and yet each time I was given one, I shooed it away like it was on fire. "I mean, thank you. That's what you're supposed to say. Thank you."

I noticed that I had subconsciously shifted my entire body toward him. I'd read all of these articles about body language and pupil dilation when people are attracted to each other, but whenever I got into a situation where it was actually useful (*Are his pupils dilated? Does he like me?*), I was always far too unfocused to take advantage.

"No, what you're supposed to do is compliment me back," he said, smiling. "That way I know where I stand."

"Ah," I said. "Well, it doesn't really tell you much if I compliment you now, does it? I mean, you know that I'm complimenting you because you've asked . . ."

"Trust me, I can still tell."

"All right," I said, while I looked him up and down. As I made a show of studying him, he stretched out his legs and lengthened his neck. He pulled his shoulders back and puffed out his chest. I admired the stubble on his cheeks, the way it made him look effortlessly handsome. My eyes felt drawn to the strength of his arms. What I wanted to say was "You have great arms," and yet, I didn't have it in me. I played it safe.

"So?" he said.

"I like your shirt," I said to him. It was a heathered gray shirt with a bird on it.

"Oh," he said, and I could hear honest to God disappointment in his voice. "I see how it is."

"What?" I smiled, defensively. "That's a nice compliment."

He laughed. He wasn't overly interested or desperate. He wasn't aloof or cool either, he just . . . was. I don't know whether he was this way with all women, whether he was able to talk to any woman as if he'd known her for years, or whether it was just me. But it didn't matter. It was working. "Oh, it's fine," he said. "But I'm not even going to try for your number. Girl compliments your eyes, your hair, your beard, your arms, your name, that means she's open to a date. Girl compliments your shirt? You're getting shot down."

"Wait—that's not—" I started, but I was interrupted.

"Ben Ross!" the cashier called out, and he jumped up. He looked right at me and said, "Hold that thought."

He paid for his pizza, thanked the cashier genuinely, and then came and sat right back down next to me on the bench.

"Anyway, I'm thinking if I ask you out, I'm going to be shot down. Am I going to be shot down?"

No, he was absolutely not going to be shot down. But I was now embarrassed and trying hard not to seem eager. I smiled wide at him, unable to keep the canary feathers in my mouth. "Your pizza is going to get cold," I told him.

He waved me off. "I'm over this pizza. Give it to me straight. Can I have your number?"

There it was. Do-or-die time. How to say it without screaming it with all of the nervous energy in my body? "You can have my number. It's only fair."

"*Elsie Porter!*" the cashier yelled. Apparently, she had been calling it for quite a while, but Ben and I were too distracted to hear much of anything.

"Oh! Sorry, that's me. Uh . . . just wait here."

He laughed, and I walked up to pay for my pizza. When I came back, he had his phone out. I gave him my number and I took his.

"I'm going to call you soon, if that's okay. Or should I do the wait-three-days thing? Is that more your style?"

"No, go for it," I said, smiling. "The sooner the better."

He put out his hand to shake and I took it.

"Ben."

"Elsie," I said, and for the first time, I thought the name Ben sounded like the finest name I'd ever heard. I smiled at him. I couldn't help it. He smiled back and tapped his pizza. "Well, until then."

I nodded. "Until then," I said, and I walked back to my car. Giddy.

JUNE

I tear the Georgie's magnet off the refrigerator and try to rip it in half, but I can't get it to succumb to my weak fingers. It just bends and stretches. I realize the futility of what I'm doing, as if removing this magnet, destroying this magnet, will ease my pain in any way. I put it back on the refrigerator door and I dial Susan.

She answers on the second ring.

"Susan? Hi. It's Elsie."

"Hi. Can you meet this afternoon to go over arrangements?"

"Arrangements?" I hadn't really thought about what Susan would want to talk about. Arrangements hadn't even occurred to me. Now, as I let it register, I realize that of course there are arrangements. There are things to plan, carefully calculated ways to grieve. You can't even mourn in peace. You must do it through American customs and civilities. The next few days will be full of obituaries and eulogies. Coffins and caterers. I'm shocked she's even contemplating me being a part of them.

"Sure. Absolutely," I say, trying to inject some semblance of get-up-and-go into my voice. "Where should I meet you?"

"I'm staying at the Beverly Hotel," she says and she tells me where it is, as if I haven't lived in Los Angeles for years.

"Oh," I say. "I didn't realize you were staying in town." She lives two hours away. She can't at least stay in her own city? Leave this one to me?

"There's a lot to take care of, Elsie. We can meet at the bar downstairs." Her voice is curt, uninterested, and cold. I tell her I will meet her there at three. It's almost one. "Whatever is convenient for you," she says and gets off the phone.

None of this is convenient for me. What would be convenient for me is to fall asleep and never wake up. That's what would be convenient for me. What would be convenient for me is to be at work right now because everything is fine and Ben will be home tonight for dinner around seven and we're having tacos. That's convenient for me. Talking to the mother-in-law I met yesterday about funeral arrangements for my dead husband isn't convenient for me no matter what time it happens in the afternoon.

I get back in bed, overwhelmed by everything I need to do before I meet with her. I'll need to shower, to get dressed, to get in the car, to drive, to park. It's too much. When Ana comes back, I'm in tears with gratitude because I know she will take care of everything.

I arrive at the hotel a few minutes late. Ana goes to park the car and says she'll be in the lobby. She says to text her if I need her. I walk into the bar area and scan for Susan. It's cold in this bar despite being warm outside. I hate air-conditioning. I moved here to be warm. The room is brand-new but made to look old. There's a chalkboard menu behind the bar that's too clean to be from the era the decorator would like you to believe. The stools are reminiscent of a speakeasy, but they aren't cracked and worn. They look pristine and unused. This is the age we live in; we are able to have nostalgia for things made yesterday. I would have loved this bar last week, when I liked things cool and clean. Now I hate it for being false and inauthentic.

I finally spot Susan sitting at a high table in the back. She is reading the menu, head down, hand covering her face. She glances up and spots me. As we look at each other for a moment, I can see that her eyes are swollen and red but her face means business.

"Hi," I say as I sit down. She does not get up to greet me.

"Hi," she says as she adjusts herself in her seat. "I stopped by Ben's apartment last night to try to—"

"Ben's apartment?"

"Off Santa Monica Boulevard. I talked to his roommate and he told me that Ben moved out last month."

"Right," I say.

"He said Ben moved in with a girl named Elsie."

"That's me," I say, excited by the prospect of her believing me.

"I gathered as much," she says drily. Then she pulls a binder from the floor and puts it in front of me. "I received this from the funeral home. It's a list of options for the service."

"Okay," I say.

"Decisions will need to be made regarding flowers, the ceremony, the obituary, et cetera."

"Sure." I don't entirely know what the "et cetera" is. I've never been in this situation before.

"I think it's best you tend to those duties."

"Me?" Yesterday she didn't even believe I had a right to be at the hospital. Now she wants me to plan his funeral? "You don't want to have any input?" I say, dubious.

"No. I won't be joining you. I think it's best you take care of this yourself. You want to be his next of kin . . ."

She trails off, but I know how she was going to end it. She was going to say, "You want to be his next of kin, you got it." I ignore her attitude and try to keep Ben—my Ben, her Ben, our Ben—in mind.

"But . . . his family should be involved."

"I am the only family Ben has, Elsie. Had. I am all he had."

"I know. I just meant . . . you should be involved in this. We should do this together."

She is quiet as she gives me a tight and rueful smile. She looks down at the utensils on the table. She plays with the napkins and saltshaker. "Ben clearly did not want me involved in his life. I don't see why I should be intimately involved in his death."

"Why would you say that?"

"I just told you," she says. "He clearly did not care enough to tell me he was getting married, or moving in with you, or whatever you two were to each other. And I . . ." She wipes a tear away with a tissue, delicately and with purpose. She shakes her head to clear it. "Elsie. I don't care to discuss this with you. You have a list of things to do. All I ask is that you inform me as to when the service will be and what will be done with his ashes."

"Ben wanted to be buried," I say. "He told me he wanted to be buried in sweatpants and a T-shirt so he'd be comfortable."

At the time, when he told me, I thought this was sweet. It didn't occur to me that I wouldn't be senile by the time he passed away, that it would be within months of that very conversation.

Her face scrunches itself around her eyes and mouth, and I can tell she's mad. The lines around her mouth become pronounced, and for the first time I can see evidence that she is an older woman. Does my mom have these lines? It's been so long since I've seen her, I don't know.

Maybe Susan doesn't realize what she's doing. Maybe she thinks she's strong enough to cut off her nose to spite her face here, to give me this funeral arranging as a punishment, but she's not. And she's already bothered.

"Everyone in our family has been cremated, Elsie. I never heard Ben say he wanted otherwise. Just tell me what is going to be done with the ashes." She looks down at the table and sighs, blowing air out of her mouth and onto her lap. "I should be going." She gets up from the table and leaves, not looking back at me, not acknowledging my existence.

I grab the binder and head toward the lobby, where Ana is

waiting patiently. She drives us home and I walk right up the front steps to my door. When I realize I've left my keys inside, I turn around and start crying. Ana soothes me as she pulls my spare key off her key ring and hands it to me. She hands it to me as if it will make everything okay, as if the only reason I'm crying is I can't get into the apartment.

JANUARY

I woke up the morning after meeting Ben to a text message from him.

"Rise and Shine, Elsie Porter. Can I take you to lunch?"

I jumped out of bed, shrieked like an idiot, and hopped in place compulsively for at least ten seconds. There was so much energy in my body I had no other way of getting it out.

"Sure. Where to?" I texted back. I stared at the phone until it lit up again.

"I'll come pick you up. Twelve thirty. What's your address?"

I sent him my address and then ran into the shower as if it was urgent. But it wasn't urgent. I was ready to go by 11:45 and I felt entirely pathetic about that. I put my hair up in a high ponytail and shimmied into my favorite jeans and most flattering T-shirt. Sitting around my house for forty-five minutes dressed and ready to go made me feel silly, so I decided to get out of my house and go for a walk. And in all of my glee and excitement, I locked myself out.

My heart started beating so fast I couldn't think straight. I'd left everything inside, my phone, my wallet. Ana had my spare key, but that wasn't going to do me much good without a phone to call her. I walked up and down the street looking for change so that I could ultimately call her on a pay phone, but it turns out, people don't really leave quarters on the ground. You'd think they would because quarters are small and sort of meaningless most of the time, but when you really need one, you realize just how ubiquitous they aren't. Then I decided to find a pay phone anyway since maybe I could rig it to call for free or there'd be a quarter stuck in the little change box. After scouring the neighborhood, I couldn't find a single one. Which left me no viable option I could think of other than breaking into my own apartment.

So that's what I tried to do.

I was on the second story of a duplex, but you could kind of get to the patio from the front stairs; so I walked up the stairs, climbed onto the railing, and tried to grab on to the rail of my patio. If I could get my hand on it and swing a leg around, I was pretty confident I could get onto the patio without much chance of falling to my death. From there, it was just a matter of crawling through the little doggie door in the screen that had been put there by the tenants before me. I had hated that damn doggie door until that very moment, when I was convinced it was my salvation.

As I continued my attempts to grab on to the patio rail, I realized that this might actually be an incredibly stupid plan, in which I was sure to be injured. If it was taking me this long to grab the rail in the first place, why on earth did I think I could easily swing my leg onto it once I reached it?

I made one final and valiant attempt to grab on before I got the cockamamie idea that it was best to go leg first. I was leg first when Ben found me.

"Elsie?"

"Ah!" I almost lost my footing, but I managed to get my leg back onto the steps, only slightly falling over in the process. I caught myself. "Hi, Ben!" I ran down the steps and hugged him. He was laughing.

"Whatcha doin' there?"

I was embarrassed, but somehow not in any threatening way.

"I was trying to break into my own apartment. I locked myself out without a phone or a wallet or anything."

"You don't have a spare key?"

I shook my head. "No. I did, at one point, but then it seemed smarter somehow for me to give it to my friend Ana, so she had it in case of emergency."

He laughed again. It didn't feel like he was laughing at me. Although, I think technically he was.

"Got it. Well, what do you want to do? You can call Ana from my phone now if you want. Or we can go get lunch and then you can call her when we get back?"

I started to answer, but he cut me off.

"Or, I'm also happy to break into your house for you. If you haven't given up on that idea yet."

"Do you think you can swing your leg over this rail onto that one?" I said. I was joking, but he wasn't.

"Absolutely, I can."

"No, stop. I was kidding. We should go get lunch."

Ben started taking off his jacket. "No, I insist you let me do this. It will look brave of me. I'll be considered a hero."

He walked closer to the rail and judged the distance. "That's actually quite far. You were going to try to do that?"

I nodded. "But I have little regard for my own safety," I said. "And a very bad sense of distance."

Ben nodded. "Okay. I'm going to jump this thing, but you have to make me a promise."

"Okay. You got it."

"If I fall and hurt myself, you won't let them call my emergency contact."

I laughed. "Why is that?"

"Because that's my mother and I blew her off for lunch today so I could see you."

"You blew off your mom for me?"

"See? It doesn't make you look very good either, letting me do it. So do we have an agreement?"

I nodded firmly. "You got it." I put out my hand to shake. He looked me in the eye and dramatically shook it, as a smile crept back onto his face.

"Here we go!" he said, and he just jumped it, like it was nothing, pulled his legs up and out, grabbed on to the patio rail, and swung his leg over.

"Okay! Now what?" he asked.

I was mortified to admit the next part of my plan. I hadn't considered how he would fare against the doggie door.

"Oh. Well. Hmm. I was just gonna . . . I was going to crawl in through the doggie door there," I said.

He looked behind him and down. Seeing it through his eyes, I realized it was even smaller than I'd thought.

"This doggie door?"

I nodded. "Yeah. I'm sorry! I should have mentioned that part first maybe."

"I cannot fit through that door, I don't think."

"Well, you could try to help me get over there," I said.

"Right. Or I could jump back over and we could call your friend Ana."

"Oh! That too." I had already forgotten that option.

"Okay, well. I might as well try once now that I'm here. Hold on."

He bent down and peeked in. His head fit in fine and he kept trying to push through. His shirt got caught in the door and was pulled up around his chest. I could see his stomach and the waistband of his underwear. I realized how physically attracted I was to him, how masculine he was. His abs looked solid and sturdy. His back was tanned and defined. His arms, flexed as he lifted himself through, looked strong and . . . capable. I had never before been attracted to the idea of being protected by someone, but Ben's body looked like it could protect me and I was surprised at the reaction it elicited in me. I wondered how I got here exactly. I barely knew this man and I was objectifying him as he broke into my apartment. He finally got both shoulders through and I could hear muffled tones of "I think, actually, I can do it!" and "Ow!" His butt disappeared and his legs slid inside. I walked around to my front door as he opened it, beaming, arms wide. I felt traditional and conventional, a damsel in distress saved by the strapping man. I thought that women who were attracted to that were stupid, but I also did, just for a moment, feel like Ben was my hero.

"Come on in!" he said. It was such a surreal reversal of how I imagined our lunch would start that I couldn't help but feel a bit exhilarated. I couldn't possibly predict what would happen next.

I stepped inside, and he looked around my apartment.

"This is a really nice apartment," he said. "What do you do?"

"Those two sentences in a row mean 'How much money do you make?'" I said. I wasn't being bitchy; at least I didn't feel like I was. I was teasing him, and he was teasing me back when he said, "Well, it's just hard for me to imagine that a woman could afford such a nice place on her own."

I gave him a look of mock indignation, and he gave me one right back.

"I'm a librarian."

"Got it," he said. "So you're doing well. This is good. I've been looking for a baby mama."

"A baby mama?"

"Sorry. Not a baby mama. What's it called when a woman pays for all the stuff for the man?"

"A sugar mama?"

He looked mildly embarrassed, and it was so charming to see. He had seemed so in control up until that moment, but seeing him even the slightest bit vulnerable was . . . intoxicating.

"Sugar mama. That's what I meant. What's a baby mama?"

"That's when you aren't married to the woman who is the mother of your child."

"Oh. No, I'm not looking for one of those."

"I don't know if anyone looks for one."

"Right. It just works out that way for them, I guess. People do look for sugar mamas, though, so watch out."

"I'll be on guard."

"Shall we go?" he said.

"Sure. Let me just grab my—"

"Keys."

"I was going to say wallet! But yes! Keys too. Can you imagine if I'd forgotten those again?" I grabbed them off the counter, and he took them delicately out of my hand.

"I'm going to be in charge of the keys," he said.

I nodded. "If you think that's best."

JUNE

I wake up to the ugly, disgusting world over and over again, each time closing my eyes tightly when I remember who I am. I finally get up around noon, not because I feel ready to face the day but because I can no longer face the night.

I walk into the living room. "Good morning," Ana says as she sees me. She's sitting on the couch and she grabs my hand. "What can I do?"

I look her in the eye and tell her the truth. "You can't do anything. Nothing you could possibly do would make this any easier."

"I know that," she says. "But there must be something I can do just to . . ." Her eyes are watering. I shake my head. I don't know what to say. I don't want anyone to make me feel better. I can't even think past this very moment in time. I can't think forward to this evening. I don't know how I'll make it through the next few minutes, let alone the next few hours. And yet, I don't know anything anyone can do to make those minutes easier. No matter how Ana acts, how hard she scrubs my house clean, how gentle she is with me, no matter if I take a shower, if I run down the street naked, if I drink every ounce of alcohol in the house, Ben is still not with me. Ben will never be with me again. I suddenly feel like I might not make it through the day, and if Ana isn't here to watch me, I don't know what I'll do.

I sit beside her. "You can stay here. Stay near me. It won't make it easier, but it will make me believe in myself more, I think. Just stay here." I'm too emotional to cry. My face and body are so consumed with dread, there's no room left to produce anything.

"You got it. I'm here. I'm here and I won't leave." She grabs me, her arm around my shoulders, squeezing me. "Maybe you should eat," she says.

"No, I'm not hungry," I say. I don't anticipate ever being hungry again. What does hunger even feel like? Who can remember?

"I know you're not hungry, but you still have to eat," she says. "If you could have anything in the whole world, what could you manage to get down? Don't worry about health or expense. Just if you could have anything."

Normally, if someone asked me that, I'd say I wanted a Big Mac. I always just want a Big Mac, the largest container of fries McDonald's has, and then a pile of Reese's peanut butter cups. My palate has never been trained to appreciate fine foods. I never crave sushi or a nice chardonnay. I crave fries and Coca-Cola. But not now. To me right now, a Big Mac might as well be a staple gun. That is how likely I am to eat it.

"No, nothing. I don't think I could keep anything down."

"Soup?"

"No, nothing."

"You have to eat at some point today. Promise me you'll eat at some point today?"

"Sure," I say. But I know I won't. I'm lying. I have no intention of carrying through on that promise. What's the point of a promise anyway? How can we expect people to stick to their word about anything when the world around us is so arbitrary, unreliable, and senseless?

"You need to go to the funeral home today," she says. "Want me to call them now?"

I hear her and I nod. That's all I can do. So it's what I do.

Ana picks up her phone and calls the funeral home. Apparently, I was supposed to call yesterday. I can hear the receptionist say something about "being behind." Ana doesn't dare pass this information along to me, but I can tell by her tone on the phone that they are giving her a hard time. Let them come at me. Just let them. I'd be happy to scream at a group of people profiting from tragedy.

Ana drives me to the office and parks the car in front, on the street. There is a parking garage underneath the building, but it's $2.50 every fifteen minutes and that's simply absurd. I refuse to encourage those overpriced assholes by using their service. This has nothing to do with my grief, by the way. I have a lifelong hatred of price gouging. It says on the sign that it's free with validation from Wright & Sons Funeral Home, but that seems awfully tacky on everyone's part. "Yes, we would like him embalmed. By the way, could you validate this for me?"

Ana finds a spot on the street easily enough. I check the passenger's side mirror and realize that my eyes are red and bloodshot. My cheeks are splotched with pink. My eyelashes are squashed together and shiny. Ana hands me her large, dark sunglasses. I put them on and step out of the car. As I catch a glimpse of myself in her mirror one last time, dressed for a meeting with large glasses on my face, I feel like Jackie Kennedy. Maybe there's a part of every woman that wants to be Jackie Kennedy, but they mean First Lady Jackie Kennedy or Jackie Kennedy Onassis. No one wants to relate to her like this.

Ana runs to the meter and goes to put quarters in but finds

herself empty. "Shit! I'm out of quarters. You head in and I'll take care of this," she says, heading back into the car.

"No," I say, reaching into my own wallet. "I have some." I put the change in the meter. "Besides, I don't think I can do this without you." Then I start crying again, blubbering, the tears falling down my face, only visible once they've made their way past the huge lenses.

JANUARY

When we got in Ben's car, he asked if I was up for an adventure and I told him that I was.

"No, I mean, a true adventure."

"I'm ready!"

"What if this adventure takes us on a road trip to a restaurant over an hour away?"

"As long as you're driving, it's fine by me," I said. "Although, I'm confused about what could possibly require us to drive an hour out of the way."

"Oh, you just leave that to me," he said, and he started the car.

"You're being very cryptic," I said. He ignored me. He reached over and turned on his radio. "You're in charge of music and possibly navigation if it comes to that."

"Fine by me," I said, as I immediately turned the station to NPR. As the low, monotonous voices started to fill the air, Ben shook his head. "You're one of those?" he said, smiling.

"I'm one of those," I said, owning it and not apologizing.

"I should have known. Pretty girl like you had to have some sort of flaw."

"You don't like talk radio?"

"I like it, I guess. I mean, I like it the way I like doctors' appointments. They serve a purpose but they aren't much fun."

I laughed, and he looked at me. He looked for just a little too long to be safe.

"Hey! Eyes on the road, Casanova!" I said. Casanova? Who was I? My dad?

Ben immediately turned back and focused on what was in front of us. "Sorry!" he said. "Safety first."

By the time we hit the freeway, he had turned off the radio.

"That's enough traffic updates for me," he said. "We will just have to entertain ourselves the old-fashioned way."

"Old-fashioned way?"

"Conversation."

"Ah, right. Conversation."

"Let's start with the basics: How long have you lived in L.A.?"

"Five years. I moved right after college. You?"

"Nine years. I moved here to go to college. Looks like we graduated the same year. Where did you go to school?"

"Oh," I said. "Ithaca. My parents both went to Cornell and made me take a tour, but when I got there, Ithaca seemed a better fit. I was originally premed, but that lasted about two months before I realized I had absolutely no desire to be a doctor."

"Why did you think you wanted to be a doctor?" We were speeding up the freeway at this point. The driving was taking up less of his attention.

"Both of my parents are doctors. My mother is the chief of staff at the hospital in my hometown, and my dad is a neurosurgeon there."

"A neurosurgeon? That's intimidating," Ben added.

"He's an intimidating guy. My mom's not easy either. They were not happy when I changed my major."

"Oh, that kind of family? The pressuring kind? Overachievers?"

"They are definitely overachievers. The thing is, I'm just not like that. I'm a work-to-live not a live-to-work type of person. I like to put in my forty hours and then go have my life."

"But that doesn't sit well with them?"

I shrugged. "They believe that life is work. It's not about joy. It's not about laughter. It's not about love, really, I don't think, for them. It's about work. I don't think my dad likes saving lives as much as he likes being at the top of a field that is constantly growing and changing. I think it's about progress for them. Library science isn't exactly cutting edge. But I mean, there isn't much they can do. My parents weren't really very engaged parents, you know? So, I think when I changed my major it was, like, this moment of . . . It was a break for all of us. They no longer needed to pretend that they understood me. I no longer needed to pretend I wanted what they had."

I hadn't ever told anyone my real feelings about that before. But I didn't see any reason to tell Ben anything but the entire truth. I was somewhat embarrassed after I said it all. I realized just how vulnerable that was. I turned and looked out my window. The traffic in the opposite direction was relentless, and yet, we were flying through town.

"That's really sad," he said.

"It is and it isn't. My parents and I aren't close. But they are happy in their way and I am happy in mine. I think that's what matters."

He nodded. "You're absolutely right. Smart and right."

I laughed. "How about you? How are your parents?"

Ben blew air out of his chest but kept his eyes forward and on the road. He spoke somberly.

"My father passed away three years ago."

"Oh, my. I'm so sorry to hear that."

"Thanks." He looked at me briefly and then returned his

eyes to the road. "He died of cancer and it was a long battle so we all knew it was coming; we were prepared for it."

"I don't know if that's good or bad."

Ben let out a brief puff of air. "I don't either. Anyway, my mom is doing well. As well as you can when you've lost the person you love, you know?"

"I can't even imagine."

"No, I can't either. I've lost a father and I know how hard that can be, but I can't even imagine losing your best friend, your soul mate. I worry about her, although she insists she's okay."

"I'm sure you can't help but worry. Do you have any brothers or sisters?" I asked.

Ben shook his head. "You?"

"No, sir." I rarely met other only children. It was nice to hear that Ben was one. When I would tell people I was an only child, I felt like I was either being pitied for not having had siblings or being judged as petulant even if I hadn't proven to be.

"Awesome! Two only children! I knew I liked you." He high-fived me sloppily as he kept one hand on the wheel.

"Do I get any hints about where we are going yet?" I asked, as he merged from one freeway onto the next.

"It's Mexican" was all I could get out of him.

After two games of Twenty Questions and one game of I Spy, we finally made it to our destination. It was a shack. Quite literally. It was a shack in the middle of the road called Cactus Tacos. I was underwhelmed, but Ben's face lit up.

"We're here!" he said as he flicked off his seat belt and opened his car door. I gathered my things, and he came around to my side. He opened the door for me before I could open it for myself.

"Why, thank you!" I said over the dinging of his car, reminding us that the door needed to be closed.

"Certainly."

I crawled out and stood next to him.

"So this is the place, huh?" I said. He shut the door behind me and the dinging relented.

"I know it doesn't look like much. But you said you were up for an adventure and these are honestly the best tacos I've ever had in my life. Do you like *horchata*?"

"What is *horchata*?"

"It's rice milk with cinnamon. Just—trust me. You gotta try one." As we walked toward the taco stand, he put his hand on the small of my back, guiding me ever so gently. It felt so comforting and so natural that it made me want to turn around into his arms. It made me want to touch more of him with more of me. Instead, I stood and stared at the menu.

"If it's okay," Ben said, moving his hand up my back and now onto my shoulder, "I'll order for you. I fully respect your right to order for yourself. It's just that I've been here many, many times and I know everything on this menu."

"Be my guest," I said.

"Do you like chicken, steak, pork?"

"No pork," I said.

"*No pork?*" Ben said, incredulous. "I'm kidding. I don't like pork either. All right!" He rubbed his hands together eagerly.

"*Perdón?*" he said through the window to the man behind the counter. "*Queria cuatro tacos tinga de pollo y cuatro tacos carne asada, por favor? Queso extra en todos. Ah, y dos horchatas, por favor.*"

The man showed him the size of the *horchatas* with a look that said, "Are you sure you want two of these?" and Ben nodded. "*Sí, sí, lo sé. Dos. Por favor.*"

I don't know what it was exactly that made Ben seem so irresistible at that moment. I don't know if it was because he seemed so knowledgeable about something I knew nothing about (Spanish), or whether it was because any time a man spoke another language it was inherently sexy to me (because that was also true). I don't know. I just know that as I stood there, unable to understand what was being communicated around me, I thought Ben Ross was the sexiest man I'd ever seen. He was so secure in himself, so sure that this would all turn out okay. That's what it was. It was the confidence. He spoke Spanish to the man at the taco stand like it never occurred to him he might sound like a complete idiot. And that was exactly why he did not sound like a complete idiot.

"Wow," I said, as he handed me my *horchata*. "That's impressive."

"I swear that's about the extent of my knowledge," he said as he unwrapped a straw and put it in my drink. "But I'd be lying if I said I wasn't hoping to impress you."

"Well, so far, so good." I took a sip of the drink. It was sweet and cold, creamy and yet easy to drink in big gulps. "Wow, this is great too."

Ben smiled as he took a sip of his own. "I'm doing okay?" he asked.

"You're doing great," I told him. I was overwhelmed, to be honest. It had been so long since I'd had a crush on someone I'd forgotten how exciting it makes everything you do.

When our tacos were ready, Ben grabbed them from the window. They came stuffed in red and white checkered cartons. He grabbed all of them and balanced them over his forearms and in his hands.

There were no places to sit at Cactus Tacos, and so Ben suggested we sit on the hood of his car.

"These tacos look messy. I'll spill *pico de gallo* all over your car."

"It's a ten-year-old Honda. I'm not exactly precious about it."

"Fine. But I feel like you should know that I'm very clumsy and messy."

"And you forget your keys a lot."

"Well, I forget everything a lot."

"So far, it's all good by me."

We sat on his hood and we talked about our jobs and if we liked living in Los Angeles, and sure enough, I dripped taco grease onto his bumper. Ben just smiled at me. Ana called me as I was feebly attempting to clean it up and I put her through to voice mail. Ben and I talked long after the tacos were gone.

Eventually, Ben asked me if I wanted dessert.

"You have somewhere else in mind?" I asked.

"No," he said. "I thought it would be lady's choice."

"Oh," I said. I was somewhat at a loss as to what to suggest. I had no idea where we were, no idea what was around us. "Actually," I said. "Are you up for another adventure?"

"Absolutely!" he said as he hopped off the hood of the car. He put out his hand for me to grab. "Where to?"

"East L.A.?" I asked, gently. While I wasn't sure where we were, I knew we were at least an hour from my place, and East L.A. was at least thirty minutes past my apartment in the opposite direction.

"East L.A. it is, my fair maiden." He helped me off the car and opened my door for me.

"Such a gentleman," I pronounced as I positioned myself to sit down.

"Wait," he said. He grabbed me around the waist and pulled me to him. "Is this okay?"

My face was up against his. I could smell his breath. It

smelled like cilantro and onions. It smelled sweet, somehow. My heart started beating faster.

"Yeah," I said. "This is okay."

"I want to kiss you," he said. "But I want to make sure you won't be embarrassed in front of the taco stand man."

I smiled at him and looked over his shoulder. The taco stand man was staring. I was, in fact, slightly embarrassed. But it was just enough to make the situation thrilling and not enough to ruin it.

"Go for it," I said to him. He did.

As he kissed me against the car, my body pushed in toward him. My arms made their way into the crooks on either side of his neck and my hands grazed the stubble on the back of his head at the hairline. His hair felt soft and oily in my hands. I felt his chest and torso push me further against the car.

He pulled away, and I looked sheepishly at the man at the taco stand. Still staring. Ben caught my eye and looked back. The taco stand man turned away, and Ben started to laugh, conspiratorially.

"We should get out of here," I said.

"I told you you'd be embarrassed," he said as he ran around to the driver's side.

Once we'd made our way back onto the freeway, I texted Ana, letting her know that I'd call her tomorrow. She texted back asking what on earth I was doing that I couldn't talk to her. I told her the truth.

"I'm on a daylong date. It's going really well so I'll call you tomorrow."

Ana tried to call me after that and I put her through to voice mail again. I realized that me being on a date probably seemed a bit odd to her. I had just seen her yesterday morning for breakfast with no plans to date anyone, let alone date them all day.

Ben and I hit traffic. The stop and go of the freeway was made even more maddening by the sweat and exhaust from all of the cars. We had been stuck on the same stretch of road for twenty minutes when Ben asked a question I had been avoiding.

"When does this mystery place close?" he asked.

"Eh . . ." I said, embarrassed to tell him we were almost certainly not going to make it.

"It's soon, isn't it?" he asked.

"It's soon. It closes at six. We've only got about a half hour. We don't need to go. I can take you some other time."

It just slipped out, the "some other time." I didn't mean to make it clear that I wanted to see him again. I mean, in my brain I assumed we would be seeing each other again, but I also wanted to maintain some sense of mystery about the whole thing. I didn't want to show my cards that soon. I turned a little red.

Ben smiled. He knew what I'd done and decided not to press it. He just took the compliment and let it alone. "Still," he said. "I want you to get whatever it is."

"Gelato," I said.

"Gelato?" he said, somewhat disbelieving. "We're racing across town for gelato?"

I hit him in the chest with my hand. "Hey! You said you wanted to do something. It's good gelato!"

"I'm just teasing you. I love gelato. Come hell or high water I'm getting you that goddamn gelato."

As traffic started to move slightly, he veered the car onto the shoulder, flew past the rest of the cars, and got in line to get off the freeway.

"Wow," I said. "Way to take control."

"Total asshole move," he said. "But this situation is dire."

He sped through back roads and dangerously ran yellow lights. He cut a few people off and honked at them as he drove by to apologize. I directed him under unfamiliar overpasses, found unheard-of drives and lanes for him to traverse, and when we finally parked the car in front of Scoops Gelato Shop, it was 6:01 p.m. Ben ran to the door just as they were locking it.

He pounded on it politely. "Please," he said, "just . . . can you open the door?"

A young Korean girl came to the door and pointed to the Closed sign. She shook her head.

Ben put his hands together in a prayer position, and she shrugged at him.

"Elsie, do me a favor, would you?"

"Hmm?" I said. I was hanging further back on the sidewalk.

"Would you turn around?"

"Turn around?"

"I'm about to beg on my knees and I don't want you to see it. I want you to think of me as a strong, virile, confident man."

I laughed, and he continued to look at me blankly.

"Oh my God, you're serious," I said, as I laughed and resigned myself to turning around.

I looked out onto the main street in the distance. I watched cars stop at red lights and cyclists speed by them. I saw a couple walking down the street with a baby stroller. Soon, I heard the jingle of a door opening and I started to turn around.

"Wait!" I heard Ben say. "Don't move yet," and so I didn't.

Two minutes later, the door jingled again and Ben came around in front of me. In his hands were two cups of gelato, both a light brown with brightly colored spoons sticking out of them.

"How did you do that?" I asked, taking one of them from him.

Ben smiled. "I have my ways."

"Seriously," I said.

"Seriously? I bribed her."

"You bribed her?" I asked, shocked. I had never known anyone to bribe someone before.

"Well, I said, 'If you can give me two cups of whatever flavor you have left, I'll give you twenty bucks extra.' So if that's a bribe, then yes, I bribed her."

"Yeah, I'd say that's a bribe."

"Somewhat corrupt," he said to me. "I hope you can forgive me."

I stared at him for a moment. "Forgive you? Are you kidding? No one has ever bribed anyone for me before!" I said.

Ben laughed. "Now you're just making fun of me."

"No," I said. "I'm entirely serious. I think it's hugely flattering."

"Oh," he said, smiling. He laughed. "Awesome." Then he took a bite of his gelato and immediately grimaced. "It's coffee," he said, as he ran to the trash can on the sidewalk and spit it out.

"You don't like coffee?"

"Coffee is like doctors' visits and NPR to me," he said.

I took his cup from his hand and held it in the palm of mine while I ate from the other. "More for me, then," I said.

We got back in his car, and neither one of us knew quite what to do next.

"The day doesn't have to end," I said. "Does it?"

"I'm glad you said that," Ben responded. "Where to next?"

"Well, I don't know," I said. "I'm not really hungry . . ."

"What if we go back to your place?" he suggested. "I promise I won't get handsy."

I let it sit in the air for a minute. "What's wrong with handsy?" I teased him. He didn't even say anything; he just threw the car in reverse and started speeding down the street.

When we got back to my apartment, Ben took my keys out of his pocket. We walked up the stairs to my door, but halfway up the stairs, Ben realized he'd forgotten something. He quickly ran back down to his car and put money in the parking meter. Then, he flashed back up the stairs to meet me and unlocked my door. Once inside, he gingerly placed the keys on my table by the door.

"They're right here when you need them," he said. "Is that a good place to remember them?"

"That's fine. Do you want anything to drink?"

"Oh, sure. What do you have?"

"Water. I should have said, 'Do you want any water?'"

Ben laughed and sat on the couch. I grabbed two glasses and went to the refrigerator to fill them, which is when I saw the big bottle of champagne sitting there, ice cold and left over from New Year's Eve.

"I have champagne!" I said and grabbed it out of the fridge. I walked to the living room and held it up in front of Ben. "Bubbly?"

He laughed. "Yeah! Let's break open the bubbly."

We ran to the kitchen and got wineglasses. I attempted to open the bottle and failed, so Ben stepped in and popped it open. The champagne sprayed all over our faces, but neither one of us much cared. He poured our glasses, and we sat down on the couch.

It was awkward for a minute. We were stuck in silence. I

drank from my glass for a bit too long, staring at the golden bubbles. Why was it awkward now? I wondered. I wasn't sure. I stood up for a minute and felt the whoosh of the alcohol to my head.

"I'll be right back," I said. "I'm just going to go . . ." What? What was I going to go do? I wasn't sure.

Ben grabbed my hand and looked at me. He stared into my eyes. His eyes looked to be pleading with me. Just like that, I threw myself onto his lap, straddling his waist. I kissed him. My arms wandered down onto his shoulders. His hands grabbed my hips. I could feel them through my jeans. He pulled me tight as he kissed me, his arms running up my back and into my hair. It felt like he was desperate to kiss me. As we moved our heads and hands in sync, my body started to ache where it wasn't being touched.

"I like you," he said to me, breathlessly.

I laughed. "I can see that," I said.

"No," he said, pulling his face away from mine for a moment, looking at me like I was important. "I like you."

Boys had told me they liked me before. They had said it in eighth grade and in high school. They had said it drunk at parties. One had said it in a college cafeteria. Some of them looked down at the ground when they mumbled it. Some of them stuttered. Each time I had told them I liked them back. And I realized now that each time I had been lying.

No man had ever made me feel this admired before, nor had I admired someone back this much before. What had Ben done in the past few hours to make me care so much? I didn't know. All I knew was that when he said that to me, I knew that he meant it. And when I heard it come out of his mouth, it felt like I'd been waiting to hear it my entire life.

"I like you too," I said. I kissed him again and he grabbed me. He put his hands around my waist and he moved me toward him, closing what little gap there was between us. He kissed my ears and jawline, sending goose bumps up the back of my neck, for what felt like hours. I finally had to stand up. There was a cramp in my hip.

When I looked at the clock, it was after 8:00 p.m.

"Wow," I said. "This is . . . that was . . . a long time."

"Are you hungry?" he asked me.

"Yeah." I nodded, realizing that I was hungry. "Are you?"

"Yeah. What should we do? Go out? Cook here? Order in?"

"Well, pizza is out. We had that last night." We hadn't eaten it together, but I knew the way I said it implied that we had. I liked hearing myself say it. I liked that I sounded like his girlfriend at that moment—which made me feel a little insane. I was ready to get monogrammed towels for us and I barely knew him.

"Right. So my vote is order Chinese or cook here, depending on what you have." He gestured toward the kitchen. "Can I look?"

I stood up and showed him the way. "Be my guest!"

We walked into the kitchen and stood in front of the refrigerator. He stood behind me, his arms around my torso, his face in my neck. I showed him what I had, and it was sparse, although had either of us been a decent cook, I'm sure we could have come up with something.

"Well, that settles it," he said. "Where's the Chinese food menu?"

I laughed and fished it out of the drawer. He looked at the menu for only a minute. "How about we split the kung pao chicken, a bowl of wonton soup, beef chow mein, and white rice?"

"Make it brown rice and you're on," I said.

"Because this is a first date, I'm going to say okay, but all subsequent dates, absolutely not. Brown rice tastes like cardboard and I simply cannot meet you halfway on that in the future."

I nodded. "I understand. We could get two different orders of rice."

"Maybe when the romance is gone we can do that, but not tonight." He turned in to the phone. "Yes, hi. I'd like to get an order of kung pao chicken, an order of beef chow mein, and wonton soup." He paused for a moment. "No. We'd like brown rice, please." He stuck out his tongue at me, and then he gave my address, his telephone number, and hung up.

When the food came, we ate it. Ana called a few more times to try to find me. Ben made me laugh over and over; he made me cackle and hiss. He made my abdomen hurt. We kissed and we teased each other; we wrestled with the remote. When it got late enough that it was do-or-die time, I spared us both any awkward misinterpretations and said, "I want you to spend the night but I'm not going to have sex with you."

"How do you know I want to have sex with you? Maybe I just want to be friends," he said. "Ever consider that?" I didn't need to respond. "Fine. So I do want to have sex with you, but I'll keep my hands to myself."

Before meeting him in my bedroom, I thought carefully and consciously of what to wear to bed. We weren't going to have sex, so lingerie or sleeping naked was clearly out of the question. And yet, it wasn't an asexual activity. I still wanted to be sexy. I settled on a pair of very small boxer shorts and a tank top. I checked myself out in the mirror before I left the bathroom, and I had to admit, I looked accidentally sexy when it was anything but an accident.

I walked into my room to find him already under my covers. His shirt was off but the blanket was covering him. I crawled in next to him and put my head on his chest. He bent his head down to kiss me and then turned to see where the light switch was.

"Oh," I said. "Check this out." I clapped loudly twice and the lights went out. "I got it as a party favor years ago." I never used the Clapper anymore. I'd honestly almost forgotten that I'd plugged it in. Ben was floored.

"You are the coolest person in the world. Just hands down. The coolest," he said.

It was pitch dark as our eyes slowly adjusted, and then there was a buzz and small flash of light. It was my phone.

"He's STILL THERE?" Ana had texted.

I turned off my phone.

"Ana, I presume," Ben said, and I confirmed. "She must be wondering who the hell I am."

"She'll know soon enough," I said. He put his finger under my chin and lifted my head toward his. I kissed him. Then I kissed him again. I kissed him harder. Within seconds our hands, arms, and pieces of clothing went flying. His skin felt warm and soft, but his body felt sturdy.

"Oh!" I said. "The parking meter. Did you put enough money in? What if you get a ticket?"

He pulled me back to him. "I'll take the ticket," he said. "I don't want to stop touching you."

As we rolled around each other, I somehow kept to my word. I did not sleep with him that night. I wanted to. It was difficult not to. Both of our bodies pleaded with me to change my mind, but I didn't. I'm not sure how I didn't. But I didn't.

I don't remember when I fell asleep, but I do remember Ben whispering, "I'm not sure if you're still awake, but . . . thank you, Elsie. This is the first time I've been too excited to go to sleep since I was a kid."

I tried to keep my eyes shut, but my mouth couldn't help but smile wide when I heard him.

"I can see you smiling," he whispered, half laughing. I didn't open my eyes, teasing him.

"Okay," he said, pulling me closer to him. "Two can play at that game."

When he left for work the next morning, I saw him take the ticket off his windshield and laugh.

JUNE

The building is cold. The air is crisp and almost sharp. I wonder if they keep it so cold because there are dead bodies here. Then I remember that Ben's body must be here. My husband is now a dead body. I used to find dead things repulsive and now my husband is one of them.

Ana and I are called into the office of Mr. Richard Pavlik. He is a tall, thin man with a face that's generic except for the fact that it has a huge mustache across it. He looks to be about sixty.

It's stuffy in Mr. Pavlik's office. I have to imagine that people are here during the worst times of their lives, so why Mr. Pavlik can't just take the extra step and make it comfortable, I'll never know. Even these chairs are terrible. They're low to the ground and oddly sunken in. My center of gravity is basically at my knees.

I try to sit forward in the chair and listen to him drone on and on about the trivial parts of my husband's death, but my back starts to hurt and I sit back in the chair. As I do, I worry the angle is unbecoming of a lady. It looks careless and comfortable, which I am not. I am neither of those things. I sit back up, rest my hands on my knees, and grin and bear it. That is pretty much my plan for the rest of my life.

"Mr. Pavlik, with all due respect," I interrupt him. "Ben did not want to be cremated. He wanted to be buried."

"Oh," he says, looking down at the pages in front of him. "Mrs. Ross indicated a cremation."

"I'm Mrs. Ross," I say.

"I'm sorry, I meant the senior Mrs. Ross." He scrunches his face slightly. "Anyway, Elsie," he says. I can't help but feel rejected slightly. I am not Mrs. Ross to him and he does not know my maiden name, so he's jumped right to first names. "In this case, Mrs. Ross is the next of kin."

"No, Richard," I say sternly. If he can take away my last name, I can take away his. "I am the next of kin. I am Ben's wife."

"I don't mean to argue otherwise, Elsie. I simply have no record of that."

"So you're saying that because I don't have a marriage certificate yet, I am not next of kin?"

Richard Pavlik shakes his head. "In situations like this, where there is a question of who is the next of kin, I have to go by official documents. I don't have anyone else close to Ben who can confirm that you two were married, and when I looked into marital records, there was no evidence of it. I hope you understand I'm in a difficult spot."

Ana sits forward in her chair and moves her hand into a fist on Richard's desk.

"I hope you understand that Elsie just got married and lost her husband within the same ten days, and instead of being on her honeymoon on some far-off private beach she's sitting here with you implying to her grieving face that she's not married at all."

"I'm sorry, Ms. . . ." Richard is uncomfortable and doesn't remember Ana's last name.

"Romano," she says, angrily.

"Ms. Romano. I really don't mean to make this uncomfortable or unpleasant for anyone. I am so sorry for your loss. All I ask is that you have a conversation with Mrs. Ross about this, because legally, I have to take my orders from her. Again, I am truly sorry for your loss."

"Let's just move on. I'll talk to Susan about the cremation later. What else do I need to go over today?" I say.

"Well, Elsie. Everything hinges on what is to be done with the body."

Don't call it the body, you asshole. That's my husband. That's the body that held me when I cried, the body that grabbed my left hand as it drove us to the movies. That's the body that made me feel alive, made me feel crazy, made me cry and shake with joy. It's lifeless now, but that doesn't mean I've given up on it.

"Fine, Richard. I'll talk to Susan and call you this afternoon."

Richard gathers up the papers on his desk and stands to see us out. He grabs his card and hands it to me. When I don't take it, he offers it to Ana, and she takes it gracefully, tucking it into her back pocket.

"Thank you so much for your time," he says as he opens the door for us.

"Fu—" I start to say to him as I am walking out the door. I plan on slamming it when I'm done. But Ana interrupts me and squeezes my hand gently to let me know I need to cool it. She takes over.

"Thank you, Richard. We will be in touch soon. In the meantime, please get back on the phone with the marital records people and sort this out," she says.

She shuts the door behind her and smiles at me. The circumstances aren't funny, but it *is* kind of funny that I almost told that man to fuck off. For a moment, I think we might both actually laugh—something I haven't done in days. But the moment passes and I don't have it in me to push the air out and smile.

"Are we going to talk to Susan?" Ana says as we are heading to the car.

"Yeah," I say. "I guess we are." At least this makes me feel like I have a purpose, however small. I have to protect Ben's wishes. I have to protect the body that did so much to protect me.

JANUARY

A t work the next day, my thoughts oscillated between focusing on tasks at hand and daydreaming. I had to promise Ana I'd drive over to her place after work to explain my absence, and I kept replaying in my head how I was going to describe him. It was always her talking to me about men and me listening. Now that I knew it would be me talking and her listening, I almost felt like I needed to practice.

I was physically present but mentally absent when Mr. Callahan cornered me. "Elsie?" he said, as he approached the counter.

Mr. Callahan was almost ninety years old. He wore polyester trousers every day in either gray or khaki. He wore a button-up shirt in some sort of plaid pattern with a cream-colored Members Only jacket to cover it.

Mr. Callahan kept tissues in his pants pockets. He kept ChapStick in his jacket pocket, and he always said "Bless you" whenever anyone within a fifty-foot radius sneezed. He came to the library almost every day, coming and going, sometimes multiple times a day. Some days, he would read magazines and newspapers in the back room until lunchtime, when he would check out a book to take home to his wife. Other days, he would come in the late afternoon to return a book and pick up a black-and-white movie on VHS or maybe some sort of opera I had never heard of on CD.

He was a man of culture, a man of great kindness and personality. He was a man devoted to his wife, a wife we at the library never met but heard everything about. He was also very old, and I sometimes feared he was on his last legs.

"Yes, Mr. Callahan?" I turned to face him and rested my elbows on the cold counter.

"What is this?" Mr. Callahan slid a bookmark in front of me. It was one of our digital library bookmarks. We had put them all over the library a week earlier to try to call attention to the digital materials we had. There was a big debate in the library about starting this initiative. We didn't have much say, to tell the truth, as we were guided by the Los Angeles Public Library system, but still, some people thought we should be doing more, some people thought we should be preserving the past. I have to say I was leaning toward preserving the past. I loved holding books in my hands. I loved smelling their pages.

"That is a bookmark about our digital library."

"What?" he said to me, asking politely but bemused.

"It's a website we have that you can go to and download materials instead of coming to the library to get them."

He nodded, recognizing what I was saying. "Oh, like if I wanted an i-book."

"An e-book, right," I said. I didn't mean to correct him.

"Wait, is it *e* or *i*?"

"*E.*"

"Oh, for heaven's sake. This whole time I've been thinking my granddaughter, Lucia, was saying iPad."

"No," I said. "She was. You read an e-book on an iPad."

Mr. Callahan started laughing. "Listen to yourself," he said, smiling. "You sound a little ridiculous."

I laughed with him. "Nevertheless," I said. "That's what it's called."

"All right, so if I get an iPad, I can read an e-book on it that I download from the library." He emphasized *iPad*, *e-book*, and *download* as if they were made-up words and I was a toddler.

"Right," I said. "That's actually quite impressive how quick you got that."

"Oh, please. I'll forget tomorrow." He touched my hand and patted it as if to say good-bye. "Anyway, it sounds like I don't want anything to do with it. Too complicated for me. I much prefer the real thing."

"Me too," I said. "But I don't know how much longer the real thing will be around."

"Long enough for me," he said, and I was struck by the sadness of realizing your own mortality. He didn't seem sad, and yet, I still felt sad for him.

My boss, Lyle, came by and told Mr. Callahan we were closing.

"Okay, okay! I'll leave," he joked, putting his hands up in surrender. I watched him walk out the door, and then I tidied up and sped away to Ana's house.

W*hat* the hell happened?! *Start* at the beginning. Who *is* this guy?" Ana said to me. I was lying on her couch.

"Ana, I don't even know how to explain it."

She sat down on the ottoman next to me. "Try."

"On Saturday night I ordered a pizza—"

"Oh my God! *He's a delivery guy?* Elsie!"

"What? No, he's not a delivery guy. He's a graphic designer. That's not . . . Just listen. I ordered a pizza but they said it would take too long to get there. So I went down to pick it up and there was this guy waiting too. That was him. That was Ben."

"Ben is the guy?"

"Ben is the guy. So I notice him, he's really cute, like too cute for me cute, you know? But he starts talking to me and it's, like, when he starts talking I just . . . Anyway, I gave him my number; he called me yesterday morning and picked me up for lunch at twelve thirty. It was the best date I've ever had. I mean, it was one of the best *days* I've ever had. He says all the right things and he's so sincere and cute and . . ."

"Sexy? Is he sexy?"

"Oh my *God* is he sexy. I can't describe it, but when I'm with him, it's like I'm with myself. I'm not worried about anything, I feel like I can say whatever I'm thinking and it won't freak him out. I'm nervous."

"Why are you nervous? This sounds *amazing*."

"It is, but this is going so fast."

"Maybe he's the one. Maybe that's why it's going so fast. Because it's right."

I was hoping she would say this. I didn't want to have to say it myself, because it seemed absurd. "No. Do you think?"

Ana shrugged. "Who knows? It could be! I want to meet this guy!"

"He's really great. I'm just . . . What if I'm getting ahead of myself? He says I'm perfect for him and he likes me and it doesn't feel like bullshit but . . . what if it's all . . ."

"An act?"

"Yeah. What if I'm being played?"

"I mean . . . being played how exactly? Did you sleep with him yet?"

I shook my head. "No, he just slept over and we slept next to each other."

"That sounds pretty sincere."

"Right, but what if he's like . . . a con man or something."

"You watch too much television."

"I know I do, but *what* if he's a con man? He's just like this really sexy, really charming, perfect man who figures out your wildest fantasies of being swept off your feet by a man who loves pizza and bribes gelato workers and is an only child and then *boom*. My money is gone."

"You don't even have very much money."

"Right, that's why I need all that I have."

"No, Elsie. I mean if he's that good of a con man, he'd target a rich person."

"Oh."

"You know what I think?" Ana moved toward me and sat so

my head was in her lap. "I think you've got a good thing going, and you're making a mountain out of a molehill. So what, it's moving fast? Just chill out and enjoy it."

"Well . . . okay . . . What if there is a limited amount of swooning in a relationship and if you use it all up too fast, then it disappears?"

Ana looked at me like I had three heads. "You're starting to stress me out. Give it a rest and stop trying to poke holes in a good thing."

I thought about this for a moment and decided she was probably right. I was freaking out about nothing at all. I did the best I could to put it out of my head.

"You good?" Ana asked me, and I nodded.

"I'm good. I'm gonna chill."

"Good," she said. "Because we need to talk about me."

I lifted my head, finally remembering the normal dynamic of this relationship and feeling much more comfortable about it. "Oh? What about?"

"Jim!" Ana could scarcely believe Jim wasn't on the forefront of my mind.

"Right! How did it go the other night?"

"I slept with him," Ana said, sounding disappointed in the act itself. "Totally not worth it. I don't know what I was thinking. I don't even like him. I think saying I wasn't going to sleep with someone made me want to sleep with someone even if I didn't really want to sleep with him. Does that make sense?"

I nodded again. Just then my phone rang. It was Ben. I showed the ringing phone to Ana, who excused herself from her own couch and I answered.

He was on his way home from work and asked if I was free.

"If you don't have plans, I could come over and see you

again tonight. I make no assumptions about sleeping over but I should be honest and tell you it's a goal of mine."

I laughed. "That sounds good. When were you thinking?"

"Have you eaten dinner yet? I could pick you up and take you out. Are you free now?"

"Oh, okay. I haven't eaten. Um . . . now? I don't know." I knew full well now was fine. I was just a little worried about looking too available, as if I had left my evening open for just this purpose. That is, in fact, exactly what I had done, but you don't ever want to admit that. "I can make that work," I said. "Want to meet me at my place in twenty minutes?"

"Yes, ma'am. I do. I'll see you then. Wear something fancy. I'm taking your ass someplace special."

"Fancy? Okay, I need thirty minutes then."

"I'll give you twenty, but I'll wait patiently in your living room for the other ten, how's that?"

I laughed. "It's a deal."

I hung up the phone and said good-bye to Ana.

"*Call me* tomorrow morning, please," she said. "And I'm saying tomorrow morning because I'm trying to be understanding, but if you get a moment to run to the bathroom and call me, I'll be waiting by the phone."

"You are my favorite person of all time," I said as I kissed her cheek.

"Not for long, I'm not," she said, and because she is a wonderful friend, there wasn't a trace of resentment. She just saw the writing on the wall.

When I got home, I ran into the bathroom. I wanted to at least get makeup on before he came in the door. I have always lived by the rule that your clothes can be a mess but if your face looks good, no one will notice. I probably believe this because I'd like to lose ten pounds but I think my face is cute. Girls that work out all day and have huge boobs but boring faces probably think the face doesn't matter if your boobs are taken care of.

Just as I had taken off my work clothes and put on a pair of black tights, the doorbell rang. I threw on a long shirt and opened the door.

"Wow," he said when he came in. He smelled great and he looked great. He was wearing dark jeans and a black button-up shirt. It was nothing special, but it somehow made him look exceptional. He leaned in to kiss me and did so gently, so as not to ruin my lipstick.

"Give me seven more minutes," I said, rushing into my room.

"You got it. I'll be on the couch here waiting patiently."

I shut my bedroom door and took off my shirt. I put on a short black sleeveless dress and black pumps, and then I added a gauzy gray cardigan to make it seem a bit less fancy. I looked in the mirror and felt that I looked a little too . . . matronly. So I pulled off the tights, put the heels back on, and walked out there.

"I think I'm under seven minutes," I said as he stood up eagerly.

"Wow."

I held out my arms in display. "Good enough for this mystery dinner?"

"You look perfect. What happened to the tights?"

"Oh." I suddenly felt whorish. "Should I put them back on?"

He shook his head. "No, not at all. Your . . . your legs look great, is all. I haven't seen you in high heels before." He came over and kissed me on the temple. It felt familiar and loving.

"Well, you've only known me since Saturday," I said as I

grabbed my purse. I took special care to make certain my keys were in there. I wasn't sure what state we would be in when we got back here, but I didn't want to create any kinks in the plan.

"Wow. You're right. It does not feel like that though. Anyway, it's not important. What is important is that you look fucking hot. Are you going to be warm enough? Fuck it. I don't care. Don't put anything else on over this."

"Wait!" I said, turning back in to the apartment as he was heading toward the door.

"Should I grab something? I hate being cold."

"If you get cold, I'll give you my jacket."

"But what if my legs are cold?"

"I'll put the jacket around your legs. Now get that beautiful ass in my car! Let's go!"

I ran right down the stairs into his front seat.

It was a warm night and we drove across town with the windows down. Once we got on the freeway, the wind from the windows made it too loud to talk so I put my head on his shoulder and closed my eyes. Before I knew it, we were parking on the Pacific Coast Highway. The dark, cool beach was to our left and high mountains to our right.

"Where are we going?" I finally asked. I could have asked earlier and he probably would have told me, but where was the fun in that?

"We are going to the Beachcomber because we can order our food sitting right over the water and I promise you won't get cold because I'll make them seat us by the fire pit."

"*There's a fire pit?*"

Ben smiled. "Would I lie to you?"

I shrugged. "How should I know?"

"Touché," he said. "Are you ready? The one caveat is that

we have to run across this two-lane highway with super-human speed."

I opened my car door and took off my heels. "Okay. I'm ready." Ben grabbed my hand and we waited until the timing was right. There were a few times we almost went, and one time I thought for sure I was going to die just standing on the edge of the freeway, but eventually, with much fanfare and me screaming, we made our way across.

When we got to the restaurant, it was somewhat empty. From the look on Ben's face, I could tell this was what he was hoping for. He asked to be seated near the fire pit, and within minutes, my legs were warmed by the fire and my shoulders were cool from the sea breeze.

As I sat there, looking out onto the ocean below us and this new person in front of me, it didn't feel like my life. It felt like I was living someone else's life for a night. I didn't usually spend my Monday nights by a fire overlooking the water, being served chilled white wine and Pellegrino. I usually spent my Monday nights eating Hot Pockets while reading a book and drinking from the tap.

"This is gorgeous," I said. I put my hands toward the flames. "Thank you for bringing me here."

"Thank you for letting me," he said, as he pulled his chair closer to me.

Ben and I discussed our days and our jobs. We talked about past relationships and our families. We talked about pretty much anything other than sex, and yet, more and more, it was becoming the only thing on my mind.

His black shirt clung to his shoulders. The way he had the sleeves rolled up halfway to his elbows exposed his hands and wrists. They were thin but sturdy. Angular but delicate. As I looked at them I wanted them to touch me. I wanted them to lift me.

"You look great tonight," I said to him as I buttered my bread. I tried to sound casual. I wasn't used to complimenting a man like that and I wasn't sure how to do it without sounding creepy. "That shirt is very flattering on you."

"Why, thank you very much!" he said as his smile widened. "Thanks."

He looked down at his plate and smiled further. He looked embarrassed.

"Are you blushing?" I teased him.

Ben shook his head. "Well, ah." He looked up at me. "I'm embarrassed to say that I went to the Gap after work and bought this shirt for our date."

I started laughing. "Before you even called me?"

"Yeah. I know. It sounds very stupid. But I just . . . I wanted to look good for you. I wanted to make it a special night and . . . to be blunt, none of my shirts looked good enough for that."

"You're not real," I said.

"Pardon me?"

"You're just . . . you're not a real person. What kind of guy is that sincere about things? And that honest? No man has ever gone out to buy a new shirt just to take me somewhere."

"You don't know that!" Ben said.

The waiter came to take our order. I ordered pasta. Ben ordered steak. That's how I could tell we both knew he would insist on paying for dinner. I wasn't going to order anything extravagant on his dime, and if he'd really thought I might succeed in paying for this, he wouldn't have ordered anything extravagant on mine.

After the waiter left, I kept at it.

"Well, sure. Okay. I don't know that, but no man has ever told me he did."

"Obviously. Only an idiot would admit it. It's too obvious that I like you. I need to reel it in."

"No, no. Please don't. It feels great."

"Being liked?" he asked, as he picked up a piece of bread and ripped it in half. He popped one whole half into his mouth. I liked that he would buy a new shirt for me but he wasn't going to eat delicately in front of me. It showed that even if he wanted to put forward the best version of himself, he was still always going to be himself.

"Being liked, yeah. And liking someone so much. Being liked by the person you like so much, is maybe more accurate."

"Do you feel like things are moving too quickly?" he asked. It jarred me. Obviously, I had been thinking about that and discussing it with Ana, but if he felt like things were going too fast, well . . . I wasn't sure what I was afraid of. I just knew that even if they were going too fast, I did not want things to slow down.

"Oh. Uh. Do you? Were you thinking that?" I looked up at him from my wineglass, trying to sound carefree and blithe. I think it worked.

"No, actually," he said matter-of-factly. I was relieved to hear it. "I think you and I are just . . . Yes, we are moving quickly but we're moving at a pace that feels natural for both of us. I think?"

I nodded, so he kept going.

"Right. So, I don't see an issue. I just wanted to make sure I wasn't coming on too strong with you. Because I don't mean to overwhelm you. I keep telling myself to cut it out. But then I keep doing it. I'm typically a pretty low-key person, but I'm just . . . not low-key about you."

I felt like butter in the microwave. I had no strength left to be cool or the type of dishonest you're supposed to be this early on.

"Are we crazy here?" I asked. "I feel like you are such a different person than anyone I have ever met and I thought about you all day today. I . . . barely know you and yet I miss you. That's crazy, right? I don't know you. I guess I'm worried that we will be so into each other so quickly that we will burn out? Sort of an acute romance, as it were."

"Kind of like a supernova?"

"Hmm?"

"It's some sort of star or explosion that's so powerful it can emit the same amount of energy that the sun will emit over its entire lifetime, but it does it in, like, two months and then it dies."

I laughed. "Yep," I said. "That's pretty much exactly what I meant."

"Well, I think it's a fair concern. I don't want to rush through this so fast that we run it into the ground. I'm not sure I think it's really possible, but better to be safe than sorry." He chewed and thought. When he was done, he had a plan. "What about this? Let's give it . . . let's say, five weeks, and we can see each other as much as we want, but no one can up the ante. We can just stop ourselves from being too intense up front. Let's just hang out and enjoy each other's company and not worry about too fast or too slow or anything. And then at the end of five weeks, we can really assess if we are crazy or not. If at the end of it, we are both on the same page, then great. And if at the end of five weeks, we have burnt out or we just aren't jiving, we've only wasted five weeks."

I laughed. "Jiving?"

"I couldn't think of a better word."

I was still laughing as he looked me, slightly embarrassed. "I can think of about ten," I said and then immediately got back to the subject. "Okay. No moving forward. No freaking out about moving too fast. Just this. That sounds great. No supernova."

Ben smiled and we shook on it. "No supernova."

It was quiet for a moment, and I broke the silence.

"We are wasting our five weeks by being quiet. I need to know more about you."

Ben took another piece of bread off of the table and spread butter on it. I was glad the intensity of the moment had worn off—that things were now casual enough for him to be spreading butter. He took a bite.

"What do you want to know?"

"Favorite color?"

"That's what you're burning to ask me?"

"No."

"So ask what you really wanna know."

"Anything?"

He splayed his hands out to show himself. "Anything."

"How many women have you slept with?"

He smiled out of the side of his mouth as if I'd pinned him down. "Sixteen," he said, matter-of-factly. He wasn't bragging or apologizing. It was higher than I was expecting, and for a second, I was jealous. Jealous that there were women out there that knew him in a way I didn't yet. Women who were closer to him, in some ways, than I was.

"You? Men?" he asked.

"Five."

He nodded. "Next question."

"Do you think you've ever been in love?"

He took another bite. "I believe I have before, yes. It wasn't a great experience for me, truthfully. It wasn't . . . . It wasn't fun," he said as if he was just realizing what the problem truly was after all this time.

"Fair enough."

"You?" he asked.

"I see how this is going. I can't ask any questions I don't want to answer myself."

"Isn't that at least fair?"

"That's fair. I have been in love once before, for most of college. His name was Bryson."

"Bryson?"

"Yes, but don't blame him for his name. He's a nice guy."

"Where is he now?"

"Chicago."

"Okay, good. Nice and far."

I laughed, and the waiter brought our meals. He placed them down in front of us, telling us not to touch them because the plates were hot. But I touched mine; it wasn't that hot. Ben looked at mine and then looked at his. "Can I eat some of yours if I give you some of mine?" he asked.

I angled my plate toward him. "Absolutely."

"There is one thing we need to sort out," Ben said as he reached over to eat some of my fusilli.

"Oh? What is that?"

"Well, if we aren't going to assess our relationship from this moment out until five weeks from now, we should probably sort out ahead of time when we are going to sleep together."

He caught me off guard because I had been hoping to sleep with him that night and then pretend that was never my intention. I was going to blame it on the heat of the moment. "What do you suggest?" I asked.

Ben shrugged. "Well, I guess our only real options are tonight or at the end of the five weeks, right? Otherwise, we'd be amping things up in the middle . . ." He was grinning as he said this. He knew exactly what he was doing. He knew I knew what he was doing.

"Oh. Okay. Well, in the interest of keeping things simple," I said, "why don't we just say tonight?"

Ben smiled out of the side of his mouth and pumped his fist. "Yeah!"

I felt good to be so desirable that a man would fist-pump the thought of getting to sleep with me. Especially because I would have fist-pumped the idea myself if I'd thought of it.

The rest of dinner felt a bit rushed. Or maybe it was just that I couldn't focus on eating now that it was in the air; it had been decided. He kissed me against his car before we got in. He had his hand on my upper thigh as we sped home. The closer we got to my house, the further it got. I could feel every inch of his hand on every inch of my thigh. It burned underneath his fingers.

We barely made it to the door before we were half-naked. He started kissing me in the driveway, and if I hadn't been a lady and stopped it, it might have happened right there in his car.

We ran up the stairs, and when I got my key into the door he was right behind me, his hand on my ass, squeezing it, whispering in my ear to hurry up. His breath was hot on my neck. The door flew open and I ran to my bedroom, holding his hand behind me.

I fell onto the bed and kicked off my shoes. I liked hearing the double clunk they made as they hit the floor. He threw his body down on top of me, his legs between mine, and he pushed my body up and further onto the bed as we kissed with my hands around his head. He kicked his shoes off. I slid under the covers with my dress still on, and he slid in next to me. Any restraint we'd shown the night before was gone, replaced with reckless abandon. I couldn't think straight. I wasn't in my own head enough to worry if I felt fat or where to move my arms. The lights were on. I never left the lights on. But I didn't even notice. I just did. I just moved. I operated on instinct. I wanted all of him, more of him, I couldn't get enough of him. His body made me feel so alive.

JUNE

I take a chance that Susan is still at her hotel. Ana brings me there and I call Susan from the lobby. I don't want to give her an opportunity to turn me away, which turns out to be a smart strategy because her tone makes it clear that she would have avoided me if she could have. Ana heads over to the bar as I take the elevator to Room 913.

As I approach her door, my palms start to sweat. I'm not sure how to convince Susan of this, how I plan on defending Ben's wishes to his own mother. It occurs to me that I just want her to like me. Take away everything that has happened, this is the woman that raised my husband. She created him out of nothing, and for that, a part of me loves her. But I can't take away everything that has happened; every moment of every day reeks of what has happened. What has happened is happening now.

I knock lightly on her door, and she opens it immediately.

"Hello, Elsie," she says. She is wearing fitted dark jeans with a thick belt, a gray shirt under a brown cardigan. She looks younger than her sixty years, in shape, healthy, but nonetheless, in grave distress. She has been crying, that much is clear. Her hair doesn't look brushed or blow-dried as usual. She's not wearing makeup. She looks raw.

"Hi, Susan," I say as I walk in.

"What can I do for you?" Her hotel room is more like a

hotel *apartment*. She has a large balcony and a sitting room filled with cream-colored everything. The carpet looks soft under my shoes, too delicate to walk on, and yet, I'm not at home enough in her company to suggest I take them off. I get the impression she'd like me to walk on eggshells around her, apologize for my very existence, and the carpet practically forces me to do just that.

"I . . ." I start. I'm not sure if it's appropriate to try for small talk in a situation like this or if it's better to just go right into it. How can you go right into it when the "it" is the remains of your husband? The remains of her son?

"I met with Mr. Pavlik this morning," I say. It seems close enough to the point without directly hitting the mark.

"Good," she says, leaning back against her couch. She is not sitting down. She is not inviting me to take a seat. She does not want me to be here long, and yet, I don't know how to make this a short conversation. I decide to just come out with it.

"Ben wanted to be buried. I thought that we discussed this," I say.

She shifts her body slightly, casually, as if this conversation is not a big deal to her, as if it doesn't terrify her the way it terrifies me. That's how I know she has no intention of hearing me out. She's not worried she's not going to get her way.

"Get to the point, Elsie," she says. She runs her hands through her long brown hair. It has streaks of gray near the top, barely noticeable unless you're staring at her like I am.

"Mr. Pavlik says that Ben's body is still to be cremated."

"It is." She nods, not offering any other explanation. Her candid voice, free from emotion, turmoil, and pain, is starting to piss me off. Her composure feels like spit in my face.

"It's not what he wanted, Susan. I'm telling you, that's not what he wanted. Doesn't that matter to you at all?" I say. I am trying to be respectful to the mother of the man that I love. "Don't you care what Ben would have wanted?"

Susan crosses her arms in front of her and shifts her weight. "Elsie, don't tell me about my own son, okay? I raised him. I know what he wanted."

"You don't, actually. You don't know! I had this conversation with him two months ago."

"And I've had conversations with him about this his entire life. I am his mother. I didn't just happen to meet him a few months before he died. Who the hell do you think you are to tell me about my own son?"

"I am his wife, Susan. I don't know how else to say it."

It doesn't sit well.

"I've never heard of you!" she says, as she throws her hands in the air. "Where is the marriage certificate? I don't know you, and here you are, trying to tell me what to do with my only child's remains? Give me a break, seriously. You are a small footnote in my son's life. I am his mother!"

"I get that you're his mother—"

She inches forward ever so slightly as she interrupts me, her finger pointed now toward my face. Her composure drains out of her body, the poise flees from her face. "Listen to me. I don't know you and I don't trust you. But my son's body will be cremated, Elsie. Just like his father's and like his grandparents'. And the next time you get the idea to try to tell me what to do about my own son, you might want to think twice."

"You gave this to me to do, Susan! You couldn't deal with it yourself and you pushed it onto me! First you try to stop me from even getting his wallet and keys, keys that are to my own home, by the way, and then you suddenly turn and push all of this off on me. And then, when I try to do it, you try to control it from behind the scenes. You haven't even left Los Angeles. You don't need to stay in this hotel, Susan. You can drive back to Orange County and be there by dinner. Why are you even still here?" I don't give her a chance to answer. "You want to torture yourself because Ben didn't tell you he got married? *Then do it!* I don't care! But don't keep going back and forth like this. I can't take it."

"I really don't care what you can take, Elsie," Susan says. "Believe it or not, I don't much care."

I try to remind myself that this is a woman in pain. This is a woman that has lost the last family member she had.

"Susan, you can try to deny it all you want. You can think I'm a crazy lunatic who is lying to you. You can cling to the idea that your son would never do anything without you, but that doesn't stop the fact that I did marry him and he did not want to be cremated. Don't have his body burned because you hate me."

"I don't hate you, Elsie. I simply—"

Now it's my turn to cut her off. "Yes, you do, Susan. You hate me because I'm the only one left to hate. If you thought you were doing a good job of hiding that, you're wrong."

She stares at me and I stare right back at her. I don't know what has given me the courage to be honest. I'm not a person inclined to stare anyone else down. Nevertheless, I hold her gaze, my lips pursed and tight, my brows weighted down on my face. Maybe she thinks I'm going to turn and walk away. I don't know. It takes so long for her to speak that the break in the silence is almost startling.

"Even if everything is as you say it is," she says. "Even if you two were married, and the marriage certificate is on its way, and you were the love of his life—"

"I was," I interrupt her.

She barely listens. "Even so, how long were you married to him, Elsie? Two weeks?" I work hard to breathe in and then breathe out. I can feel the lump in my throat rising. I can feel the blood in my brain beating. She continues. "I hardly think two weeks proves anything," she says.

I think about turning around and just leaving her there. That's what she wants. But I don't do it. "You wanna know something else about your son? He would be livid, to see what you're doing. Heartbroken and positively livid."

I leave her hotel room without saying good-bye. As I walk out the door, I look behind me to see a dirt stain the size of my shoe on her pristine white carpet.

Two hours later, Mr. Pavlik calls to tell me Susan has taken over burial plans.

"Burial plans?" I ask, not sure if he is mistaken.

There is a pause, and then he confirms. "Burial plans."

I wish it felt like a victory but it doesn't. "So what do I need to do?" I ask.

He clears his throat and his voice becomes tight. "Uh," he says. "I don't believe anything else is required of you, Elsie. I have Mrs. Ross here and she has decided to take care of the rest."

I don't know how I feel about this. Except tired. I feel tired.

"Okay," I say to him. "Thank you." I hang up the phone and set it down on the dining room table.

"Susan kicked me out of the funeral planning," I tell Ana. "But she's having him buried. Not cremated."

Ana looks at me, unsure of how to react. "Is that good or bad?"

"Good?" I say. "It's good." It is good. His body is safe. I did my job. Why am I so sad? I didn't want to pick out a casket. I didn't want to choose flowers. And yet, I have lost something. I have lost a part of him.

I call Mr. Pavlik right back.

"It's Elsie," I say when he answers. "I want to speak."

"Hmm?"

"I want to speak at his funeral."

"Oh, certainly. I'll speak to Mrs. Ross about it."

"No," I say sternly. "I am speaking at the funeral."

I can hear him whispering and then I hear hold music. When he comes back on he says, "Okay, Elsie. You're welcome to speak if you'd like to." He adds, "It will be Saturday morning in Orange County. I'll send you further details shortly," and then he wishes me well.

I get off the phone, and as much as I want to congratulate myself for standing up to her, I know that, if Susan had said no, I wouldn't have been able to do much about it. I'm not exactly sure how I gave her all the power, but I gave it to her. For the first time, it doesn't feel like Ben was just alive and well a second ago. It feels like he's been gone forever.

Ana heads back to her place to walk her dog. I should offer for her to bring the dog here, but I get the impression Ana needs a few hours every day to get away from me, to get away from this. It's the same thing. I am this. When she gets back, I'm in the same place I was when she left. She asks if I've eaten. She doesn't like the look on my face.

"This is absurd, Elsie. You have to eat something. I'm not messing around anymore." She opens the refrigerator. "You can have pancakes. Eggs? It looks like you have some bacon." She opens the pack of bacon and smells it. It's clearly putrid judging from the look on her face. "Never mind, no bacon. Unless . . . I can go get some bacon! Would you eat bacon?"

"No," I say. "No, please do not leave me to get bacon."

The doorbell rings, and it's so loud and jarring that I almost jump out of my skin. I turn and stare at the door. Ana finally goes to answer it herself.

It's a goddamn flower deliveryman.

"Elsie Porter?" he says through my screen door.

"You can tell him there's no one here by that name," I say to Ana. She ignores me and opens the screen to let him in.

"Thank you," she says to him. He gives her a large white bouquet and leaves. She shuts the door and places it on the table.

"These are gorgeous," she says. "Do you want to know who they're from?" She grabs the card before I answer.

"Are they for the wedding or the funeral?" I ask.

Ana is quiet as she looks at the card. "The funeral." She swallows hard. It wasn't nice of me to make her say that.

"They are from Lauren and Simon," Ana says. "Do you want to thank them or should I?"

Ben and I used to double-date with Lauren and Simon. How am I supposed to face them myself? "Will you do it?" I ask her.

"I'll do it if you'll eat something. How about pancakes?"

"Will you just run point on everyone?" I ask. "Will you tell everyone the news? I don't want to tell them myself."

"If you make me a list," she says. She pushes further. "And you eat some pancakes."

I agree to eat the damn pancakes. If you don't put maple syrup on them, they taste like nothing. I think I can choke down some nothing. As for the list, it's a silly task. She knows everyone I know. They are her friends too.

She starts to grab bowls and ingredients, pans and sprays. Everything seems so easy for her. Each movement doesn't feel like it might be her last, the way mine feel. She just picks up the pancake mix like it's nothing, like it's not the heaviest box in the world.

She sprays cooking spray on a pan and lights the burner. "So, we have two things we have to go over this morning and neither of them are pretty."

"Okay."

When she's got the first pancake under control she turns to me, the spatula wet with batter and dangling in her hand on her hip. I stare at it while she talks, wondering if it will drip onto the kitchen floor.

"The first one is work. What do you want to do? I called them on Monday, told them the situation and bought you a few days but . . . how do you want to handle it?"

Honestly, I don't even remember why I am a librarian. Books? Seriously? That's my passion?

"I don't know if I can go back," I say at first, meaning it.

"Okay," she says, turning back to the stove. The batter doesn't fall off the spatula until the last minute, until I have almost given up on it falling to the floor. It makes a small splatter at her foot, but she's oblivious.

"I know I need to, though," I add. "If only because I'm not exactly rolling in dough." Being a librarian meant that when I graduated, my starting salary was higher than the rest of my peers', but it didn't grow as quickly and I am now merely making a decent living. I'm certainly not in a position to quit my job.

"What about Ben's . . . ?" Ana can't finish the question. I don't blame her. I can barely ask it myself in my own head.

"He had a good amount of money saved," I say. "But I don't want it."

"Well, wouldn't he want you to have it?" My pancake is done, and she delivers it to me on the table with containers of butter, maple syrup, jam, and confectioners' sugar. I push them aside. The thought of tasting something sweet right now makes my mouth sour.

"I don't know, but . . . I think it puts me in a weird position. We weren't married long. None of his family has ever heard of me. I don't want a windfall of cash right now," I say. "Not that it's a windfall, it's just more than I had saved. Ben wasn't a big spender."

Ana shrugs. "So, then maybe you should call your boss and work out when you're going back? Assuming you're going back?"

I nod. "You're absolutely right. I should." I do not want to. I wonder how long I could go before they fired me. It would be so indelicate of them to fire a widow, to fire a grieving woman, and yet, I'd leave them no choice.

"And speaking of calling people . . ." Ana flips what I hope is a pancake she's making for herself. I said I'd eat, but I'm not eating two huge pancakes. I can barely stomach this piece of shit in front of me.

"Wow, you're really going for it this morning, aren't you?" I say.

She plates the pancake, which I think is a pretty good sign she's going to eat it herself. If it was for me, she'd put it on my plate, right? "I don't mean to push you. I just think the longer you put this off, the more uncomfortable it will be. Your parents, no matter how difficult your relationship is, they need to know what has happened to you in the past few days."

"Okay," I say. She's right. Ana sits down next to me and starts on her pancake. She loads it up with butter and maple syrup. I am astonished that she can have an appetite during a time like this, that things like taste and pleasure are on her mind.

I wipe my chin and set down the napkin. "Who do you want me to call first? Let's just get this shit over with."

Ana puts down her fork. "That's my girl! You're taking life by the balls."

"I don't know if that's the case. I'm merely getting this bullshit out of the way so I can go in my room and cry for the rest of the day."

"But you're trying! You're doing the best you can."

"I guess I am," I say and grab the phone. I look to her with my eyebrows raised and the phone tilted in my hand. "So?"

"Call work first. That's an easier conversation. It's just logistics, no emotion."

"I like that you think the conversation with my parents will contain emotion."

I dial the phone and wait as it rings. A woman picks up; I can recognize that it's Nancy. I love Nancy. I think Nancy is a great woman, but as she says, "Los Angeles Library, Fairfax Branch, Reference Desk, how may I help you today?" I hang up.

JANUARY

The library was technically closed for Martin Luther King Day, but I agreed to work. We'd had a group of people, most likely high school students or fancy little rebels, come in and place the entire World Religions section out of order over the weekend. They threw books on the floor, they hid them in other sections, under tables. They rearranged the titles in no discernible order.

My boss, Lyle, was convinced that this was some sort of terrorist act, meant to make us here at the Los Angeles library really think about the role of religion in modern government. I was more of the mind that the act was harmless tomfoolery; the World Religions section was the nearest to the back wall, the furthest from view. I'd caught a number of couples making out in the library in my few years there, and they had all been in the World Religions section.

No one else was working that day, but Lyle told me that if I chose to come in and re-sort the World Religions section, he'd give me a day off some other time. This seemed like great currency to me, and since Ben was going to have to work that day anyway, I came in. I tend to like alphabetizing, which I realize makes absolutely no sense, but it's true nonetheless. I like things that have a right and a wrong answer, things that can be done perfectly. They don't often come up in the humanities. They are normally relegated to the sciences. So I've always liked the alphabet and the Dewey decimal system for being objective standards in a subjective world.

Cell phone reception is terrible at the library, and since it was empty, I had a spookily quiet day, a day spent almost entirely in my own mind.

Around three, as I found myself pretty much done piecing together the World Religions section like some three-dimensional puzzle, I heard the phone ring. I had been ignoring the phone the few times it rang that day, but for some reason, I forgot all that and ran to answer it.

I don't typically answer the phone at work, I'm often with people or filing or working on larger projects for the library, so when I answered this time, I realized it completely slipped my mind what I was supposed to say.

"Hello?" I said. "Uh. Los Angeles Fairfax Library. Oh, ah. Los Angeles Public Library, Reference Branch. Fairfax Branch, Reference Desk."

By the end of it, I'd remembered there was no need for me to answer the phone in the first place, making this that much more of a needless embarrassment.

That's when I heard laughing on the other end of the phone. "Ben?"

"Uh, uh, Fairfax. Reference. Uh," he said, still laughing at me. "You are the cutest person that ever lived."

I started to laugh too, relieved that I had embarrassed myself only in front of Ben, but also embarrassed to have embarrassed myself in front of Ben. "What are you doing? I thought you were working today."

"I was. Working today. But Greg decided to let us all go home a half hour ago."

"Oh! That's great. You should come meet me here. I should

be done in about twenty minutes or so. Oh!" I said, and I was overcome with a great idea. "We can go to a happy hour!" I never got out of work in time to go to a happy hour, but the idea had always intrigued me.

Ben laughed. "That sounds great. That's kind of why I'm calling. I'm outside."

"What?"

"Well, not outside exactly. I'm down the street. I had to walk until I could get service."

"Oh!" I was thrilled to know that I'd be seeing Ben any minute and drinking two-dollar drafts within the half hour. "Come down to the side door. I'll open it."

"Great!" he said. "I'll be there in five."

I took my time heading to the side door, passing the circulation desk and front door on my way back there. I'm glad that I did because as I passed the front door, I heard a tapping on the door and looked up to see Mr. Callahan standing sad and confused, with his hands cupped around his eyes and fixed against the glass.

I walked up to the door and pushed it open. It was an automatic door turned off for the holiday, so it gave great resistance, but I got it open just enough to let Mr. Callahan in. He grabbed my arm with his shaking, tissue paper–like hands and thanked me.

"No problem, Mr. Callahan," I said. "I'm going to take off in about ten minutes and the library is closed, but is there something you wanted?"

"It's closed?" he asked, confused. "What on earth for?"

"Martin Luther King Day!" I answered.

"And you still let me in? I am a lucky man, Elsie."

I smiled. "Can I help you get anything?"

"I won't be but just a minute, now that I know you're in a hurry. Can I have a few minutes in the Young Adult section?"

"The Young Adult section?" It wasn't my business why, but this was out of character for Mr. Callahan. The fiction section, sure, new releases, definitely. World Wars, Natural Disasters, Sociology. All of these were places where you could find Mr. Callahan, but Young Adult was never his style.

"My grandson and his daughter are coming this week and I want to have something to read with her. She's getting too old to find me particularly entertaining, but I thought if I got a really good yarn to her liking, I could convince her to spend a few minutes with me."

"Great-granddaughter? Wow."

"I'm old, Elsie. I'm an old man."

I laughed instead of agreeing with him. "Well, be my guest. It's over to the left, behind the periodicals."

"I'll only be a minute!" he said as he headed back there, slow like a turtle but also just as steady.

I headed to the side door to find Ben wondering what the hell I'd been doing.

"I've been here for two minutes and twenty-seven seconds, Elsie!" he joked as he stepped in.

"Sorry, Mr. Callahan came to the front door and I had to let him in."

"Mr. Callahan is here?" Ben's face lit up. He had never met Mr. Callahan but had heard me talk about him, about how I found his devotion to his wife to be one of the more romantic real-life sentiments I had ever witnessed. Ben always said when he was ninety, he'd treat me the same way. I had only known Ben for about three weeks, so while it was a sweet thing to say, it was also foolhardy and arrogant. It was naïve and intoxicating. "Can I meet him?"

"Sure," I said. "Come help me put a few last books in order

and we can go find him." Ben came with me to finish up, contributing in no way to my reordering of the books. He hung back and read the spines as I told him all about finding *Buddhism: Plain and Simple* stuck up in a nook of the ceiling.

"How did you get it down?" he said, only half listening to me. His attention seemed focused on the stacks.

"I didn't," I told him. "It's right there." I pointed above us to the thin, white book stuck precariously between the metal grid and the popcorn panel. He walked toward me, standing right over me. Our bodies were so close that his shirt was touching mine. The skin on his arm just barely touched mine. I could smell his deodorant and his shampoo, smells that had become sensual to me because of how often I smelled them in sensual situations. His neck was craned upward, checking out the book in the ceiling.

"Those tricky bastards," Ben marveled, then he turned back to face me. He could now appreciate how close we were. He looked at me and then looked around us.

"Where's Mr. Callahan?" he asked. He asked it in a way that clearly let me know he was asking something else entirely.

I blushed. "He's a few walls over," I said.

"Seems pretty private back here," he said. He didn't move toward me to grab me. He didn't need to.

I giggled, girlishly. "It is," I said. "But it would be—"

"Right," he said. "That would be . . ."

Was it getting hotter? I honestly thought maybe it was getting hotter. I thought it was getting hotter and quieter, as if the air itself was becoming more intense around us.

"It would be crazy," I said, matter-of-factly, doing my best to stop this before it started. He wouldn't. I knew he wouldn't. Right there in the library? I was certain that I was the only one actually considering it. And so I put my foot down. I stepped away slightly, put the book in my hand into its place on the shelf, and announced that we needed to go check on Mr. Callahan.

"Okay," Ben said, putting his hands up in surrender. He then put one arm out as if to invite me to lead us there. I walked in front of him, and when we were almost out of the World Religions stacks, he teased me.

"I would have done it," he said.

I smiled and shook my head. I had never felt so desirable, had never realized how feeling that desirable made me feel like I could do anything in the world.

We found Mr. Callahan right where he'd said he'd be.

"What is all of this?" Mr. Callahan said to me as he saw us coming up to meet him. "I thought there would be a few books back here. This section is bigger than the new releases!"

I laughed. "There are a lot of young adult books lately, Mr. Callahan. Kids love reading now."

He shook his head. "Who knew?" Mr. Callahan already had a book in his hand.

"Mr. Callahan, I'd like you to meet Ben." I gestured to Ben, and Mr. Callahan grabbed Ben's outstretched hand.

"Hello, son," he said and took his hand back. "Strong grip on you, good to see."

"Thanks," Ben said. "I've heard a lot about you and I wanted to meet the man behind the legend."

Mr. Callahan laughed. "No legend here. Just an old man who forgets things and can't walk as fast as he used to."

"Is that for you?" Ben asked, gesturing to the book.

"Oh, no. My great-granddaughter. I'm afraid I'm a bit lost in this section. This book takes up a whole shelf, though, so I figured it's pretty popular." Mr. Callahan held up a copy of a supernatural franchise. The kind of book that gets the kids reading in the first place, even if it is insipid, so I couldn't knock it. He had the third book in his hand, and I had a hunch he couldn't tell that the whole shelf was actually four different installments with similar covers and motifs. His fine vision probably was not what it used to be, and they probably all looked the same.

"That's actually the third one," I said. "Did you want me to find the first one?"

"Please," he said.

Ben gingerly grabbed the book out of his hand. "If I may, Mr. Callahan." He put the book back in place and stopped me from picking up the first of the series.

"I'm categorically against all books about vampires in love with young women. Those books always make it seem like being bitten to the point of death is a form of love."

I looked at Ben, surprised. He sheepishly looked back at me. "What?"

"No, nothing," I said.

"Anyway," he continued, focused on Mr. Callahan. "I'm not sure it's the best influence for your great-granddaughter. I can only assume you want her to grow up believing that she can do anything, not just sit around lusting for the undead."

"You're exactly right about that," Mr. Callahan said. When Mr. Callahan was a child, he was probably raised to believe that women were made to follow men, to stay home and darn their socks. Now, he was an old man who had changed with the times, who wanted to reinforce for his great-granddaughter that she should not stay home and darn socks unless she wanted to. It occurred to me that you could see a lot in a lifetime if you stuck around as long as Mr. Callahan. He had lived through times I'd only read about.

Ben grabbed a bright blue book from the display. "Here you go. Just as popular, ten times more awesome. It's got love in it, but the love is secondary to actual character development, and you really love these characters. The girl is a hero. I don't want to spoil anything, but bring tissues."

Mr. Callahan smiled and nodded. "Thank you," he said. "You just saved me a tongue-lashing from her mother."

"It's a really good book," Ben said. "I read it in two days."

"Can I check it out, Elsie? Or . . . how does that work if you're closed?"

"Just bring it back in three weeks, Mr. Callahan. It will be our secret."

Mr. Callahan smiled at me and tucked the book into his coat, as if he were a criminal. He shook Ben's hand and walked away. After he cleared the front door I turned to Ben.

"You read young adult novels?"

"Look, we all have our idiosyncrasies. Don't think I don't know that you drink Diet Coke for breakfast."

"What? How did you even know that?"

"I pay attention." He tapped his temple with his pointer finger. "Now that you know my deepest, most embarrassing secret, that I read young adult novels written mostly for thirteen-year-old girls, do you still like me? Can we still go out, or have you just about had enough?"

"No, I think I'll stick with you," I said, grabbing his hand. The phone rang again, and Ben ran and picked it up.

"Los Angeles Public Library, Fairfax Branch, Reference Desk, how may I help you?" he said arrogantly. "No, I'm sorry. We're closed today. Thanks. Bye."

"Ben!" I said after he hung up. "That was unprofessional!"

"Well, you can understand why I didn't trust you to do it."

JUNE

What was that all about?" Ana says as she finishes her pancake.

"I . . . I got a little overwhelmed there. I just wasn't ready for it." I pick up the phone and dial again.

"Los Angeles Public Library, Fairfax Branch, Reference Desk, how may I help you?" It is still Nancy. Nancy is round and older. She's not a professional librarian. She just works the desk. I shouldn't say "just." She does a lot of work and is kind to everyone. I can't imagine Nancy saying an unkind thing about a single person. She's one of those people that can be sincere and neighborly. I've always found the two to be at odds, personally.

"Hey, Nancy, it's Elsie."

She lets out a blow of air and her voice deepens. "Elsie, I'm so sorry."

"Thank you."

"I can't even imagine—"

"Thank you." I cut her off. I know that if she keeps talking, I will hang up again. I will roll into a ball and heave tears the size of marbles. "Is Lyle around? I need to talk to him about coming back in."

"Absolutely. Absolutely," she says to me. "One second, sweetheart."

It's a few minutes before Lyle answers, and when he does, he steamrolls the conversation. I can only assume it's because he's more loath to have this conversation than I am. No one wants to be the person telling me of my responsibilities right now.

"Elsie, listen. We get it. You take as much time as you need. You have plenty of vacation days, sick days, personal time saved up," he says, trying to be helpful.

"How much my-husband-died time do I have?" I ask, trying to lighten the mood, trying to make this okay for everyone. But it's not okay for everyone, and the joke lands like a belly flop. You could fit a city bus in the length of the awkward pause between us. "Anyway, thank you, Lyle. I think it's best that I get back into my routine. Life has to go on, right?" I am all talk right now. Life can't go on. That's just a thing people say to other people because they heard it on daytime TV. It doesn't exist for me. It never will. There will be no moving on. But people not living in the valley of a tragedy don't like to hear this. They like to hear you "buck up." They want to say to your friends, to your co-workers, to the people you used to ride elevators with, that you're "handling it well." That you're a "trooper." The more crass of them want to say you're a "tough bitch" or a "hard as nails motherfucker." I'm not, but let them think it. It's easier on all of us.

"Well, great. You just let me know the day."

"The funeral is tomorrow morning and I'll take the rest of the weekend to rest. How about Tuesday?" I say.

"Tuesday sounds fine," he says. "And Elsie?"

"Yeah?" I say, wanting to get off the phone.

"May he rest in peace. We can never know God's plan for us."

"Uh-huh," I say and hang up the phone. This is the first time someone has mentioned God to me, and I want to wring Lyle's fat neck. To be honest, it seems rude to even mention it to me. It's like your friend talking about how much fun she had at the party you weren't invited to. God has forsaken me. Stop rubbing it in how great God's been to you.

I put the phone down on the kitchen table. "One down," I say. "Can I take a shower before the next one?" Ana nods.

I head into the shower and turn on the faucet, wondering how I'm going to start this conversation, wondering how it can possibly go. Are my parents going to offer to fly out here? That would be terrible. Are they not going to offer to come out here at all? That would be even worse. Ana knocks on the door, and I turn off the water. I'm sure she thinks that I'll never get out of here on my own, and I don't want to give her any more to worry about than I already have. I can get myself out of the damn shower. For now.

I put on a robe and grab the phone. If I don't do it this second, I won't do it, so let's do it.

I dial their home phone. My father answers.

"It's Elsie," I say.

"Oh, hi, Eleanor," my father replies. I feel like he's spitting in my face by saying my full name, reminding me that I am not who they intended. On my first day of school in kindergarten, I told everyone to call me Elsie. I told my teacher it was short for Eleanor, but in reality, I had liked the name ever since I saw Elsie the Cow on ice cream cartons. It was a couple of months before my mother figured out what exactly was going on, but by that time, try as she might, she could not get my friends to call me Eleanor. It was my first true rebellion.

"Do you and Mom have a minute to talk?" I ask.

"Oh, I'm sorry. We're on our way out. I'll call you some other time. Is that okay?" he says.

"No, actually, I'm sorry. I need to speak with you now. It's rather important."

My father tells me to hold on.

"What is it, Eleanor?" My mother is now on the phone.

"Is Dad on the line too?"

"I'm here. What did you want to say?"

"Well, I believe I told you about a man I was seeing. Ben."

"Uh-huh," my mother says. She sounds like she's distracted. Like she's putting on lipstick or watching the maid fold the laundry.

"Well," I start. I don't want to do this. What good comes of this? What good comes of me saying it out loud? Of hearing it through their ears? "Ben was hit by a car and passed away."

My mother gasps. "Oh my God, Eleanor. I'm sorry to hear that," she says.

"Jesus," my dad says.

"I don't know what to say," my mother adds. But she can't stand not saying something so she pulls something out of her ass. "I trust you've informed his family." My parents see death every day, and I think it has made them numb to it in a lot of ways. I think it's made them numb to life too, but I'm sure they'd just say I'm too sensitive.

"Yeah, yeah. That's all taken care of. I just wanted you to know."

"Well," my mother says, still pulling words out of thin air. "I imagine this is a hard time for you, but I hope you know that we feel for you. I just . . . My word. Have you had time to process? Are you doing okay?"

"I'm not okay, exactly. The other thing I wanted to tell you is that Ben and I were married in a private ceremony two weeks ago. He died as my husband."

It's out of my mouth. I have done my job. Now all I have to do is get off the phone.

"Why did you marry someone you barely knew?" my father asks, and there it is, off and running.

"Your father's right, Eleanor. I don't even know . . ." My mother is livid. I can hear it in her voice.

"I'm sorry I didn't tell you," I say.

"Forget telling us!" she says. "What were you thinking? How long had you known this man?"

"Long enough to know that he was the love of my life," I say, defensively.

They are silent. I can tell my mom wants to say something.

"Just go ahead," I say.

"I knew your father for four years before I agreed to even go on a date with him, Eleanor. We dated for another five before we got married. You can't possibly know enough about a person after a few months."

"It was six months. I met him six months ago," I say. God, even I know this sounds paltry and embarrassing. It makes me feel so stupid.

"Precisely!" my dad pipes in. "Eleanor, this is terrible. Just terrible. We are so sorry you have been hurt like this, but you will move on. I promise."

"No, but, Charles," my mom interjects. "It's also important that she understands that she needs to take more time with her decisions. This is exactly—"

"Guys, I don't want to talk about this right now. I just thought you should know I'm a widow."

"A widow?" my mother says. "No, I don't think you should consider yourself a widow. Don't label yourself like that. That's only going to make it more difficult to rebound from this. How long were you two married?" I can hear the judgment in her voice.

"A week and a half," I say. I'm rounding up. How sad is that? I'm fucking rounding up.

"Eleanor, you are going to be okay," my father tells me.

"Yes," my mother says. "You will be fine. You will get back up on your feet. I hope you haven't taken too much time off work at the library. You know with state budget cuts, it really isn't the time to be compromising your job. Although, I was talking to one of my friends on the board of the hospital, and she mentioned that her daughter is a law librarian. She works directly with some very high-powered attorneys on some really impressive cases. I could call her, or give you her number if you'd like. They are a bicoastal firm."

I've always known that my mother will take any opportunity to remind me that I can be better than I am now. I can be more impressive than I am now. I have the potential to do more with my life than I am doing now. And I didn't necessarily think she'd waste this opportunity out of fear of being insensitive and gauche, but I don't think I realized how seamlessly she'd be able to do it. I can hear, as she speaks, how far I have strayed from their plan for me. This is what happens when you are your parents' only child, when they wanted more but couldn't have any, when they procreated for the purpose of building mini-versions of themselves. This is what happens when they realize you aren't going to be like them and they aren't sure what to do about it.

It always bothered me until I moved out here, away from them, out of sight of their disapproving stares, their condescending voices. It didn't bother me again until right now. I have to assume it's because I didn't need them again until right now. And as much as I may say that nothing will make this better, I'm inclined to think that feeling supported by my parents would have made this just a little bit easier to bear.

"No, thanks, Mom," I say and hope that the conversation will end there. That she will give up and just resolve to sell harder next time.

"Well," my dad says. "Is there anything you need from us?"

"Nothing, Dad. I just wanted you guys to know. I hope you have a good rest of your night," I say.

"Okay, I'm sorry for your loss, Eleanor." My mother hangs up her end of the line.

"We really wish you the best, Elsie," my dad says. It catches me off guard, hearing the name out of his mouth. He is trying. It means that he is trying. "We just . . . we don't know how to . . ." He breathes audibly and restarts. "You know how your mother is," he says, and he leaves it at that.

"I know."

"We love you," he says, and I say, "I love you too," out of social convention rather than feeling.

I hang up the phone.

"It's done now," Ana says to me. She grabs my hand. She holds it to her heart. "I'm so proud of you for that one. You handled yourself really, really well." She hugs me, and I throw my face into her body. Ana's shoulder is a soft place to cry, but I've heard urban legends about the safety of a mother's arms and that sounds pretty good right now.

"Okay," I say. "I think I'm going to go lie down."

"Okay," she says. She cleans the plates from the table. Hers is an empty plate covered in maple syrup. Mine is clean but full of pancake. "If you're hungry, let me know."

"Okay," I say, but I am already in my room, already lying down, and I already know I won't be hungry. I look up at the ceiling and I don't know how much time passes. I remember that his cell phone still exists somewhere. That the number didn't die when he did. And I call it. I listen to him over and over, hanging up and dialing again.

JANUARY

It was a rainy and cold Saturday night. Well, cold for Los Angeles. It was fifty degrees and windy. The wind had started to sway the trees and make the rain fall sideways. It was only five o'clock but the sun had already set. Ben and I decided to go to a wine bar not too far from my house. Neither one of us cared that much about wine, but it had covered valet parking, so it seemed the most dry of the nearby options.

We made our way to the table, taking off our wet coats and mussing with our hair. It had been so cold outside that the inside felt warm and cozy, as if we were sitting at a campfire.

I ordered a caprese salad and a Diet Coke. When Ben ordered a pasta dish and a glass of Pinot Noir, I remembered that the whole point of this place was the wine bar.

"Oh," I said. "Cancel the Diet Coke. I'll have the same." The waiter grabbed our menus and walked away.

"You don't have to order wine if you don't want wine," Ben said.

"Well," I said to him. "When in Rome!"

Our glasses came shortly after, filled halfway with dark red. We swirled the glasses under our noses, smiling at each other, neither of us having any idea what we were doing.

"Ah," Ben said. "A faint smell of blackberry and . . ." He sipped his drink in a reserved, taste-tester sort of way. "It has a woodsy quality to it, don't you think?"

"Mmmm," I said, sipping mine and pretending to contemplate. "Very woodsy. Very full-bodied."

We both laughed. "Yes!" Ben said. "I forgot *full-bodied*. Wine people love saying things are *full-bodied*."

He started to chug his down. "Honestly," he said, "it all tastes the same to me."

"Me too," I said, as I sipped mine again. Although, I had to admit that while I couldn't speak to the tannins or the base notes or whatever else people that know wine know, it tasted wonderful. After a few more sips, it started to feel wonderful.

Our food had just been served when Ben's phone rang. He put it through to voice mail as I took a bite of my salad. He started to eat his pasta and his phone rang again. Again, he ignored the call. I finally caved and asked.

"Who is that?" I said.

"Oh," he said, clearly wishing I hadn't asked. "It's just a girl that I dated a while ago. She drunk-dials sometimes."

"It's not even seven thirty."

"She's a bit . . . What is the correct way to say this? She is . . . a party girl? Is that the polite way to say that?"

"I guess it depends on what you're trying to say."

"She's an alcoholic," he said. "That's why I stopped dating her."

He said it so matter-of-factly that it caught me off guard. It almost seemed silly because it was so serious.

"She calls from time to time. I think she's trying to booty-call me."

I wanted to laugh again at him using the expression *booty-call*, but deep down, I was starting to get jealous and I could feel the jealousy moving its way closer and closer to the surface.

"Ah" was all I said.

"I've told her I'm with someone. Trust me. It's annoying more than anything else."

The jealousy was now hot on my skin. "Okay."

"Are you upset?"

"No," I said, breezily, as if I truly wasn't upset. Why did I do this? Why not just say "Yes"?

"Yes, you are."

"No."

"You're doing that thing."

"No, I'm not."

"Yep, your chest is getting red and you're speaking in clipped tones. That means you're mad."

"How would you even know that?"

"Because I pay attention."

"Okay," I said finally. "I just . . . I don't like it. This woman you used to date—which by the way, let's just acknowledge means you used to sleep with—I don't know if I like that she's calling you to do it again."

"I know. I agree with you. I told her to stop," he said to me. He didn't seem angry but he did seem defensive.

"I know. I know. I believe you, I just . . . Look, we said we would be exclusive for these five weeks, but if you don't want to . . . ."

"What?" Ben had long ago stopped eating his pasta.

"Never mind."

"Never mind?"

"When was the last time you saw her?" Why I asked this question, what I thought it proved, I do not know. You don't ask questions you don't want the answers to. I never learned this.

"What does that matter?"

"I'm just asking," I said.

"It was a bit before I met you," he said, looking down into his wineglass, sipping it to hide from me.

"How much of a 'bit' are we talking about?"

Ben smiled, embarrassed. "I saw her the night before I met you," he said.

I wanted to reach across the table and wring his neck. My face flushed with jealousy. My chest felt like my lungs were a bonfire. I didn't have a good reason. I couldn't rationalize it. I wanted to yell at him and tell him what he had done wrong, but he hadn't done anything wrong. Nothing at all. It didn't even make sense for me to be this jealous. I just . . . I wanted to believe that Ben was mine. I wanted to believe that no one had made him smile until I did, no woman had made him yearn to touch her until I had. Suddenly, the woman calling took on a personality of her own in my head. I saw her in a red dress with long black hair. She probably wore black lace bra and panty sets. They probably always matched. In my head, her stomach was flat. In my head, she liked to be on top. Instead of admitting my jealousy, instead of telling the truth, I scoured the facts and tried to find a way to blame him.

"I just don't know how much I believe you're really pushing her away. I mean, a woman doesn't call over and over if she knows she's going to be rejected."

"It's my fault she's a drunk?"

"No—"

"You're telling me you don't know any women that are so confident in their attractiveness that they don't ever hear *no*?"

"So now you're saying this woman is hot?" I challenged.

"What does that have to do with this?"

"So she is," I said.

"Why are you being so insecure right now?"

What. The. Fuck.

It wasn't necessary. I could have stayed at the table. I could have finished my meal and told him to take me home and stay at his place. I could have done lots of things. I had plenty of options. But at the time it felt like I had one option and that option was to take my coat, put it on, call him an asshole under my breath, and walk out.

It wasn't until I was standing in the rain without the valet ticket that I started to realize all of the other options I had. I saw him through the restaurant's front window. I saw him look around for a waiter. I saw him flag one down and hand over a wad of cash. I saw him grab his jacket. I just stood outside in the cold rain, hugging my jacket tighter around myself, shivering a bit and wondering what I was going to say to him when he came out. I was starting to feel pretty stupid for walking out. I was starting to feel like the stupidity of my walking out had eclipsed his insensitivity.

As he headed out to the front door, I saw through the window that he checked his phone and it was lit up again. I saw him put the call through to voice mail for the third time in ten minutes, and I grew angry again. Jealousy was so ugly. It made me feel so ugly.

I felt the gust of warm air as he opened the door and came out. When it shut, I went back to being freezing cold again.

"Elsie—" he started to say. I couldn't read this tone. I didn't know if he was going to be contrite, defensive, or irritated, so I interrupted him.

"Look," I said, closing my jacket tighter, raising my voice to be heard above the sounds of car wheels speeding through shallow puddles. "I may not be conducting myself all that well right now, but that's a hell of a thing to say to me!"

"You can't just walk out on me in the middle of a goddamn restaurant!" he yelled. I hadn't seen him yell like that before.

"I can do whatever I—"

"No!" he said. "You can't. You can't punish me for something that happened before I met you and you can't punish me for what Amber—"

"Don't say her name!"

"This is not a big deal!" he said to me. "If you knew the way I think about you and the way I think about her, this would not be a big deal." He was choking over his words as the rain snuck into his mouth.

"What does that even mean?" I said. "Don't you think that if the situation were reversed—"

"I would be jealous, yeah. To think about another guy touching you, or you . . . touching him. Yeah. I'd be jealous."

"See?"

"But I wouldn't leave you there in the middle of a restaurant looking like an idiot. I wouldn't worry you like that."

"Oh, c'mon. You weren't worried."

"Yes, Elsie, yes, I was."

"What did you think was going to happen?"

"I don't know!" he said, raising his voice again. I was so cold. The rain was so loud. "I thought maybe that this was . . ."

"Over?"

"I don't know!"

"It's not over," I said. "Just because I got upset doesn't mean that I don't want . . ." Suddenly, I wanted to hold him and make sure he knew I wasn't going anywhere. His vulnerability was so tender and touching, I almost couldn't stand it. I put my hand out and smiled at him. "Besides," I said. "We can't break up for another few weeks."

He wasn't smiling. "It's not funny," he said, his shoulders hunched, combating the rain. "I don't want to lose you."

I looked him straight in the eye and I told him what I couldn't believe he didn't already know. "Ben Ross, I'm not leaving you." Before I could even get out the last syllable, he had thrown his body against mine, his lips against my mouth. It was sloppy and imperfect. Our teeth hit, making the side of my lip sting. But it was the moment I knew Ben loved me. I could feel it. I could feel that he loved me in a raw and real way, when it's not all rainbows and butterflies, when sometimes it's fear. I could feel his fear in that kiss and I could feel the desperation in his relief. It was intoxicating and it made me feel just a little less alone. The way we felt about each other, it made him do stupid things too.

He pulled away from me, finally, and yet all too soon. I had almost forgotten that we were in public, that we were in the rain. "I'm sorry," he said, putting his thumb to the blood on his lip.

"No," I said, taking a tissue out of my jacket and dabbing his lip myself. "I'm sorry." He put his hand on my wrist and moved my hand away from his lips. He kissed me again, gently.

"You're very sexy," he said to me, as he fished his phone out of his jacket pocket. He pressed a few numbers and said finally, "Hi, you've reached the voice mail of Ben Ross. Please leave a message and I'll call you back. If this is about what I'm doing later tonight, I am busy. Don't bother asking because the answer is that I am busy. From now on, I will always be busy." He hung up the phone and looked at me.

"You didn't have to do that," I said. Ben smiled at me.

"No," he said, taking the valet ticket out of his pocket. "I really do hope she stops calling. It's not going to happen. I have a huge crush on someone else."

I laughed at him as he handed the ticket to the valet.

"It's you, by the way," he said plainly, as he pulled his jacket up over my head to protect me from the rain.

"I figured," I said.

"So are you still starving?" he asked. "Because I am and we certainly can't go back in there."

JUNE

Hi, you've reached the voice mail of Ben Ross. Please leave a message and I'll call you back. If this is about what I'm doing later tonight, I am busy. Don't bother asking because the answer is that I am busy. From now on, I will always be busy."

"Hi, you've reached the voice mail of Ben Ross. Please leave a message and I'll call you back. If this is about what I'm doing later tonight, I am busy. Don't bother asking because the answer is that I am busy. From now on, I will always be busy."

"Hi, you've reached the voice mail of Ben Ross. Please leave a message and I'll call you back. If this is about what I'm doing later tonight, I am busy. Don't bother asking because the answer is that I am busy. From now on, I will always be busy."

I listen over and over again until I know the inflections and pauses by heart, until I can hear it even when it's not playing. And then I dial again.

This time I don't get to the message. Susan picks up.

"Elsie! Jesus! Just stop it, okay? Leave me alone. I can't take it anymore! He's going to be buried! Just like you wanted. Now stop."

"Uh . . ." I say, too dumbfounded to even know how to respond.

"Good-bye, Elsie!"

She hangs up the phone.

I sit there stunned, simply staring straight ahead, eyes unfocused, but resting on one spot on the ceiling. She could have turned off the ringer, I think. She could have turned off the phone. But she didn't. She wanted to scream at me instead.

I dial Ben's number again and she picks up. "Damn it!" she says.

"You want to sit there and pretend you knew everything about your son, you go ahead. Live the lie if you want to. But don't try to bring me down with you. I am his wife. He had been scared to tell you about me for six months. Six months of him going to your house with the intention of telling you that he had fallen in love and six months of him not doing it because he thought you were too distraught to handle it. So yes, he hid it from you. And I let him because I loved him. You want to be pissed at him. *Go ahead.* You want to be in denial about what happened. *Go right ahead.* I really don't care anymore, Susan. But I lost my husband and I will call his fucking phone over and over and over if I want to because I miss his voice. So turn it off if you have to, but that's your only option."

She's quiet for a minute, and I want to hang up but I also want to hear what she has to say for herself.

"It's funny to me that you think six months is a long period of time," she says. And then she hangs up.

My fury sends me up out of my bedroom. It throws shoes on my feet. When Ana asks what I'm doing, my fury tells her I'll be back later. It pushes me out the front door, into the June heat, and then it leaves me there.

I stand outside, unsure of how I feel or what to do. I stand there for a long time, and then I turn around and walk right back inside. There's no walking away from this problem. There's no cooling off from this.

I have to pick out an outfit for tomorrow," I say when I come back in.

"No, you don't," Ana says. "I pulled out what you're wearing. You shouldn't have to think about that."

"What am I wearing?" I look at her, grateful and confused.

"I tried to find the perfect balance of sex appeal and decorum, so you're wearing that long sleeveless black shift dress I found with black pumps. And I bought you this." Ana pulls something out from under the couch. It occurs to me this couch has been her bed for days now, when I'm not using it to avoid my own.

She returns and hands me a box. I set it down in front of me and pull off the top. Inside the box is a small black hat with a thin, short black veil. It's a morbid gift, a gift you can't really say "thank you" for or say you always wanted. But somehow, this small gift fills a small chunk of the huge hole in my heart.

I slowly move toward it, delicately removing it from the box. The tissue paper crinkles around it. I move the box from my knees onto the floor and I put the hat on. I look to Ana to help me set it straight, to make it right. Then I walk into the bathroom and look at myself in the mirror.

For the first time since Ben died, I look like a widow. For the first time since I lost him, I feel like I recognize the person in the mirror. There I am, grief-stricken and un-whole. Widowed.

It's such a relief to see myself this way. I have felt so insecure in my widowness that seeing myself look like a widow comforts me. I want to run to Susan and say, "Look at me. Don't I look like a woman that lost her husband?" If I look the part, everyone will believe me.

Ana is behind me in the bathroom. Her shoulders are hunched; her hands are clasped together, fingers intertwined. She is clearly unsure if she's made a huge mistake in giving me the type of gift one hopes never to receive. I turn to her and take off the hat. She helps me set it down.

"Thank you," I say, holding her shoulder. For some reason, I don't need to rest my head on it right now. "It's beautiful."

Ana shrugs, her head sinking slightly as her shoulders sag in. "Are you sure? It's not too much? It's not too . . . macabre?"

I don't actually know what *macabre* means, so I just shake my head. Whatever bad thing she thinks this gift might be, she is wrong. Given the circumstances, I love it.

"You are a friend that I could never . . ." I choke on the words, unable to look her in the eye. "No one deserves a friend as wonderful as you," I say. "Except maybe you."

Ana smiles and seizes my temporarily not-miserable mood to slap the back of my thighs. "What can I say, kid? I love ya. Always have."

"Should I try on the whole thing?" I ask, suddenly somewhat eager for an old-fashioned game of dress-up. Ana and I used to play dress-up in college, each of us going into the bathroom to try to come up with the most ridiculous outfits for the other one to wear. This is different; this is much, much sadder, but . . . this type of dress-up is where life has taken us and Ana is on board.

"Do it. I'll wait out here."

I run into my bedroom to see that she's set aside my dress and shoes. I put them on quickly, adding a pair of black panty hose to complete the ensemble and mitigate the inherent sexiness of the veil and bare legs.

"Is it appropriate to be a sexy widow?" I call out to her while I put on my second shoe.

Ana laughs. "I've never actually seen one in person," she replies.

I step out of the door and into the hallway. When I do, I slip on the heel of my shoe and my ankle gives in. I fall flat on my ass. There is a moment when Ana stares at me not knowing what to do. She doesn't know if I'm going to laugh or cry. I think she's petrified that I will cry because this is certainly something to cry about, but I don't want to cry right now. As I look back at her, I can feel the laugh starting in my belly. I can feel it ripple through my body and then, here it is. It overtakes me.

"Oh God," I say through tears and sharp breaths. "Oh!"

Ana starts laughing loudly now too. "BAHHAHAHHHA-HAHA!" she cackles. She throws herself on the floor next to me. "I don't know why," she says and breathes in sharply. "I don't know why that was so funny."

"Oh, but it was," I say as I laugh with her. I think if she wasn't here, I would have been able to stop laughing sooner, but hearing her laugh makes me laugh. My laugh grows wild and unpredictable. It grows loud and free. She is wiping her eyes and gaining her composure, but as she looks me in the eye she loses it again. When I finally get ahold of myself, I'm light-headed.

"Oooh," I say, trying to cool down. It feels so good. I can feel it in my abdomen and my back. Then I get a glimpse of myself in the mirror again and I remember why I'm here. Why I'm in the middle of the floor on a Friday afternoon dressed in black. Ben is gone. And I hate myself for laughing. I hate myself for forgetting, even for ten seconds, the man I have lost.

Ana can tell the mood has shifted; the vacation from our misery has ended and I, once again, need to be maintained. She gets up off the floor first, dusting her ass off, and gives me a hand. I rise awkwardly, flashing my underwear at her while trying to stand up like a lady. No, like a lady isn't enough. Like a widow. Widows require even more poise. Widows don't accidentally flash their underwear at anyone.

I t doesn't get much shittier than this.

It's hot in the morning when Ana and I leave Los Angeles. It feels even hotter in Orange County. It feels stickier, sweatier, more terrible in every way. Southern California is always warmer than the rest of the country, and it's supposed to be less humid. But on this June morning, it's hot as hell and I'm dressed in all black.

We weren't late arriving here, but we weren't early. We weren't the type of early that you imagine the wife of the deceased to be. Susan stares at me as I make my way graveside. She was probably a full forty-five minutes early. What I want to tell her is that we aren't early because I almost didn't come, because I refused to get into the car. Because I threw myself on my own front lawn and told Ana that I honestly believed that if I went to his funeral, Ben would never come back. I told her, black mascara running down my face, that I wanted to stay there and wait. "I can't give up on him," I said to her, as if attending his funeral would be a betrayal and not a commemoration.

The only reason we were on time is that Ana picked me up off the ground, looked me in the eyes, and said to me, "He's never coming back. Whether you go or you don't go. So get in the car, because this is the last thing you can do with him."

Ana now stands next to me, wearing a black pantsuit. I

would hazard to guess she did this to allow me to shine today, as if this were my wedding. Susan is wearing a black sweater and black skirt. She is surrounded by young men in black suits and a few older women in black or navy dresses. We are standing outside in the grass. The heels of my high heels are digging into the grass, making me sink into the ground as if on quicksand. Moving my legs means pulling the heels up out of the ground as if they were mini-shovels. I'm aerating the graveyard grounds.

I can hear the pastor speaking; rather, I can hear that he is speaking, but I cannot make out the words. I believe he is the pastor that tended to Ben's father's service a few years ago. I do not know his denomination. I do not know how religious Susan really is. I just know he's speaking about an afterlife I'm not sure I believe in, about a God I don't trust. I am standing with my head down, glancing furtively at the people around me I don't know. I don't think I ever imagined attending my husband's funeral, whether it was specifically Ben's or the fictional idea of a husband I held on to until I met Ben. But if I did, I would have expected to know the people at the funeral.

I look over and see people I can only assume are aunts and uncles, cousins or neighbors. I stop trying to guess who they are because guessing makes me feel like I didn't know Ben. But I did know Ben, I just hadn't met this part of him yet.

My side of the funeral looks like a frat at a school dance. It's Ben's friends and former roommate. It's men who have one nice suit, who eat pizza every night, and play video games until they go to bed. That's who Ben was when he was here, it's who Ben surrounded himself with. It's good that they are here now, however nameless and faceless they feel in this crowd. Ana stands next to me, one of the only women our age in attendance. Ben wasn't friends with a lot of women, and ex-girlfriends would be out of place. Some of my friends offered to come, the ones that had met him a few times or gone out with us. I had told Ana to tell them, "Thanks, but no thanks." I wasn't sure how to react to them in this context. I wasn't sure how to be their host at a place where I felt like a guest.

As the pastor's voice dies down, I can sense that my turn to speak is coming. I am relieved when his hand gestures first to Susan.

Susan moves toward the top of the grave and opens a manila folder. Should I have brought a manila folder? I barely prepared anything. Thinking of what to say was so awful, so ulcer-inducing, that I simply didn't do it. I couldn't do it. I decided I was going to wing it. Because nothing could be worse than lying in bed thinking of what to say over your husband's dead body, right? At least that's what I thought until I saw Susan's perfectly preserved manila folder. She hadn't cried on it or ripped it up. She hadn't folded the corners over and over out of fear. It is straight as a board. I bet the paper inside isn't even scribbled on. I bet it's typed.

"I want to start by saying thank you to everyone in attendance today. I know this is not the way anyone wants to spend a Saturday morning." She half chuckles to herself, and the rest of us make a noise resembling a snort so that she can move on. "Some of you were with me a few years ago when Ben and I commemorated Steven, and I know I said then that Steven would have wanted us to enjoy this day. He would have wanted us to smile. I happened to have known that for a fact because Steven and I talked about it before he passed. We lay in the hospital together, when we knew it wasn't going to get any better, when we knew the end was near, and he told me, as I told you then, 'Make it fun, Susie. My life was fun, make this fun too.' I wasn't able to spend Ben's last moments with him." Her face starts to scrunch and she looks down. She regains her composure. "But in many ways he took after his father, and I can tell you, Ben would have wanted the same thing. He had fun in life, and we should do our best to find the fun in his death. It's senseless and painful, but it can be happy and I promise to try to make today a day of celebration of who he was. I thank God for every day I had with him, with both of them. We can lament that Ben is gone, but I'm trying to, I'm choosing to, I'm . . ." She laughs a rueful laugh. "I'm doing my best to instead think of Ben's time in my life as a gift from God. One that was shorter than I'd like, but miraculous nonetheless." She makes eye contact with me for a short period of time, long enough for both of us to notice, and then her eyes are back to the page. "No matter how many days we had with him, they were a gift. So in the spirit of celebration, I wanted to tell you all a story about one of my favorite, favorite Ben moments.

"He was eighteen and leaving for college. As many of you know he went to college close by, only an hour or two away, but it was much farther than he had ever been from me and I was terrified. My only son was moving away! All summer long I was crying on and off, trying to hide it from him, trying not to make him feel guilty. The day came to take him to school. Well, actually, wait." She stops, no longer reading from the paper. "The other part of this you need to know is that we have a guest bathroom in the house that we never use. No one ever uses it. It was this big family joke that no one had set foot in the guest bathroom for years. We have a bathroom downstairs that guests always use and an extra bathroom upstairs that I had deemed the guest bathroom and insisted it had to be redone and gorgeous because guests would use it, but no guest ever used it. I've never even had to clean it. Anyway . . ." she continues.

"As Steven and I are moving Ben in, we bring in the last of his stuff and I just start bawling my eyes out, right in front of his new roommate and his parents. It had to be mortifying for him, but he didn't show it. He walked me out to the car and he hugged Steven and I, and he said, 'Mom, don't worry. I'll come back next month and stay a weekend, all right?' And I nodded. I knew that if I didn't leave that minute, I'd never be able to. So I got in the car and Steven and I had started to drive away when Ben gave me one last kiss and said, 'When you get sad, check the guest bathroom.' I asked him to explain what he meant, but he smiled and repeated himself, so I let it go, and when I got home, I ran in there." She laughs. "I couldn't wait another minute, and as I turned on the light, I saw that he had written 'I love you' across the mirror in soap. At the very bottom it said, 'And you can keep this forever because no one will ever see it.' And I did, it's still there now. I don't think a single other person has ever seen it."

I look down at the ground just in time to see the tears fall off my face and onto my shoes.

JANUARY

It was the day before our five-week deal was up. For the past four weeks and six days, Ben and I had been spending all of our time together, but neither one of us was allowed to mention words like *boyfriend, girlfriend,* or more specifically, *I love you.* I was very much looking forward to tomorrow. We had spent the day in bed, reading magazines (me) and newspapers (him), and he had been trying to convince me that it was a good idea to get a dog. This all started because of the pictures of dogs for adoption in the classifieds.

"Just look at this one. It's blind in one eye!" Ben said as he shoved the newspaper in my face. His fingertips were covered in gray ink. All I could think was that he was getting the ink all over my white sheets.

"I see him!" I said back, putting down my magazine and turning toward Ben. "He's very, very cute. How old is he?"

"He's two! Just two years old and he needs a home, Elsie! We can be that home!"

I grabbed the newspaper from him. "*We* can't be anything. *We* aren't talking about anything that would progress our relationship in any way, shape, or form. Which a dog most certainly does."

Ben grabbed the paper back. "Yes, but that ends tomorrow and this dog might get adopted today!"

"Well, if he gets adopted today then he's okay, right? We

don't need to step in and help him," I said, smiling at him, teasing him.

"Elsie." Ben shook his head. His voice turned purposefully childish. "Before, when I said that I was worried that the dog wouldn't find a good home, I wasn't being entirely honest about how I felt about this dog."

"You weren't?" I said, falsely shocked.

"No, Elsie. I wasn't. And I think you knew that."

I shook my head. "I knew no such thing."

"I want this dog, dammit! I don't want anyone else to have it! We have to get it today!"

We had been joking up until then, but I was starting to feel that if I said I'd go get it that day, he'd put his clothes on and be in the car within minutes.

"We can't get a dog!" I said, laughing. "Whose house would it even live at?"

"Here. It would live here and I would take care of it."

"Here? At my house?"

"Well, I can't keep him at my house! It's a shithole!"

"So, really, you want *me* to get a dog and you want to play with it."

"No, I will take care of the dog with you and it will be *our* dog."

"You are cheating. This is . . . this is progressing the relationship. This is a huge . . . just a huge . . . I mean . . ."

Ben started laughing. He could see that he was making me nervous. The conversation had started to teeter on moving-in territory, and I was way too eager to discuss the idea. So eager that it embarrassed me and I did everything I could to hide it.

"Fine," he said, putting one arm around me and the other behind him on the pillow. "I won't talk about this at all today. But if Buster is still around tomorrow, can we discuss it?"

"Buster? You want to name the dog Buster?"

"I didn't name the dog! It says in the ad that his name is Buster. If it were up to me, we'd name the dog Sonic. Because that is an awesome name."

"I'm not getting a dog and naming it Sonic."

"Fine, how about Bandit?"

"Bandit?"

"Evel Knievel?"

"You would end up calling it Evel for short. That's terrible."

Ben was laughing at himself. "Please don't tell me you'd want to name a dog Fluffy or Cookie."

"If I was going to have a dog, I'd name it something based on what it looked like. You know? Really take into account the personality of the dog."

"Has anyone else told you you're the most boring woman on the planet?" Ben asked me, smiling.

"They have now," I said. "What time is it? We have to meet Ana soon, I think."

"It's five forty-seven p.m.," he said.

"Ah!" I jumped up off the bed and into a pair of jeans. "We're already going to be late!"

"We're meeting her at six?" Ben asked, not moving. "She's always late."

"Yes! Yes! But *we* still have to be on time!" I was reaching around the side of the bed searching for my bra. I didn't like the way my breasts looked in certain positions, and I found myself running around the room with one arm covering them.

Ben got up. "Okay. Can we just check to see if she'll be there on time?"

I stopped looking a moment to stare at him. "What? No. We have to leave now!"

Ben laughed. "Okay, I will get us there at six oh five," he said as he put his pants on and threw a shirt on over them. He was suddenly ready to go, and I was nowhere near it.

"Okay! Okay!" I ran into the bathroom to see if I'd left my bra there. Ben followed me in, helping me. He found it before I did and threw it at me. "Don't cover your boobs on my account. I know you think they look bad when you are bent over, but you're wrong. So next time just let 'em hang free, baby."

I looked at him in stunned silence. "You are so fucking weird," I said.

He picked me up like I weighed three pounds. My body was straight against his, my legs tight together, my arms on his shoulders. He looked at me and kissed my collarbone. "I'm weird for loving you?"

I think he was just as shocked he'd said it as I was. "To love parts of you, I meant." He put me down. "I meant, to love parts of you." He blushed slightly as I found a shirt and put it on. I smiled at him like he was a child who had very adorably hidden my car keys.

"You weren't supposed to say that," I teased him as I put on mascara and got my shoes.

"Ignore it please!" He was now waiting by the door for me.

"I don't think I can ignore it!" I said as we exited my front door.

We got in the car and he started the engine. "I really am sorry about that. It just came out."

"You broke the rules!" I said again.

"I know! I know. I'm already embarrassed. It's . . ." He trailed off as we headed down the street. He was pretending to be focused on driving, but I could tell all of him was focused on this sentence.

"It's what?"

Ben sighed, suddenly serious. "I made up the whole five-week thing because I was afraid I'd tell you I loved you too soon and you wouldn't say it back and I'd be embarrassed, and now here I am, I waited all these days to tell you and I . . . I still told you too soon and you didn't say it back and I'm embarrassed." He played the end off like a joke, but it wasn't a joke.

"Hey," I said, grabbing his arm. He was stopped at a red light. I turned his head and looked him in the eye. "I love you too," I said. "Probably before you did. I've been waiting to say it all month, practically."

His eyes looked glassy, and I couldn't tell if he was tearing up or he was perfectly fine. Either way, he kissed me and held my gaze until the cars behind us honked. Ben immediately started paying attention to the road again.

"I had this whole plan!" He laughed. "I was going to wake up early tomorrow and go into the bathroom and write 'I love you' on the mirror with a bar of soap."

I laughed. "Well, you can still do that tomorrow," I said, rubbing his hand. "It will mean just as much to me then."

Ben laughed. "Okay then, maybe I will." And he did. I left it there for days.

JUNE

I can't help but feel for Susan after her eulogy. She has made me love my husband even more than I did when he was alive.

Susan walks to her place along the grave, and the pastor asks for me to make my way to the front. I can feel myself sweating out of nervousness on top of the sweat already there from the heat.

I pull my heels out of the ground and stand at the top of Ben's grave. For a minute, I just stare at the box, knowing what is inside, knowing just days earlier that body had put a ring on my finger. Knowing even more recently, that body had gotten on a bike and headed up the street to get me cereal. That body loved me. They say that public speaking and death are the top two most stressful events in a person's life. So I forgive myself for being so scared I almost faint.

"I," I start. "I . . ." I stop. Where do I even begin? My eye catches the casket in front of me again, and I stop myself from looking at it directly. I will fall to pieces if I keep thinking about what I'm doing. "Thank you for coming. For those of you who don't know me, I want to introduce myself. My name is Elsie and I was Ben's wife."

I gotta breathe. I just gotta breathe.

"I know that you've probably all heard by now that Ben and I eloped just a few days before he passed away and I . . . know that puts us all in a difficult position. We are strangers to each other, but we share a very real loss. I had only been dating Ben a short while before we got married. I didn't know him for very long. I admit that. But the short amount of time that I was his wife," I say, "was the defining part of my life.

"He was a good man with a big heart, and he loved all of you. I've heard so many stories about you. I've heard, Aunt Marilyn, about the time you caught him peeing in your backyard. Or Mike, he told me about when you two were little and you used to play cops and robbers, but you both were robbers so there weren't any cops. These stories were part of why I grew to love him in such a short span of time, and they're part of what makes me feel so close to all of you."

I want to look these people in the eye when I say their names, but to tell the truth, I'm not entirely sure which of the older ladies is Marilyn and which of the young men is Mike. My eyes scan the people looking at me and then they move briefly to Susan. She has her head down, tucked in her chest.

"I guess I just want you all to know that at the end of his life, he had someone who loved him deeply and purely. He had someone who believed in him. I took good care of him, I promise you I did. And I can tell you, as the last person to see him alive, I can tell you, he was happy. He had found a happy life for himself. He was happy."

Susan catches my eye as I step back into place. This time she nods and puts her head back down. The pastor steps back up to lead, and my brain drifts to somewhere else, anywhere else but here.

As I stand next to Ana, she puts her arm around me and gives me a squeeze. The pastor offers Susan and me small shovels to spread dirt on the casket. We both step forward and take them, but Susan grabs the dirt with her hand instead and gently throws it on Ben's casket, so I do the same thing. We stand there, together but separate, side by side, dusting the dirt off our hands. I find myself jealous of the dirt that will get to spend so many years close to Ben's body. As I dust off the last of the dirt and Susan starts to move back toward her place in the crowd, our hands graze each other, pinkies touching. Out of reflex, I freeze, and when I do, she grabs my hand, if only for a split second, and squeezes it, never looking at me. For one second, we are together in this, and then she goes back to her spot and I retreat to mine. I want to run up to her. I want to hug her and say, "Look at what we could be to each other." But I don't.

I head back to the car and try to ready myself for the next phase of this day. I break it down into baby steps in my head. I just need to sit here in the front seat as Ana drives us to Susan's house. I just have to put one foot out of the door after she parks. Then the other foot. I just have to not cry as I head into her home. I just have to give a consternated smile to the other mourners as we walk in together. That's as far as I get before we are parked outside of Susan's house, one in a long line of cars against the sidewalk. Do the neighbors know? Are they looking at this invasion on their street and thinking, Poor Susan Ross. She lost her son now too?

I get out of the car and straighten my dress. I take off my hat with the veil and leave it on the front seat of Ana's car. She sees me do this and nods.

"Too dramatic for interiors," she says.

If I open my mouth I will cry and spill my feelings all over this sidewalk. I simply nod and tighten my lips, willing the knot in my throat to recede, to let me do this. I tell myself I can cry all night. I can cry for the rest of my life, if I can just get through this.

When I find myself in front of Susan's house, I am shocked at the sheer size of it. It's too big for one person; that much is obvious from the street. My guess is she knows that already, feels it every day. It's a Spanish-style house in a brilliant shade of white. At night, it must serve as a moon for the whole block. The roof is a deep brown with terra cotta shingles. The windows are huge. Bright, tropical-looking flowers are all over her front lawn. This house isn't just expensive; it takes a lot of upkeep.

"Jesus, what did she do? Write Harry Potter?" Ana says as we stare at it.

"Ben didn't grow up crazy rich. This all must be recent," I say, and then we walk up the brick steps to Susan's open front door. The minute I cross the threshold, I'm thrown into the middle of it.

It's a bustling house now full of people. Caterers in black pants and white shirts are offering people things like salmon mousse and shrimp ceviche on blue tortilla chips. I see a woman walk by me with a fried macaroni and cheese ball, and I think, If I ate food, that's what I'd eat. Not this seafood crap. Who serves seafood at a funeral reception? I mean, probably everyone. But I hate seafood, and I hate this funeral reception.

Ana grabs my hand and pulls me through the crowd. I don't know what I was expecting from this reception, so I don't know whether I'm disappointed or not.

Finally, we make our way to Susan. She is in her kitchen, her beautiful, ridiculously stocked kitchen, and she is speaking to the caterers about the timing of various dishes and where things are located. She's so kind and understanding. She says things like "Don't worry about it. It's just some salsa on the carpet. I'm sure it will come out." And "Make yourself at home. The downstairs bathroom is around the corner to the right."

The guest bathroom. I want to see the guest bathroom. How do I run upstairs and find it without her knowing? Without being terribly rude and thoughtless? I just want to see his handwriting. I just want to see new evidence that he was alive.

Ana squeezes my hand and asks me if I want a drink. I decline, and so she makes her way over to the bar area without me. Suddenly, I am standing in the middle of a funeral dedicated to my husband, and yet, I am not a part of it. I do not know anyone here. Everyone is walking around me, talking next to me, looking at me. I am the enigma to them. I am not a part of the Ben they knew. Some of them stare and then smile when I catch them. Others don't even see me. Or maybe they are just better at staring. Susan comes out from the kitchen.

"Should you go talk to her?" Ana asks, and I know that I should. I know that this is her house, this is her event, and I am a guest and I should say something.

"What do I say in a situation like this?" I have started saying "situation like this" because this situation is so unique that it has no name and I don't feel like constantly saying, "My new husband died and I'm standing in a room full of strangers making me feel like my husband was a stranger."

"Maybe just 'How are you?'" Ana suggests. I think it's stupid that the most appropriate question to ask the mother of my dead husband on the day of his funeral is the same question I ask bank tellers, waiters, and any other strangers I meet. Nevertheless, Ana is right. That is what I should do. I breathe in hard and hold it, and then I let it out and I start walking over to her.

Susan is speaking with a few women her own age. They are dressed in black or navy suits with pearls. I walk up and wait patiently next to her. It's clear that I want to cut in. The women leave pauses in the conversation, but none feel big enough for me to jump in. I know that she can see me. I'm in her sight line. She's just making me wait because she can. Or maybe she's not. Maybe she's trying to be polite and this isn't about me.

Honestly, I've lost perspective on what's about me and what isn't so . . .

"Hi, Elsie," she says to me as she finally turns around. She turns her back away from her friends, and her torso now faces mine. "How are you?" she asks me.

"I was just about to ask you that," I say.

She nods. "This is the most fucked-up day of my life," she says. The minute the word *fuck* comes out of her mouth, she becomes a real person to me, with cracks and holes, huge vulnerable spots and flaws. I see Ben in her, and I start to cry. I hold back the tears as best I can. Now isn't the time to lose it. I have to keep it together.

"Yeah, it's a hard day," I say, my voice starting to betray me. "Your speech was . . ." I begin, and she puts her hand out to stop me.

"Yours too. Keep your chin up. I know how to get through these things, and it's by keeping your chin up."

This is about all I get from Susan, and I'm not sure if it's a metaphor or not. She is pulled away by new arrivals that want to prove what good people they are by "being there for her." I walk back over to Ana, who is now near the kitchen. The waiters are running back and forth with full and empty trays, and as they do, Ana keeps pulling bacon-wrapped dates off the full ones. "I did it," I say.

She high-fives me. "When was the last time you ate?" she says, devouring the dates as she asks.

I think back to the pancake and know that if I tell the truth, she's going to force-feed me hors d'oeuvres.

"Oh, pretty recently," I say.

"Bullshit," she says as another waiter comes through with shrimp. She stops him, and I cringe.

"No," I say, perhaps too boldly. "No shrimp."

"Dates?" she says, handing her napkin over to me. It still has two left. The dates are big, and the bacon looks thick around them. They are gooey from the sugar. I don't know if I can do it. But then I think about all the seafood here and I know this is my best bet. So I take them and eat them.

They. Are. Decadent.

And suddenly my body wants more. More sugar. More salt. More life. And I tell myself, That's sick, Elsie. Ben's dead. This is no time for hedonism.

I excuse myself and head upstairs, away from the food and toward the guest bathroom mirror. I know where I'm going as I walk up the stairs, but I'm not consciously moving there. I feel pulled there. As I get further up the stairs, I can hear a number of voices chattering and people chewing. There are quite a few people hanging out in the guest room. Everyone has come up to see the bathroom mirror. I don't turn the corner and go into the room. I stand at the top of the stairs, not sure what to do. I want to be alone with the mirror. I can't bear to see his handwriting with an audience. Do I turn back around? Come back later?

"That eulogy was convincing," I hear a man's voice say.

"No, I know. I'm not saying it wasn't convincing," says another voice, this one higher, womanly, and more committed to the conversation.

"What are we talking about?" comes a third voice. It's gossipy, and I can tell just by the tone, the speaker's got a drink in her hand.

"Ben's widow," says the woman.

"Ohh, right. Scandal," the third voice says. "They weren't even married two weeks, right?"

"Right," says the man. "But I think Susan believes her."

"No, I know Susan believes her," the woman says. "I believe her too. I get it. They were married. I'm just saying, you know Ben, you know the way he loved his mom. Don't you think he would have told her if this was the real deal?"

I slowly step away, not wanting to be heard and not wanting to hear whatever comes next. As I walk down the steps to find Ana, I catch a glimpse of myself in one of Susan's mirrors. For the first time, I don't see myself. I see the woman they all see, the woman Susan sees: the fool who thought she was going to spend her life with Ben Ross.

FEBRUARY

It was a Tuesday night and Ben and I were tired. I had had a long day at the library, pulling together a display of artifacts of the Reagan administration. Ben had gotten into an argumentative discussion with his boss over a company logo that Ben was lead on. Neither one of us wanted to cook dinner, neither one of us wanted to do much of anything except eat food and go to bed.

We went out for dinner at the café on the corner. I ordered spaghetti with pesto. Ben got a chicken sandwich. We sat at one of the wobbly tables out front, with two wobbly chairs, and we ate alfresco, counting the minutes until it was appropriate to go to sleep.

"My mom called me today," Ben said, pulling red onions out of his sandwich and placing them on the wax paper underneath.

"Oh?"

"I just . . . I think that is part of why I am stressed out. I haven't told her about you."

"Well, don't worry about it on my account. I haven't told my parents about you either."

"But this is different," he said. "I am close with my mom. I talk to her all the time, I just, for some reason, I don't want to tell her about you."

I was confident enough by this point that I had Ben's heart, that the issue here was not me.

"Well, what do you think is stopping you?" I asked, finishing my pasta. It had been watery and unsatisfying.

Ben put his sandwich down and wiped the excess flour off his hands. Why on earth do fancy artisan sandwiches have flour on them?

"I'm not sure. I think part of it is that I know that she will be happy for me but concerned . . . er . . ."

"Concerned?" Now I was starting to think maybe I *was* the issue here.

"Not concerned. When my dad died, I spent a lot of time with my mom."

"Naturally," I said.

"Right, but also, I was worried about her. I wanted to make sure she always had someone around. I didn't want her to be alone."

"Sure."

"And then as time went on, I wanted to give her a chance to move on herself. To meet someone else, to find her new life. To really . . . leave the nest, kind of."

I chuckled slightly, subtly, to myself. What kind of son wants to help his own mother leave the nest?

"But she just didn't."

"Right. Well, everyone is different," I said.

"I know, but it's been three years and she's still in that same house, alone. My mom had the exterior of the house redone after my dad died. I think to keep busy maybe? I don't know. She got money from the life insurance policy. When that was done, she added an extension. When that was done, she had the front yard redone. It's like she can't stop moving or she'll implode. But she hasn't changed much about the place inside, really. It's mostly as my father left it. Pictures of him everywhere. She still wears her wedding ring. She isn't moving on."

"Mmm-hmm," I said, listening.

"I'm worried that my meeting you, meeting this fantastic girl who is perfect for me . . ." he said, "I'm worried it will be too much. I'm worried she'll feel left behind. Or . . . that I'm moving on too quickly or something. There's nothing left in the house to change. And I feel like she's about to"—he didn't say it lightly—"crash."

"You feel like you need to stagnate because she is stagnating? Or that you need to keep her at bay for now until she settles?"

"Kind of. For some reason, I just think, when I tell my mom I'm in a really great relationship, some part of her isn't going to be ready for that."

"I guess I don't understand why it's so dramatic. I mean, you've dated other girls before."

"Not girls like you, Elsie. This is . . . you are different."

I didn't say anything back. I just smiled and looked him in the eyes.

"Anyway." He went back to his sandwich, finishing it up. "When I tell my mom about you, it's going to be serious because I'm serious about you and I don't know . . . I'm worried she'll take it as a rejection. Like I'm no longer there for her."

"So I'm a secret?" I asked, starting to feel bothered and hoping I was misunderstanding.

"For now," he said. "I'm being such a baby, scared of my mom. But if you don't have a problem with it, I just want to be delicate with her."

"Oh, sure," I said, but then felt myself speaking up. "But not forever, right? I mean, you'll tell her eventually." I didn't say the last part as a question and yet, that's exactly what it was.

Ben nodded as he finished chewing. "Absolutely!" he said. "When the time is right, I know she'll be thrilled." He rolled up the wax paper from his sandwich. He pitched it toward the trash can and missed. He laughed at himself, walked over, picked up the ball of paper, and put it in the trash can. By the time he grabbed my hand and started to lead us back to my place, I had come around to his way of seeing it.

"Thank you, Elsie. For understanding and not thinking I am a gigantic douchey mama's boy."

"You're not scared your mom will be mad at you," I said. "That would make you a gigantic douchey mama's boy. You're just scared to hurt her feelings. That makes you sensitive. And it's one of the reasons I love you."

"And the fact that you understand that about me and it's a reason you love me, makes you the coolest girl in the world," he said, as he put his arm around me and kissed my temple. We walked awkwardly down the block, too close together to walk gracefully.

When we got to my apartment, we brushed our teeth and I washed my face, both of us using the sink in our own perfectly timed intervals. We took off our jeans. He took off his shirt and handed it to me silently, casually, as if it were now an impulse. I took it and put it on, as he turned on the one bedside lamp and picked up a book with a wizard on the cover. I got in beside him and put my head on his shoulder.

"You're going to read?" I asked.

"Just until my brain stops," he said, and then he put the book down and looked at me. "Want me to read to you?" he offered.

"Go for it," I said, thinking that it sounded like a nice way to fall asleep. My eyes were closed by the time he got to the end of the page, and the next thing I knew it was morning.

JUNE

I tell Ana I want to go, and within seconds, we are headed for the door.

"What's the matter?" Ana asks.

"No, nothing. I'm just ready to leave," I say. Ana's keys are in her hand, and my hand is on the doorknob.

"You're leaving?" Susan asks. I turn to see her a few feet behind me.

"Oh," I say. "Yes, we're going to make the drive back to Los Angeles." What is she thinking right now? I can't tell. She's so stone-faced. Is she happy I'm leaving? Is this all the evidence she needs that I don't belong in their lives?

"Okay," she says. "Well." She grabs my hand and squeezes it. "I wish you the best of luck, Elsie."

"You too, Susan," I say. I turn around and catch Ana's eye, and we walk out the door. It isn't until my feet have hit the cement in her driveway that I realize why I am so bothered by what she just said, aside from how disingenuous it was.

She thinks she'll never see me again. It's not like I live in Michigan. She could easily see me if she wanted to. She just doesn't want to.

When we get home, I run to the bathroom and shut the door. I stand against it, holding the knob still in my hand. It's over. Ben is over. This is done. Tomorrow people will expect me to start moving on. There is no more Ben left in my life. I left him in Orange County.

I lock the door behind me, calmly walk over to the toilet, and puke bacon-wrapped dates. I wish I had eaten more in the past few days so I'd have something to give. I want to expel everything from my body, purge all of this pain that fills me into the toilet and flush it down.

I open the bathroom door and walk out. Ana is standing there, waiting.

"What do you want to do?" she asks.

"I think, really, I'm just going to go to sleep. Is that okay? Do you think that's bad? To go to sleep at"—I look at the clock on my cell phone; it is even earlier than I thought—"to go to bed at seven oh three p.m.?"

"I think you have had a very hard day and if you need to go to sleep, that's okay. I'm going to go home and let my dog out and I'll be back," she says.

"No." I shake my head. "You don't need to, you can sleep in your own bed."

"Are you sure? I don't want you to be alone if you—"

"No, I'm sure." I don't know how she's been sleeping here for all of these days, living out of a backpack, going back and forth.

"Okay." She kisses me on the cheek. "I'll come by in the morning," she adds. She grabs her things and heads out the door, and when it closes, the apartment becomes dead and silent.

This is it. This is my new life. Alone. Quiet. Still. This isn't how it was supposed to go. Ben and I had mapped out our lives together. We had a plan. This wasn't the plan. I've got no plan.

FEBRUARY

Ben called me from the car to tell me he would be late. Traffic was backed up.

"I'm stuck on the 405. Nobody's moving and I'm bored," he said to me. I had been at lunch with Ana and had just left and made my way home.

"Oh no!" I said, opening up my front door and placing my things on the front table. "How far away are you?"

"With this traffic I can't even tell, which sucks because I want to see you," he said.

I sat down on the couch and kicked my shoes off. "I want to see you too! I missed you all morning." Ben had spent the night with me and left early to make the visit down to Orange County. He had planned on telling his mother about us and wanted to do it in person.

"Well, how did it go?" I asked.

"We went out to breakfast. She asked a lot about me. I kept asking about her, but she kept turning the conversation back to me and there just . . . there wasn't an opening to say it. To tell her. I didn't tell her."

He didn't say the phrase "I'm sorry," but I could hear it in his voice. I was disappointed in him for the first time, and I wondered if he could hear it in mine.

"Okay, well . . . you know . . . it is what it is," I said. "Is traffic moving? When do you think you'll be home? Er . . . here. When do you think you'll be here?" I had started to make this mistake more and more often, calling my home his home. He spent so much time here, you'd think he lived here. But paying rent in one place and spending your time in another was just the way things were done when you were twenty-six and in love. Living together was something entirely different, and I was showing my hand early by continuing to make that mistake.

"You keep doing that!" he teased me.

"Okay, okay, it was a mistake. Let's move on."

"The freeway is clearing up so I should be there in about a half hour, I think. Then I think I'll move in, in about four months. We will get engaged a year after that and married within a year after that. I think we should have time alone together before we have kids, don't you? So maybe first kid at thirty. Second at thirty-three or thirty-four. I'm fine to have three if we have the money to do it comfortably. So, with your biological clock, let's try for the third before thirty-eight or so. Kids will be out of the house and in college around fifty-five. We can be empty-nested and retired by sixty-five. Travel around the world a few times. I mean, sixty is the new forty, you know? We'll still be spry and lively. Back from world travel by seventy, which gives us about ten to twenty years to spend time with our grandkids. You can garden, and I'll start sculpting or something. Dead by ninety. Sound good?"

I laughed. "You didn't account for your midlife crisis at forty-five, where you leave me and the kids and start dating a young preschool teacher with big boobs and a small ass."

"Nah," he said. "That won't happen."

"Oh no?" I dared him.

"Nope. I found the one. Those guys that do that, they didn't find the one."

He was cocksure and arrogant, thinking he knew better, thinking he could see the future. But I loved the future he saw and I loved the way he loved me.

"Come home," I said. "Er, here. Come here."

Ben laughed. "You have to stop doing that. According to the plan, I don't move in for another four months."

JUNE

I lie in bed all morning until Ana shows up, and she tells me to get dressed because we are going to the bookstore.

When we walk into the behemoth of a store, I follow Ana along as she picks up books and puts them down. She seems to have a purpose, but I don't much care what it is. I leave her side and walk toward the Young Adult section. There I find a trio of teenage girls, laughing and teasing each other about boys and hairstyles.

I run my fingers over the books, looking for titles that I now own on my own bookshelf, their pages torn and softened by Ben's fingers. I look for names I recognize because I got them from work and brought them home to him. I never guessed correctly, the books he'd want to read. I don't think I ever got one right. I didn't have enough time to learn what he liked. I would have learned though. I would have studied it and learned it and figured out who he was as a book reader if I'd just been given enough time.

Ana finds me eventually. By the time she has, I'm sitting on the floor next to the E-F-G section. I stand up and look at the book in her hand. "What'd ya get?"

"It's for you. And I already paid for it," she says. She hands it to me.

The Year of Magical Thinking by Joan Didion.

"Are you fucking kidding me?" I say, too loudly for a bookstore, even though I realize that's not the same as a library.

"No," she says. She's taken aback by my reaction. Hell, so am I. "I just thought, you know, it's a really popular book. There are people out there going through what you are going through."

"You mean there are millions of misguided friends buying books for their sad friends."

She ignores me.

"There are other people that have gotten through this, and I wanted you to know that if all those stupid people can do it, you, Elsie Porter, can do it. You are so strong and so smart, Elsie. I just wanted you to have something in your hand you could hold and know that you can do this."

"Elsie Ross," I say, correcting her. "My name is Elsie Ross."

"I know," she says, defensively.

"You called me Elsie Porter."

"It was an accident."

I stare at her and then get back to the issue at hand.

"There is no getting through this, Ana. But you won't ever understand that because you've never loved someone like I love him."

"I know that," she says.

"No one could. Certainly not a goddamn book."

My job is books, information. I based my career on the idea that words on pages bound and packaged help people. That they make people grow, they show people lives they've never seen. They teach people about themselves, and here I am, at my lowest point, rejecting help from the one place I always believed it would be.

I walk out of the bookstore.

I walk down streets with cracked pavement. I walk down neighborhood roads. I walk through large intersections. I wait at stoplights. I press the walk signals over and over. I avoid eye contact with everyone in front of me. I get hot. I take my sweatshirt off. I get cold and I put it back on. I cross through traffic jams by weaving in between cars, and somehow, I find myself in front of my house, looking up at my door. I don't know how long I've been walking. I don't know how long I've been crying.

I see something at my door, and from a distance I think maybe it's the marriage certificate. I run up to it and am disappointed to see it's just the *Los Angeles Times*. I pick it up, aware of the fact that I have been so unaware of current events since the current event. The first thing I notice is the date. It's the twenty-eighth. That can't be right. But it has to be. I highly doubt that the *L.A. Times* printed the date wrong and I'm the only genius that figured it out. All of the days have been blurring together, bleeding from one into the next. I didn't realize it was so late in the month. I should have gotten my period days ago.

MARCH

Y ou're a goddess," he said to me, as he lay down on his back, sweaty in all the right places, his hair a tangled mess, his breathing still staccato.

"Stop it," I said. I was light-headed and my body felt hollow. I could feel sweat on my hairline and upper lip. I tried to wipe it away, but it kept coming back. I turned toward him, my body naked next to his. My nerves were overly sensitive. I could feel every place his body was touching mine, no matter how subtle or irrelevant.

It was quiet for a moment, and he grabbed my hand. He pulled our clasped hands onto his bare stomach and we rested them there. I closed my eyes and drifted off. I was awakened by his snoring and realized that we should not be napping in the middle of the day. We had movies to see and plans to get dinner. I got up and cracked a window. A chill quickly took over what was a muggy room.

"Ugh, why did you do that?" Ben groaned. I stood next to him and told him we had been sleeping long enough. He pulled me back down to the bed. He put his head on my chest as he tried to wake up.

"I have to say, I am really glad you went on that NuvaRing thing," he said, once he was alert. "I don't have to worry about anything. I can just fall asleep after."

I laughed. So much of Ben's happiness was based on his love for sleep. "It's not in the way or anything?" I asked.

He shook his head. "No, not at all. It's like it's not there, honestly."

"Right," I said. "But it is there."

"Right."

"You saying that just made me paranoid."

"About what?"

"You can't feel it at all? What if it fell out or something?"

Ben moved his body upright. "How would it fall out? That's absurd."

He was right. That was absurd. But I wanted to check just in case.

"Hold on."

I walked to the bathroom and shut the door. I sat down and braced myself but . . . it wasn't there.

My heart started beating rapidly and my face began to turn hot. The whole room felt hot. My hands were shaking. I didn't say anything. I couldn't. And soon enough, Ben knocked on the bathroom door.

"You okay?"

"Uh . . ."

"Can I come in?"

I opened the door, and he saw my face. He knew.

He nodded. "It's gone, right? It's not there?"

I shook my head. "I don't know how! I don't understand how." I felt like I had ruined both of our lives. I started crying.

"I'm so sorry, Ben! I'm so sorry! I don't understand how this could have happened! It's not . . . I did exactly what I was supposed to! I don't know how it would have just *fallen* out! I don't! I don't!"

Ben grabbed me. By this time he had put his underwear back on. I was still naked as he clutched me.

"It's going to be okay," he said. "We have plenty of options."

To me, when a man tells you that you have options, he means you can get an abortion.

"No, Ben," I said. "I can't do that. I can't. Not . . . not when it's yours."

Ben started laughing. Which was weird because there was nothing funny about it.

"That's not what I meant. At all. And I agree. We won't do that."

"Oh," I said. "Then what are you talking about?"

"Well, we don't know how long it's been gone, right?"

I shook my head, embarrassed. This was completely my fault. How could I be so incredibly careless?

"So, we can get the morning after pill for this one. But we might not be out of the woods for anything days ago."

"Right. Right."

"So, if it ends up that next month, your period is late and you are pregnant, then I'm going to grab your hand and take you with me to the courthouse right across the street from my office. We're getting a marriage license and I will marry you right then and there in front of the judge. That doesn't scare me. Diapers scare me. But spending my life with you doesn't scare me. Not one bit. And trust me, I do not want a baby right now. We can't afford it. We don't have a lot of time. We don't have the resources. But you bet your fucking ass that if you're pregnant, we will figure out a way to make it work and we'll look back on it and say that you losing that NuvaRing was the smartest thing we ever did. So don't cry. Don't stress. Whatever happens happens. I'm here. I'm not going anywhere. We are in this together and we will be fine."

No one had ever said that to me before. I didn't know what to say.

"Does that work for you? I want to make sure you feel the same way," he said.

I nodded.

"Okay. Just for the record, I hope you're not pregnant because—" He started laughing. "I am not ready to be a dad."

"Me neither," I said and then corrected myself. "To be a mom, I mean." It was quiet for a while. "When is your lease up?" I asked.

"It's month to month." He smiled.

"I think you should move in."

"I thought you'd never ask."

And then, for some masochistic and stupid reason, we had sex again.

JUNE

I am sitting in the bathroom, not sure what to do. My period is nowhere to be found. And for the first time since Ben died, I find myself excited about something. Scared, for sure. Nervous, most definitely. I am anxious in every conceivable interpretation of the word.

What if I'm pregnant? Maybe my life with Ben isn't over. Maybe Ben is here. Ben could be living inside me. Maybe our relationship isn't a ghost. What if my relationship with Ben is a tangible piece of the world? What if Ben is soon to be living and breathing again?

I run to the pharmacy down the street, the very same one that Ben biked to when he was getting my cereal. Normally, I avoid this street, I avoid this store, but I have to know. I have to know as soon as possible whether this is real. I know that having a baby won't solve anything, but it could make this better. It could make this easier. It will mean that Ben will never truly leave my life. I yearn for that feeling so badly that I can't take my usual detour. I take the most direct route.

I run past the intersection where I lost him, the intersection that fractured my life from one long joyride to a series of days, hours, and minutes that are insufferable. As I fly through the crosswalk, I hear a small crunch under my feet and I am too scared to look down. If I see a Fruity Pebble, I might just drop to the middle of the road, willing cars to run me over, and I can't do that now. I might have a baby inside me.

I get into the pharmacy and I run right past the food section. I know that it was the last place Ben did anything. I know he stood in that aisle and he picked a box of cereal. I can't look at it. I head to the family planning aisle and I buy four boxes of pregnancy tests. I rush to the cashier and tap my foot impatiently as the line moves slowly and inconsistently.

When it is finally my turn, I pay for them, and I know the cashier thinks he knows what's going on, a woman my age buying boxes of pregnancy tests. He probably thinks he gets me. He doesn't. No one could ever understand this.

I run home and race into the bathroom. I'm nervous and I don't have to pee, so it takes me quite a while to finally pee on a stick. I do two just to be sure. I figure I have the other two left over if I need them.

I set them down on the counter and look at the time. I have two minutes. Two minutes until I know what the rest of my life is going to look like.

Then I start to realize, I have to be pregnant. What are the chances I'm not? I must be. I messed up my birth control, I had unprotected sex multiple times, and it's just a coincidence that my period, which is never late, is now late? That doesn't make any sense. My period is days late. That can only mean one thing.

It means I'm not alone in this. It means Ben is here with me. It means my life, that felt empty and miserable, now feels difficult but manageable. I can be a single mother. I can raise this child by myself. I can tell this child all about his father. About how his father was a gentle man, a kind man, a funny man, a good man. If it's a girl, I can tell her to find a man like her father. If it's a boy, I can tell him to be a man like his father. I can tell him his father would have been so proud of him. If he's gay, I can tell him to be like his father *and* find a man like his father—

which would be the best of all worlds. If she grows up to be a lesbian, she won't need to be or find anyone like her father, but she'll still love him. She'll know that she came from a man that would have loved her. She'll know she came from two people that loved each other fiercely. She'll know not to settle for anything less than a love that changes her life.

I can tell her about the time we met. She'll want to know. She'll ask over and over as a child. She'll want to keep pictures of him framed around the house. She'll have his nose or his eyes, and just when I least suspect it, she'll say something that sounds like him. She'll move her hands in a way that he did. He'll live on in her and I won't be alone. I won't be without him. He's here. He didn't leave me. This isn't over. My life isn't over. Ben and I are not over. We have this. We have this child. I will dedicate my life to raising this child, to letting Ben's body and soul live on through this child.

I grab the sticks, already knowing what they say, and then I drop to my knees.

I am wrong.

There is no child.

No matter how many sticks I use, they keep saying the same thing. They keep telling me Ben is gone forever and that I am alone.

I don't move from the bathroom floor for hours. I don't move until I feel it. I am bleeding.

I know it's a sign that my body is fully functioning, that I am physically fine. But it feels like a betrayal.

I call Ana. I say I need her and I'm sorry. I tell her she is all I have left.

PART TWO

AUGUST

Are things easier with time? Maybe. Maybe not. The days are easier to get through because I have a pattern to follow. I'm back at work. I have projects to occupy my mind. I can almost sleep through the night now. In my dreams, Ben and I are together. We are free. We are wild. We are what we were. In the mornings, I ache for my dreams to be real, but it's a familiar ache, and while it feels like it might kill me, I know from having felt it the day before that it won't. And maybe that's how some of my strength comes back.

I rarely cry in public anymore. I've become a person about which people probably say, "She's really bounced back quite nicely." I am lying to them. I have not bounced back nicely. I've just learned to impersonate the living. I have lost almost ten pounds. It's that dreaded last ten that magazines say every woman wants to lose. I suppose I have the body I've always wanted. It doesn't do me much good.

I go places with Ana, to flea markets and malls, restaurants and cafés. I've even started to let her invite other people. People I haven't seen for ages. People who only met Ben a few times. They grab my hand and say they're sorry over brunch. They say they wish they could have known him better. I tell them, "Me too." But they never know what I mean.

But when I'm alone, I sit on the floor of the closet and smell his clothes. I still don't sleep in the middle of the bed. His side of the room is untouched. If you didn't know any better, you'd think two people lived in my apartment.

I haven't moved his PlayStation. There is food in the refrigerator that he bought, food I will never eat, food that is rotting. But I can't throw it out. If I look in that refrigerator and there are no hot dogs, it will just reinforce that I am alone, that he is gone, that the world I knew is over. I'm not ready for that. I'd rather see rotting hot dogs than no hot dogs, so they stay.

Ana is very understanding. She's the only person that can really get a glimpse of this new life I lead. She stays at her place now, with an open invitation for me to come over anytime I can't sleep. I don't go over. I don't want her to know how often I can't sleep.

If I can't have Ben, I can have being Ben's widow, and I have found a modicum of peace in this new identity. I wear my wedding ring, even though I no longer insist people call me by my married name. I am Elsie Porter. Elsie Ross only existed for a couple weeks, at most. She was barely on this earth longer than a miniseries.

I still have not received the marriage certificate, and I haven't told anyone. Every day I rush home from work, expecting it to be waiting for me in the mailbox, and every day, I am disappointed to find a series of credit card offers and coupons. No one alerted the national banks that Ben is dead. If I didn't have other things to be miserable about, I'm pretty sure this would set me off. Imagine being the kind of woman that gets over her dead husband only to find his name in her mailbox every day. Luckily, Ben never leaves the forefront of my mind, so I can't be provoked into remembering him. I am always remembering him.

I read somewhere to watch out for "triggers," things that will remind you of your loss right out of the blue. For instance, if

Ben loved root beer and had this whole thing about root beer, then I should stay away from soda aisles. But what if I went into a candy store and saw, unexpectedly, that they had root beer and I started crying right there in the store? That would be a trigger. The reason why this is completely irrelevant to me is that root beer doesn't remind me of Ben. Everything reminds me of Ben. Floors, walls, ceilings, white, black, brown, blue, elephants, cartwheels, grass, marbles, Yahtzee. Everything. My life is trigger after trigger. I have reached a critical mass of grief. So, no, I don't need to avoid any triggers.

The point, though, is that I am functional. I can get through each day without feeling like I'm not sure I'll make it to midnight. I know when I wake up that today will be just like the day before, devoid of honest laughter and a genuine smile, but manageable.

Which is why when I hear my own doorbell at 11:00 a.m. on a Saturday and I look through my peephole, I think, God *dammit*. Why can't everyone just leave *well enough* alone?

She's standing outside my door in black leggings, a black shirt, and a gray, oversize, knit vesty-sweater thing. She's over sixty fucking years old. Why does she always look so much better than I do?

I open the door.

"Hi, Susan," I say, trying hard to sound like I'm not pissed she's here.

"Hi." Although, just from the way she greets me, I feel like this is a different woman than the one I met almost two months ago. "May I come in?"

I open the door fully and invite her in with my arm. I stand by the door. I don't know how long she plans on staying, but I don't want to imply she should stay longer than she wanted.

"Could we talk for a minute?" she asks.

I lead us into the living room.

As she sits, I realize I should offer her something to drink. Is this a custom in all countries? Or just here? Because it's stupid. "Can I get you anything to drink?"

"Actually, I wanted to ask if you'd like to go to lunch," she says. Lunch? "But first, I wanted to bring you something."

She pulls her purse from over her shoulder onto her lap and sorts through it, pulling out a wallet. It's not *a* wallet. I know that wallet; its leather worn down in places by my husband's fingers and molded around his butt. She hands it over to me, losing her balance slightly as she leans so far forward. I take it from her softly. It might as well be a Van Gogh, that's how delicately I am approaching it.

"I owe you an apology, Elsie. I hope you can forgive me. I offer no excuses for my behavior. The way I spoke to you, there is no excuse for being so cold and, truthfully, cruel. I treated you so poorly that I . . . I'm embarrassed about my actions." I look at her and she keeps talking. "I am incredibly disappointed in myself. If someone treated my child the way I treated you, I would have killed them. I had no right. I just . . . I hope you can understand that I was grieving. The pain in front of me felt so insurmountable, and to learn that my only child didn't feel comfortable telling me about you . . . I couldn't face that too. Not at that time. I told myself you were crazy, or lying, or . . . I blamed you. You were right when you said I hated you because you were the only one around to hate. You were right. And I knew it then, that's why I tried so hard to . . . I wanted to make it better, but I just couldn't. I didn't have it in me to be a kind person." She stops for a minute and then corrects herself. "Even a decent person."

She looks at me with tears in her eyes, a look of somber and grave regret across her face. This sucks. Now I can't even hate her.

"It's awful to say, but I just . . . I wanted you as far away from me and as far away from Ben as possible. I think I thought if you'd just go away, then I could deal with the loss of my son and I wouldn't have to face the fact that I lost a part of him a long time before he died."

She looks down at her own knees and shakes her head. "That's not . . . that's not what I came here to talk about. Never mind. Anyway, I wanted you to have his wallet and this."

She pulls his wedding ring out of her purse.

I was wrong.

I do have triggers.

I start crying. I put that wedding ring on him myself, my hand shaking while his was steady as a rock. I remember seeing it on him the next day thinking that I never knew how sexy a wedding ring was on a man until it was my ring, until I put it there.

She comes over to me on the couch and holds me. She takes my left hand and she puts the ring into it, balling my fingers up into a fist as she holds me.

"Shh," she says. "It's okay." She puts her head on top of mine. My head is buried in her chest. She smells like a sweet, flowery, expensive perfume. She smells like she's worn the same perfume for forty years, like it's molded to her. Like it's hers. She is warm and soft, her sweater absorbing my tears, whisking them away from my face and onto her. I can't stop crying and I don't know if I ever will. I feel the ring in my hand, my palm sweating around it. My fist is so tight that my fingers start to ache. I let my muscles go, falling into her. I can hear myself blubbering. I am wailing loudly; the noises coming out of me feel like blisters. Once I have calmed, once my eyes have gotten control of themselves again, I stay there. She doesn't let go.

"He loved you, Elsie. I know that now. My son wasn't a very romantic person, but I doubt you ever knew that. Because he was clearly very romantic with you."

"I loved him, Susan," I say, still stationary, inert. "I loved him so much."

"I know you did," she says. "He kept a copy of his proposal in his wallet. Did you know that?"

I perk up. She hands the paper to me, and I read it.

"Elsie, let's spend our lives together. Let's have children together and buy a house together. I want you there when I get the promotion I've been shooting for, when I get turned down for something I've always hoped for, when I fall and when I stand back up. I want to see every day of your life unfold. I want to be yours and to have you as my own. Will you marry me? Marry me."

"Will you marry me?" is crossed out and replaced with the more forward statement. "Marry me."

This isn't how he proposed. I don't even know what this is. But it feels good to know he struggled with how to ask me. This was one of his attempts. His handwriting was so very bad.

"I found it in his wallet when I went through it. That's when I got it. You know? Like it or not, you are the truth about Ben. He loved you fiercely. And just because he didn't tell me, doesn't mean he didn't love you. I just have to keep telling myself that. It's a hard one to make sense of, but anyway, you should have these things. He would want that." She smiles at me, grabbing my chin like I am a child. "I am so proud of my son for loving you this way, Elsie. I didn't know he had it in him."

It feels nice to think that maybe Susan could like me. I am

actually overwhelmed by how nice that thought feels. But this is not the Susan I know. And it makes me feel uneasy. If I'm being honest, part of me is worried she's going to wait until my defenses are down and then sock me in the stomach.

"Anyway, I would love to get to know you," she says. "If that is okay with you. I should have called before I came up here, but I thought"—she laughs—"I thought if I was you, I'd tell me to fuck off, so I didn't want to give you the chance."

I laugh with her, unsure of what exactly is going on and how to respond to it.

"Can I take you to lunch?" she asks.

I laugh again. "I don't know," I say, knowing my eyes are swollen and I haven't showered.

"I wouldn't blame you for asking me to leave," she says. "I was awful, when I think about it from your point of view. And you don't know me at all, but I can tell you that once I realize I'm wrong, I do everything to make it right. I've thought about this for weeks and I wouldn't be here if I wasn't ready to do better. I really do want to get to know you and I'd love to just . . . start over." She says "start over" like it's a refreshing thought, like it's something people can actually do. And because of that, I start to feel like maybe it is possible. Maybe it's easier than it feels. We will just start over. Let's try again.

"Yeah," I say. "We can try again."

Susan nods. "I'm so sorry, Elsie."

"Me too," I say, and it isn't until I say it that I realize I mean it. We sit there for a minute, considering each other. Can we do this? Can we be good to each other? Susan seems convinced that we can, and she's determined to take the lead.

"All right," she says. "Let's get composed and head out."

"You are much better at composure than I am."

"It's a learned trait," she says. "And it's entirely superficial. Hop in the shower, I'll wait here. I won't poke through anything, I promise." She puts her hands up in the air to signify swearing.

"Okay," I say, getting up. "Thank you, Susan."

She closes her eyes for just half a second and nods her head.

I head into the bathroom, and before I shut the door, I tell her she's welcome to poke through anything she likes.

"Okay! You may regret this," she says. I smile and get in the shower. While I'm washing my hair, I think of all the things I have been meaning to say to her for weeks. I think of how I've wanted to tell her the pain she caused me. I've wanted to tell her how wrong she was. How little she really knew her own son. How unkind she has been. But now that she's here, and she's different, it doesn't seem worth it.

I get dressed and come out into the living room, and she's sitting on the sofa, waiting. Somehow, she's put me in a better mood.

Susan drives us to a random restaurant she found on Yelp. "They said it was private and had great desserts. Is that okay?"

"Sure," I say. "I'm always up for someplace new."

Our conversation, when not about Ben, doesn't flow as freely. It is awkward at times, but I think both of us know that is to be expected.

I tell her that I am a librarian. She says that she loves reading. I tell her that I am not close with my parents; she says she is sorry to hear that. She tells me she's been working on occupying her time with various projects but can't seem to stick to something longer than a few months. "I realized I was too fixated on the house so I stopped renovating, but truthfully, renovating is the only thing that keeps me occupied!" Eventually, the conversation works its way back to the things we have in common: Ben, dead husbands, and loss.

Susan tells me stories about Ben as a child, about embarrassing things he did, tricks he tried to play. She tells me how he would always ask to wear her jewelry.

The visual of Ben in women's jewelry immediately cracks me up.

She drinks her tea and smiles. "You have no idea! He used to always want to dress up as a witch for Halloween. I would explain to him that he could be a wizard, but he wanted to be a witch. I think he just wanted to paint his face green."

We talk about Steven and how hard it was for her to lose him, how much of Steven she used to see in Ben, how she feels like maybe she suffocated Ben, trying too hard to hold on to him because Steven was gone.

"I don't think so," I say. "At least, from my point of view, Ben really loved you. He worried about you. He cared about you. We talked about you a lot. He . . ." I don't know how much I should tell her about Ben's intentions and worries, about why he never told her about me. But it feels so good to talk to someone that knew him as well as I did, that knew him better than I did. It feels good to have someone say, "I know how much it hurts," and believe them. It all just rolls off my tongue and into the air faster than I can catch it.

"He was scared that if you knew that he was with someone, in a serious relationship, that you would feel left out, maybe. Not left out, but . . . like he was moving on and there wasn't a place for you. Which wasn't true. He would always have a place for you. But he thought that if you heard about me, that you'd feel that way and he didn't want that. He kept putting it off. Waiting for the right time. And then the right time never came and things with us progressed to the point where it was weird he hadn't told you already, which made him feel bad. And then it just became this big thing that he wasn't sure how to handle. He loved you, Susan. He really, really did. And he didn't tell you about me because he was thinking of you, however misguided. I'm not going to say I totally understood it. Or that I liked it. But he didn't keep it from you because you didn't matter. Or because I didn't matter. He just, he was a guy, you know? He didn't know how to handle the situation gracefully so he didn't handle it at all."

She thinks about it for a minute, looking down at her plate. "Thank you," she says. "Thank you for telling me that. That's not what I thought happened . . . It's not necessarily good news, but it's not entirely bad, right?" She is unsure of herself, and it's clear that she is grappling with this. She's trying very hard to be the Susan I'm seeing, but my guess is, she's not quite there yet. "Are we at a place where I can make a gentle suggestion?" she says. "From one widow to another?"

"Oh. Uh . . . sure."

"I poked," she says. "In my defense, you did say it was okay, but really, I'm just nosy. I've always been nosy. I can't stop myself. I tried to work on it for years, and then I just gave up around fifty. I just resigned myself to it: I am nosy. Anyway, I poked. Everything of Ben's is still in its place. You haven't moved a thing. I looked in the kitchen. You have food rotting in the fridge."

I know where this is going and I wish I'd told her she could not make a gentle suggestion.

"I'd like to help you clear some things out. Make the place yours again."

I shake my head. "I don't want to make it mine, it's ours. It was ours. He . . ."

She puts her hand up. "Okay. I'm dropping it. It's your place to do with what you want. I just know, for me, I waited too long to move Steven's things into storage and I regret that. I was living in this . . . shrine to him. I didn't want to move his little box of floss because I thought it meant I was giving up on him—which I realize sounds crazy."

"No, that doesn't sound crazy."

She looks me in the eye, knowing that I am doing the same thing, knowing that I am just as lost as she was. I want to convey to her that I like where I am in this. I don't want to move forward.

"It is crazy, Elsie," she says. It is pointed but kind. "Steven is alive in my heart and nowhere else. And when I moved his things out of my eyesight, I could live my life for me again. But you do what you want. You're on no one's timetable but your own."

"Thank you," I say.

"Just remember that if you wade too long in the misery of it, you'll wake up one day and find that your entire life is built around a ghost. That's it. I'm off my soapbox. I'm in no place to tell you your business. I just feel like I know you. Although, I realize I don't."

"No." I stop her. "I think you do."

After lunch, Susan drops me off at my apartment and kisses me on the cheek. Before I jump out of her car and make my way up my own steps, she says to me, "If you ever need anything at all, please don't hesitate." She laughs in a sad way, as if it's funny how pathetic what she is about to say truly is. "You're the only person I have left to be there for," she says.

I unlock my door and settle in, staring at Ben's wedding ring on the counter. I think about what Susan said. We were or are, technically, family. What happens to the relationship you never had with your mother-in-law when your husband dies?

I sit down, holding Ben's wallet in my hands, rubbing the worn edges. I take off my wedding ring, put his around my ring finger, and slide mine back on to hold it in place. His doesn't fit. It's a thick band many sizes too large, but it feels good on my finger.

I look around the house, now seeing it through Susan's eyes. So many of Ben's things are strewn about. I see myself twenty years from now, sitting in this very place, his things stuck, frozen in time. I see myself how I'm afraid others will see me. I am a Miss Havisham in the making. And for the first time, I don't want to be that way. For a fleeting minute, I think that I should move Ben's things. And then I reject the idea. Ben's things are all I have left. Though it does occur to me that maybe Susan knows what she's talking about. Susan seems at peace but hasn't lost that sadness about her. As long as I have that sadness, I still have Ben. So if Susan can do it, maybe I can too.

I go to the refrigerator and pick up the hot dogs. The package is soft and full of liquid. Simply moving it from its place on the shelf has elicited some foul, rancid reaction. The entire kitchen starts to reek. I run to the garbage cans outside, the liquid from the bag dripping on my floor on the way out. As I put the lid on the garbage can and walk back in to clean up and wash my hands, I laugh at how ridiculous it is that I thought Ben lived on through rancid hot dogs. The hot dogs are gone and I don't feel like I've lost him, yet. Score one for Susan.

When Monday comes, I feel the familiar relief of distraction. I go to work, eager to start research on the new display case for this month. Most months, Lyle tells me what to feature, but lately he's been letting me choose. I think he's still scared of me. Everyone here treats me with kid gloves. At certain times I find it charming or at least convenient; at other times I find it irritating and naïve.

I choose Cleopatra for this month, and start pulling together facts and figures that I can show easily with photos and replicas. I am hovering over a book containing images of what the currency looked like in her time, trying to decide how relevant that is, when I am stopped by Mr. Callahan.

"Hi, Mr. Callahan," I say, turning toward him.

"Hello, young lady," Mr. Callahan says.

"What can I help you with?"

"Oh, nothing. I find myself a bit bored today is all," he says slowly and deliberately. I get the impression his mind moves faster than his body can at this point.

"Oh! Nothing striking your fancy?"

"Oh, it's not that. I've just been stuck in the damn house for so long, walking back and forth to the library. I don't have anywhere else to go! Nothing else to do. The days are all starting to fade away."

"Oh," I say. "I'm sorry to hear that."

"Would you have lunch with me?" he asks. "I'm afraid if I don't spend time with someone or do something interesting my brain is going to . . . decay. Atrophy. You know . . . just . . . wither away." I pause before answering, and he fills the void. "There's only so many goddamn sudoku puzzles a man can do, you know? Excuse my language."

I laugh and put the book down. I look at my watch and see that his timing is almost perfect. It's 12:49 p.m. "I would love to, Mr. Callahan," I say.

"Great!" He clasps his hands together in a rather feminine way, as if I've given him a pair of pearl earrings. "If we are going to have lunch together, though, Elsie, you should call me George."

"All right, George. Sounds like a plan."

Mr. Callahan and I walk to a sandwich shop nearby, and he insists on buying my lunch. To tell the truth, I have left-over pizza waiting for me in the office refrigerator, but it didn't seem appropriate to mention that. As Mr. Callahan and I sit down at the small café table, we open our sandwiches.

"So, let's hear it, miss. Tell me something interesting! Anything at all."

I put down my sandwich and wipe the mayonnaise from my lips. "What do you want to know?" I ask.

"Oh, anything. Anything interesting that's happened to you. I don't care if it's sad or funny, scary or stupid. Just something. Anything I can go home and recount to my wife. We're starting to bore each other to tears."

I laugh like I think Mr. Callahan is expecting, but to tell the truth, I want to cry. Ben never bored me. God, how I wish I'd had time to find him positively mind-numbing. When you love someone so much that you've stuck around through all the interesting things that have happened to them and you have nothing left to say, when you know the course of their day before they even tell you, when you lie next to them and hold their hand even though they haven't said one interesting thing in days, that's a love I want. It's the love I was on target for.

"You look sad," he says, interrupting my one-person pity party. "What's the matter?"

"Oh, I'm fine," I say. "I just . . . got a funny bit of mustard I think."

"No." He shakes his head. "You've looked sad for some time. You think I don't see things because I'm an old fart, but I do." He brings his finger to his temple and taps it. "What is it?"

What's the point in lying? Who benefits from it anyway? Propriety says not to discuss such intense matters in public, but whom does that serve? This man is bored and I am broken. Maybe I'll be a little less broken in telling him about it. Maybe he'll be a little less bored.

"My husband died," I say. I say it matter-of-factly, trying to work against the intensity of the conversation.

"Oh," he says, quite surprised. "That's heartbreaking to hear. It is interesting, like I asked, but just terrible. I didn't realize you were married."

"You met him," I say. "A few months ago."

"No, I remember. I just didn't realize you were married."

"Oh, well, we had only just married when he died."

"Terrible," he says, and he grabs my hand. It's too intimate to feel comfortable, and yet, it doesn't feel inappropriate. "I'm sorry, Elsie. You must be in such pain."

I shrug and then wish I could take it back. I shouldn't shrug about Ben. "Yes," I admit. "I am."

"Is that why you were gone for a while before?" he says,

and my face must change. It must convey some sort of surprise because he adds, "You're my favorite person here and I'm here every day. You think I don't notice when my favorite person isn't around?"

I smile and bite into my sandwich.

"I don't know you very well, Elsie," he says. "But I do know this: You are a fighter. You've got chutzpah. Moxie. Whatever it is."

"Thank you, Mr. Callahan." He gives me a disapproving glance. "George," I correct myself. "Thank you, George."

"No thanks needed. It's what I see. And you will be okay, you know that? I know you probably don't think it now, but I'm telling you, one day you'll look back on this time and think, Thank God it's over, but I got through it. I'm telling you."

I look doubtful. I know I do because I can feel the doubt on my face. I can feel the way it turns down the corners of my mouth.

"You don't believe me, do you?" he asks, picking up his sandwich for the first time.

I smile. "No, I'm not sure I do, George. I'm not even sure I want that."

"You're so young, Elsie! I'm eighty-six years old. I was born before the Depression. Can you even imagine that? Because I'll tell you, during the Depression nobody could imagine me still living now. But look at me! I'm still kicking! I'm sitting here with a gorgeous young lady, having a sandwich. Things happen in your life that you can't possibly imagine. But time goes on and time changes you and the times change and the next thing you know, you're smack in the middle of a life you never saw coming."

"Well, maybe."

"No, not maybe." His voice gets stern. He's not angry, just firm. "I'm going to tell you something no one who is still alive knows. Well, except my wife, but she knows everything."

"Okay," I say. I am done with my sandwich and he has barely started his. I am usually the one done last, but I now realize that's because I am rarely the one listening.

"I fought in World War Two. Suited up right in the beginning of 1945. Toughest time of my life. Honest to God. It just wreaked havoc with my faith in God, my faith in humanity. Everything. I'm not a man fit for war. It doesn't sit well with me. And the only thing that got me through was Esther Morris. I loved her the minute I saw her. We were eighteen years old, I saw her sitting with her friends on the sidewalk across the street, and I just knew. I knew she would be the mother of my children. I walked across the street, I introduced myself, I asked her out, and six months later we were engaged. By the time I found myself in Europe, I thought for sure I wasn't going to stay long. And I was right, because I was only there for about eight months before I was shot."

"Wow," I say.

"I was shot three times. Twice in the shoulder. One grazed my side. I remember being in that medical tent, the nurse hovering over me, the doctor rushing to my side. I was the happiest man on earth. Because I knew they'd have to send me home and I'd see Esther. I couldn't believe my luck that I could go home to her. So I recovered as fast as I could and I came back. But when I got home, Esther was gone. No sign of her."

He sighs, but it seems more a sigh of old age than one of heartbreak.

"I still don't know where she went. She just up and left me. Never told me why. I heard rumors from time to time that she'd taken up with a salesman, but I don't know if that's true. I never saw her again."

"Oh God," I say, now grabbing George's hand. "That's awful. I'm so sorry."

"Don't be," he said. "I waited around for years for her to come back. I wouldn't leave the town we lived in, just in case she came lookin' for me. I was devastated."

"Well, sure," I say.

"But you know what?"

"Hmm?"

"I took each day as it came, and it led me to Lorraine. And Lorraine is the love of my life. Esther is a story I tell young women in libraries, but Lorraine makes me feel like I could conquer the world. Like the universe was made for me to live in it. The minute I met her, she just set my world on fire. I forgot about Esther just as fast as she forgot about me, once I met Lorraine."

"I don't want Ben to be a story I tell young women in libraries though. He was more than that. That's what I'm afraid of! I'm afraid that's what he'll end up," I say.

George nods. "I know. I know. You don't have to do it exactly like I did. I'm just trying to tell you that your life will be very long with zigzags you can't imagine. You won't realize just how young you are until you aren't that young anymore. But I'm here to tell you, Elsie. Your life has just begun. When I lost Esther, I thought my life was over. I was twenty. I had no idea what was in store for me. Neither do you."

George is done talking, and so he finishes his sandwich and we sit in silence. I contemplate his words, remaining convinced that living any part of the years I have before me would be a betrayal to the years behind me.

"Thank you," I say, and I mean it. Even if I can't recover from loss like he did, it's nice to know that someone did.

"I should thank you!" he says. "I am certainly not bored."

That afternoon, I further compile research on Cleopatra. It occurs to me that Cleopatra had two great loves and look how they vilified her. At least she had a son and a dynasty to commemorate Caesar. At least she could put him on coins and cups. She could erect statues in his honor. She could deify him. She had a way to make his memory live on. All I have are Ben's dirty socks.

When I leave work on Friday afternoon and head home for the empty weekend in front of me, it occurs to me that I could call Susan. I could see how she is. I think better of it.

I walk in my front door and put my things down. I go into the bathroom and start running the shower. As I'm disrobing, I hear the cell phone in the back pocket of my pants vibrating against the floor. I fumble to get it, and as I answer, I see that it is my mother.

"Hi," she says.

"Oh. Hello," I answer.

"Your father and I just wanted to see how you were doing. See how you were . . . uh . . . dealing with things?" she says. Her euphemism irritates me.

"Things?" I challenge.

"You know, just . . . we know you are having a hard time and we were sitting here thinking of you . . . I just mean . . . how are you?"

"I'm fine, thank you." I am hoping this conversation will be over shortly, so I don't bother turning off the shower.

"Oh good! Good!" Her voice brightens. "We weren't sure. Well, we are just glad to hear you are feeling better. It must have been a strange feeling to be caught up in the grief of his family, to be in the middle of all of that."

I turn the shower off and lose my energy. "Right," I say. What's the point of explaining that I was his family? That this is my grief? That when I said I was fine I just said that because it's something people say?

"Good," she says. I can hear my father in the background. I can't make out any of what he is saying, but my mother starts to get off the phone. "Well, if you need anything at all," she says. She always says this. I don't even know what she means by it.

"Thanks." I shut off the phone, turn the faucet back on, and get under the water. I need to see Ben. I need just a minute with him. I need him to show up in this bathroom and hug me. I just need him for a minute. One minute. I step out of the shower, grab my towel and my phone.

I call Susan. I ask her if she'd like to have lunch tomorrow and she says she's free. We agree on a place halfway between us, and then I put on a robe, get in bed, smell Ben's side, and fall asleep. The smell is fading. I have to inhale deeper and deeper to get to it.

Susan has suggested a place in Redondo Beach for lunch. Apparently, she and Ben came here often over the years. Sometimes, before Steven died, they would all meet up here for dinner. She warns me not to expect much. "I hope you're okay with chain Mexican restaurants," she says.

The restaurant is decorated with bulls, hacienda-style tiles, and bright colors. It's aggressively cheesy, wearing tacky like a badge of honor. Before I even reach Susan's table, pictures of margaritas have accosted me about nine times.

She's sitting in front of a glass of water when I find the table. She gets up immediately and hugs me. She smells the same and looks the same as always: composed and together. She doesn't make grief look glamorous, but she does make it look bearable.

"This place is awful, right?" She laughs.

"No!" I say. "I like any place that offers a three-course meal for nine ninety-nine."

The waiter comes to drop off a bucket of tortilla chips and salsa, and I nervously reach for them. Susan ignores them for the moment. We order fajitas.

"And, you know what?" Susan says to the waiter. "Two margaritas too. Is that okay?" I'm already face-deep in tortilla chips, so I just nod.

"What flavor?" he asks us. "Original? Mango? Watermelon? Cranberry? Pomegranate? Cantalo—"

"Original is fine," she says, and I wish that she'd asked me about this one too because watermelon sounded kind of good.

He gathers our sticky red menus and leaves the table.

"Shit. I meant to ask him for guacamole," she says after he leaves, and she starts to dig into the chips with me. "Sir!" she calls out. He comes running back. I can never get waiters' attention once they've left the table. "Can we get guacamole too?" He nods and leaves, and she looks back at me. "My diet is a joke." Who can count calories at a time like this? I feel good that Susan can't either.

"So," she says. "You mentioned it on the phone but I don't understand. Your mom said she thought you'd be over it by now?"

"Well," I say, wiping my hand on my napkin. "Not necessarily. She just . . . she called and asked how I was handling 'things.' Or 'the thing'—you know how people use that terminology like they can't just say 'Ben died'?"

Susan nods. "The euphemisms," she says. "As if you won't remember that Ben is dead if they don't say it."

"Right! Like I'm not thinking about it every moment of the day. Anyway, she just asked and I said I was fine, like . . . I'm not really fine, but it's just a thing you say. Anyone that asked me that would know that when I said 'Fine' I meant 'Fine, considering the circumstances.'"

"Right." The basket is now empty, and when the waiter comes to drop off the margaritas, Susan asks him to fill it up.

"But my mom honestly thought I was fine, I think," I say. "I think she was hoping I'd say I was fine and that if I did say that, it would mean that she didn't need to do anything and I was back to my old self. Like nothing ever happened."

"Well, to her, nothing did happen." Susan takes a sip of her margarita and winces. "I'm not much of a drinker, I'm afraid. I just thought it would be festive of us. But this . . . is a bit strong, no?"

I take a sip of mine. "It's strong," I say.

"Okay! I thought I was being a baby. Anyway—you were saying?"

"Actually, I think you were saying."

"Oh. Right. Nothing happened to her. You two rarely talk, right?"

"Right."

"It seems like she's just one of those people that can't empathize or even sympathize. So, she doesn't know how to talk to you because she doesn't understand you."

I don't talk about my family often, and when I do, I speak in short sentences and dismissive comments. But Susan is the first person to see what's going on and give it a name. Or . . . at least a description. "You're right," I tell her.

"Don't worry about your parents. They are going to do what they would want someone to do for them, and it's going to be entirely different than what you need. And I say, give up trying to make the two fit. Not that I'm some expert. I just noticed that when Steven died there was a large difference between what I wanted from people and what they wanted to give me. I think people are so terrified of being in our position that they lose all ability to even speak to us. I say let it go."

By the time she's done talking, my margarita is gone. I'm not sure how that happened. Our fajitas come, sizzling and ostentatious, if fajitas can be ostentatious. They are just so big and require so many plates and people to bring them. There is the plate for the side dishes, the pans of chicken and vegetables, the case for tortillas, both corn and flour, and the condiments of guacamole, cheese, salsa, and lettuce. Our table looks like a feast fit for a king, and the chicken is frying so loudly on the skillets that I feel like the whole restaurant is looking.

"It's a bit much, isn't it?" Susan asks demurely. "I think it's great though, the way they bring it to you like it's a presentation. There's absolutely no need for them to have the chicken still grilling on the table. None at all."

The waiter comes back to check on us. Susan orders us each another margarita. "Watermelon for me," I interject. Susan agrees. "That sounds good; watermelon for me too."

We talk over our steaming lunches about politics and families; we talk about traffic and movies, news and funny stories. I want to be able to talk to Susan about things other than life and death, other than Ben and Steven. It seems possible. It seems like I could know her regardless of the tragedy between us. But Ben is what we have in common, and so the conversation will always come back to Ben. I wonder if it's unhealthy to fixate out loud. If being obsessed with Ben's death is something I'm only supposed to do in my own head. I also wonder how much I can truly rely on her.

"Do you have a plan for when you're going to stop his mail?" she asks me casually, while she is picking at what's left off the hot plate in front of her with her fork.

I shake my head. "No," I say. "I don't even know really how to do that." That's not all of the truth. The other fact is that I'm scared that would cause the post office to hold the marriage certificate too since it will have his name on it. I don't want to have his mail stopped until I have it.

"Oh, it's easy. We can do it today if you want," she says.

"Oh," I say, trying to think of a way to stop her and realizing I have no real excuse but the truth. "Well, I'm still waiting for the marriage certificate," I say. "I don't want to stop the mail in case they try to hold that too."

"What do you mean?" she says, peeling an onion off the plate and putting it in her mouth with her hands.

"It hasn't come yet and since both of our names will be on it, I'm worried they might keep it with his old bills and stuff instead of sending it through to me."

"It hasn't come yet?" Her voice indicates that there must be some misunderstanding. For so long, I've been worried to tell anyone that it hadn't come yet. I've thought they'd think I was lying about our marriage. I was afraid they would use it to convince themselves of the one thing I'm scared to be: not relevant. But Susan's voice doesn't convey a moment of doubt. She sounds only concerned about a clerical error or logistical mistake. It doesn't even occur to her to question whether I've been completely full of shit. I have to admit that she's come so far since I met her. She must move so quickly through emotional turmoil.

"No, I don't have it yet. I've been checking the mail every day, opening up even the most innocuous of envelopes. It's nowhere."

"Well, we need to start calling people, figuring out where it is. Have you called the county to check and see if it's at least in their records?"

"No," I say and shake my head. Honestly, I hadn't thought it was that big of a deal until I said it out loud. I hadn't wanted to face the logistical nightmare of figuring this out.

"Well, that's got to be the first step. You need to find out if the original license made it to the county."

"Okay," I say. Her concern is making me concerned.

"It's okay," she says and grabs my hand. "We'll figure it out."

The way she says "we," that she doesn't say "You will figure it out," makes me feel like I'm not alone. It makes me feel like if I can't get myself out of this, she will get me out of this. It makes me feel like I'm high on a tightrope, losing my balance, but seeing the net underneath me. "We" will figure this out. Ana has made similar sentiments to me, but all those times I knew that she couldn't help me. She could hold my hand, but she couldn't hold me up. For the first time, I feel like it's not up to only me. Nothing is up to only me.

"So you'll call on Monday?" she says. "Call the county and find out?"

I nod. It's clear she's assuming we got married in Los Angeles County and I don't have it in me to correct her. Part of me wants to. Part of me wants to revel in the truth with her. Tell her everything. But I know it's not that simple. I know that our newfound connection is still too tenuous for the whole truth.

"Should I ask for the check?" she asks me.

I laugh. "I think I need to wait out that last margarita," I say, and she smiles.

"Dessert then!"

She orders us fried ice cream and "dessert" nachos. We sit there, spoons in the ice cream, licking the chocolate around the bowls. It's what I imagined sisters did with their mothers when their fathers were away on business. When I get in the car, I think of a few things I forgot to say and I find myself looking forward to seeing Susan again to tell her.

Ana has been patient with my recovery, expecting nothing, supporting everything, but I can tell that I am starting to wear on her. Being my friend means she is pulled into this even though it has nothing to do with her. I can only assume that, after a while, even the most understanding and empathetic of people would start to wonder just how long it will be before we can have honest to God fun again. Fun that doesn't end in a sorrowful look from me, fun that isn't laced with what I have lost. She knew me before Ben, she knew me during Ben, and now she knows me after Ben. She's never said it, but I would imagine the me she knew before Ben was probably her favorite.

Ana said she'd be at my place at eight to pick me up, but she calls at seven asking if I mind if she brings this guy she has been seeing.

"Who have you been seeing?" I say. I didn't know she was seeing anyone.

"Just this guy, Kevin." She laughs, and I suspect he's right there next to her.

"I'm just some guy?" I hear in the background, confirming my suspicion. I can hear her shush him.

"Anyway, is that okay? I want him to meet you," she says.

"Uh, sure," I say, taken aback. You can't say no in a situation like this. It's rude and weird, but I wonder, if the rules of propriety allowed it, what I would have said.

"Cool," she says. "Be there at eight to pick you up. You still want to go to that ramen house?"

"Sure!" I overcompensate for my apprehension by being outwardly perky and excited. It feels obvious to me, but she doesn't seem to notice. Maybe I've been getting really good at hiding my emotions, or maybe she's not paying attention.

APRIL

Ben and I were waiting in the front of the movie theater for Ana. She was twenty minutes late and the tickets were on her credit card. The movie was starting in seven minutes. Ben was one of the only people I knew that looked forward to the previews more than the actual movie.

"Can you call her again?" he asked me.

"I just called her! And texted. She's probably just parking."

"Ten bucks she hasn't left the house yet."

I slapped him lightly across the chest. "She's left the house! C'mon. We won't be late for the movie."

"We're already late for the movie."

He said this would happen. I said it wouldn't happen, but here we were, just like he said we would be. He was right.

"You're right."

"There she is!" Ben pointed toward a woman running through the food court to the movie theater. There was a man behind her.

"Who is that?" I asked.

"How would I know?"

Ana slowed herself as she reached us. "I'm sorry! I'm sorry!"

"I'm sure you had a good reason," Ben said to her. You could hear in his voice that he had no expectation of a good reason. Ana jokingly glared at him.

"Marshall, this is Elsie and Ben." The man behind her extended his hand to us, and we each shook it. "Marshall is going to join us."

"All right, well, let's get to it, shall we? We're already missing previews!" Ben said.

"Well, I still need to print the tickets. Will you guys go get us some popcorn?"

Ben looked at me incredulously and rolled his eyes. I laughed at him. "I want a Diet Coke," I said.

Ben and Marshall ran ahead to the concession as Ana and I picked up the tickets from the kiosk.

"Who is this guy?" I said to her. She shrugged. "I don't know. He keeps asking me out and I finally just relented and invited him here to get it over with."

"So it's true love, I guess," I said. She picked up the tickets and started walking toward Ben and Marshall.

"True love, schmoo love," she said. "I'm just trying to find someone that doesn't bore me to tears for a little while."

"You depress me," I said, but I wasn't paying attention to her when I said it. I was looking at Ben, who was asking the cashier for more butter on his already buttered popcorn. I was smiling. I was grinning. I was in love with the weirdo.

"No, you depress me," she said.

I turned to her and laughed. "You don't think that one day you'll meet 'the One'?"

"Love has made you sappy and gross," she said to me. We had almost met up with Ben and Marshall when I decided to tell her the news.

"Ben's moving in," I said. She stopped dead in her tracks and dropped her purse.

"What?"

Ben saw her face and caught my eye. He knew what was

going on, and he smiled at me mischievously as he put a handful of popcorn into his mouth. I smiled back at him. I picked up Ana's purse. She pulled me aside by my shoulders as Ben watched, standing next to a very confused Marshall.

"You are crazy! You're basically sending yourself to a prison. You wake up, he's there. You go to sleep, he's there. He's going to always be there! He's a great guy, Elsie. I like him a lot. I'm happy that you two found each other, but c'mon! This is a death sentence."

I just looked at her and smiled. For the first time, I felt like I had something over her. Sure, she was stunning and gorgeous and lively and bright. Men wanted her so badly they'd hound her for dates. But this man wanted me, and unlike Ana, I had felt what it was like to be wanted by someone you wanted just as badly. I wanted that for her, but there was a small part of me that felt victorious in that I had it and she didn't even know enough to want it.

SEPTEMBER

A na and Kevin are only three minutes late. She opens my door with her own key. Ana looks hot. Really hot, spared-no-expense, pull-all-the-punches hot. I am dressed like I'm going to the grocery store. Kevin is right behind her, and while I am expecting some overly tailored douche bag with hair better than mine, I find a much different person.

Kevin is short, at least shorter than Ana. He's about my height. He's wearing jeans and a T-shirt; looks like he got the grocery store memo too. His face is nondescript. His skin is mostly clear but somewhat muddled; his hair is a shade of brown best described as "meh," and he looks like he neither works out nor is a slovenly couch potato.

He leans toward me, around Ana. "Kevin," he says, shaking my hand. It's not a bold handshake, but it's not a dead fish. It's polite and nice. He smiles and I smile back. I see him take in his surroundings, and I start to look around my house as well, as an impulse. I see my living room through his eyes. He no doubt knows about me, knows that my husband is dead, knows that Ana is my best friend; maybe he knows that I feel like he is trying to take her away from me. As he looks, I feel self-conscious about all of Ben's things around us. I want to say, "I'm not some crazy woman. It's just too hard to put these away yet." But I don't, because saying you're not crazy makes you seem crazy.

"Shall we?" Ana says. Kevin and I nod. Within a few sec-

onds we are out the door. We cram into Kevin's Honda. I offer
to take the backseat, and I squeeze myself into it by ducking
and crunching behind the passenger-side door. Why do two-
door cars exist? It is the most cumbersome of all tasks to try to
wedge yourself into the backseat of one.

On the way to the restaurant, Ana is clearly trying to give
Kevin and me a common thread upon which to build a relationship. It feels so strange. I get the distinct impression that
Ana is trying to make sure Kevin and I get along. She's trying
to make sure I like Kevin. She's never done that before. She's
never cared. Most of the time, meeting me is their death knell.
She uses me to let them know that she doesn't need alone time
with them, that we are all friends. This isn't that. She's not
kicking him out the door. She's inviting him inside.

"How did you guys meet?" I ask from the backseat.

"Oh, at yoga," he says, paying attention to the road.

"Yeah, Kevin was always in my Tuesday night class and he was
just so bad"—she laughs—"that I had to personally help him."

"I've tried to explain to her that instructors are supposed to
help their students, but she seems to think she was doing me
a favor," he jokes, and I laugh politely as if this is hilarious. I'm
missing whatever it is this guy has going for him. "Worked out
in my favor though, since it got her to ask me out."

"Can you believe that, Elsie?" Ana says, half turning her face
toward me in the backseat. "I asked him out."

I thought he'd been joking.

"Wait," I say, leaning forward. "Kevin, Ana asked you out?"

Kevin nods as he enters the parking garage and starts to look
for a parking space.

"Ana has never asked anyone out the entire time I've known
her," I tell him.

"I've never asked anyone out in my entire life," she clarifies.

"So why Kevin?" I ask and immediately realize that I have not phrased it in a polite way. "I just mean—what made you change your mind? About asking people out, I mean."

Kevin finds a spot and parks the car. Ana grabs his hand. "I don't know." She looks at him. "Kevin's different."

I want to vomit. I go so far as to make a vomit noise as a joke to them, but neither of them finds it funny. They aren't even paying much attention to me. I realize, as I try to climb out of the backseat of this shitty little car without injuring myself, that Kevin has hijacked my dinner plans with Ana and they are just letting me come along as a courtesy. I am a third wheel.

You try being a widow and a third wheel. You will never feel more alone.

We get to the restaurant, and it seems pretty cool, actually. Kevin and Ana are having a good time regardless of whether I am.

"How long have you two been dating?" I ask. I'm not sure what to expect, or rather, I don't expect anything.

"Uh"—Kevin starts to think—"just about a month?" he says.

Ana looks somewhat uncomfortable. "More or less," she says, and then she changes the subject. How could my best friend have been dating someone for the past month and never mentioned him to me? I refuse to believe that she talked about him and I wasn't listening. That's not who I am, even now. I try to listen to other people. How could Ana go from a person who would never settle down, never care about a man, to a woman who asks a man out and invites him to crash dinner with her best friend? And she did this all on her own time, never mentioning it to me, as if it were a side project of self-development that she didn't want to reveal until it was complete.

After dinner, they drive me back to my house and say good

night. Kevin kisses me on the cheek sweetly and looks me in the eye when he says it was nice to meet me. He says he hopes to see me again soon, and I believe him. I wonder if maybe the thing that Kevin has going for him is that he is very sincere. Maybe Ana is attracted to how genuine he is. If that's the case, I can understand.

I call her a few hours later, and my call goes through to voice mail. I'm sure they are together. I try again in the morning, and she puts me through to voice mail again but texts me and says she'll call later. She's still with Kevin. Kevin is different. I can feel it. I can see it. It makes me nervous. I've already lost Ben. I can't lose Ana. She can't change her personality and priorities now. I'm just barely hanging on.

She calls me Sunday afternoon and offers to come over. When she gets here, the first words out of her mouth are "What did you think of him? Adorable, right?"

"Yeah," I say. "He was really sweet, I liked him a lot." This isn't entirely untrue. Even if I don't see exactly what about him is exceptional, he still seemed perfectly nice and likable.

"Oh, Elsie! I'm so glad to hear you say that. I've been nervous for you two to meet and he was over yesterday afternoon and asked if he could join our dinner and I wasn't sure how to—" She cuts herself off. "I'm just really glad you liked him."

"He was cool. He seems a bit"—how do I say this?—"out of character for you though, am I right?"

She shrugs. "Something just clicked in me," she says. "And I realized that I want to love someone, you know? I mean, everyone wants to love someone, right? I think I just mean, I finally feel ready to be with one person. And of all the people I've dated in the past, I think the problem was that I wasn't into *them*. I was just into how much they were into me. But Kevin is different. Kevin wasn't even into me. We would stay after and I would be helping him with his poses and touching him in these ways, you know how yoga is. And most men perk up when you get that close, they make it sexual when it isn't sexual, but not Kevin. He was just really genuinely trying to get the pose right. So I started kind of . . . trying to make it sexual . . . just to see if I could get his attention, but he was just really focused."

So I was kind of right. It's the sincerity that has made her smitten.

"And I think I just . . . I want to be with someone that approaches things like that. That doesn't think of me as a thing to possess or obtain. So I asked him out and he said yes and it made me so nervous, but I was proud of myself that I did it, and then from our first date, I just felt this . . . connection . . ."

I start to get mad because a strong connection on first dates is for Ben and me. It's not common, it doesn't just happen to everyone. And she's watering it down. She's making it seem like it's not mine anymore.

"I don't understand why you didn't mention it sooner," I say.

"Well." Ana starts to grow uncomfortable. "I just . . . you are dealing with your own stuff and I didn't think you wanted to hear about this," she says, and that's when it hits me. Ana pities me. Ana is now the one in love; Ana is the happy one; I am the sad one; the lonely one, the one to whom she doesn't want to rub it in.

"What made this 'click' just happen?" I ask. My words are sharp; my voice is bitter.

"What?" she asks.

"It's interesting that you just 'changed' like that. You go from being this . . . kind of . . . from someone who . . ." I give up on trying to name it. "Well to turn around now and be the poster child for love. What made you change your mind?"

"You," she says. She says it as if it will pacify me, as if I should be happy. "I just realized that life is about love. Or at least, it's about loving someone."

"Do you hear yourself? You sound like a Valentine's Day card."

"Whoa, okay," she says as a reaction to the anger in my voice. "I'm sorry. I thought you'd be happy for me."

"Happy for you? My husband died and I'm sitting here miserable and alone, but you've learned from this whole experience how to love. *Congratulations, Ana! We're all really happy for you.*"

She is stunned, and unfortunately, because it is a silent stunned, I am able to continue.

"Let's all celebrate for Ana! She's found true love! Her life wasn't perfect enough with her perfect apartment and her perfect body and all of these men chasing her, but now, she's evolved enough to see in my husband's death a life lesson about the importance of love and romance."

Ana is now almost in tears, and I don't want her to cry but I can't stop myself.

"Was it love at first sight? This romance of yours? Are you going to get married next week?"

By now, all I have as evidence of how much Ben loved me is how quickly he knew he wanted to marry me. I honestly think that if Ana says Kevin has already started talking about marriage I will lose the only piece of life I have left in me.

"No." She shakes her head. "That's not it."

"Then what is it, Ana? Why are you doing this to me?"

"What am I doing to you?" she finally explodes. "I haven't done anything *to you*. All I did was meet someone I like and try to share it with you. Just like you did months ago to me and I was happy for you!"

"Yeah, well, you weren't widowed at the time."

"You know what, Elsie? You don't have to be a widow every second of every day of your life."

"Yes, Ana, I do."

"No, you don't. And you think you can just tell me to fuck off because you think I don't know anything, but I know you better than anyone. I know you sit here at home alone and think about what you've lost. I know it consumes you. I know that you keep his things around like they are a fucking medal for how tortured you are."

"You know what—" I start, but she interrupts me.

"No, Elsie. I'll tell you what. Everyone may tiptoe around you, myself included, but at some point someone needs to remind you that you lost something you only had for six months. Six months. And I'm not saying this isn't hard, but it's not like you're ninety and you lost your life partner here. You need to start living your life and letting other people live theirs. I have the right to be happy. I didn't lose that right just because your husband died."

It's quiet for a moment, as I look at her with my mouth wide open in shock.

"And neither did you," she adds, and she walks out the door.

I stand there for a few minutes after she leaves, frozen. Then I reanimate. I walk into the back closet and find the pillow I stuffed in a trash bag right after he died, the pillow that smells like him. I just stand there, smelling it through the open hole at the top of the bag, until I can't smell anything anymore.

Ana calls me over and over again during the week, leaving messages that she's sorry. That she should never have said those things. She leaves text messages saying much the same. I don't answer them, I don't answer her. I don't know what to say to her because I'm not mad at her. I'm embarrassed. I'm lost.

I did only know Ben for six months. I didn't even celebrate a birthday with him. I only spent January to June with him. How well can you really love someone if you haven't seen him through an August or an autumn? This is what I was afraid of. I was afraid that because I hadn't known Ben *long*, I hadn't known him *well*. I think I needed someone to say it to me before I could really think about it. And after thinking about it, over the course of the week I avoid Ana, I decide that that theory is wrong. It doesn't matter how long I knew him. I loved him. I still love him.

Then I think that maybe it is time to start putting his things away, because if I did love him, if our love was real, and it did matter, then what is the harm in putting some of his things in boxes? Right? I'll be okay, right?

I don't call Ana to help me. I'm not sure I could look her in the eye. Instead, I call Susan. When she answers the phone, she immediately asks about the marriage certificate, and I have to admit that I have not called the county yet. I tell her that I didn't have enough time, but that is a lie. I did have the time.

I just know that if they tell me they do not have a record of our marriage, I will not be able to move his things into storage. I know it will make me hold on tighter to his old clothes and toothbrush. I need to believe the government knows we were married. Otherwise, I'll have to prove it to myself in arbitrary and pathetic ways. I am trying to move forward. I am trying to make arbitrary and pathetic things of the past.

MAY

Ben was sweaty. It was a hot spring day. I had all of the windows open in the apartment; the door had been open for the past few hours as we hauled things up the front stairs. There was no point in turning on the air conditioner. All the cold air would have just flown right out the front door. I threw Ben a bottle of water as he headed down the stairs for another round of boxes.

"Thanks," he said to me as he hit the sidewalk.

"Almost done!" I said.

"Yeah, but then I have to unpack everything!"

"Well, sure, but we can do that slowly, you know? Over the course of a few days if you want."

Ben made his way to the moving truck and started pushing boxes toward the back edge. I played with a few of them to see which one was lightest, and then I took that one. I knew that the proper way to face a challenge was head-on, and in that spirit, I should have taken the heavy ones first, but my arms had started to quiver and my legs were feeling unreliable. It had been a full day of unpacking and unloading, after a full night of packing and loading. I was starting to phone it in, and I was all right with that.

With the lightest box, a box that was still rather heavy, in my hands, I made my way up the stairs. As I got to the door, Ben called to me. "What did you do?" he asked. "Take the lightest box you could find?"

"It's not all that light, you know! You should pack better next time!"

"I'm hoping there won't be a next time," he yelled up at me. I was inside, setting the lightest heavy box down on the floor. I was trying to bend from the knees or whatever, but I finally just plopped it down on top of the others using what muscles I had left in my back.

"I just mean if we move someplace together." I was waiting at the door, holding the screen open for him. He walked up the stairs, straight past me, and put down his box. We started to walk out together. We were both out of breath, albeit me more so than him.

"This hasn't taught you anything about the perils of moving?" he asked, as he rushed ahead.

"No, you're right," I said. "We should stay here forever. I don't ever want to move another thing."

The sun started to set as we brought in the last of it. This was the beginning of something. We could both feel it. It was us against the world.

"Do you think you'll be able to handle my dirty dishes?" he asked with his arm around me, kissing my head.

"I think so," I replied. "Do you think you can handle the fact that I always want it to be ninety degrees in the house?"

"No," he said. "But I will learn."

I kissed his neck because it was as far as I could reach. My calves didn't have the power to get me any higher. Ben moaned. It made me feel powerful to elicit that type of reaction without even meaning to. It made me feel like one of those women that oozes sex appeal in even the simplest of tasks. I felt like the Cleopatra of my apartment.

I rubbed my nose further into his neck. "Stop it," he said

falsely, as if I was doing something tawdry. "I have to return the truck by seven."

"I wasn't trying anything!" I said.

"Yes, you were! I'm too tired!"

"I wasn't trying anything, really. I'm tired too."

"Okay! Fine!" he said, grabbing me and pulling me toward my bedroom. Our bedroom. It was now filled with his stuff on the floor and resting against the walls.

"No, really. I'm so tired."

And just like that the tides shifted. "Fine! I'll do all the work," he said. He laid me on the bed and lowered himself on top of me. "I love you," he said, kissing my cheeks and my neck. "I love you so much. I feel like the luckiest guy in the world."

"I love you too," I said back to him, but I don't know if he heard me. He had started to focus on other things.

Thirty minutes later, I was naked and leaning over him, resting his head on a pillow and asking if he wanted me to take him to the hospital.

"No! No," he said. "I think I just threw out my back."

"Isn't that what old men do?" I teased him.

"Look at how much crap I lifted today!" He winced in pain. "Can you get me my underwear?"

I got up and gave it to him. Then I put on my own. I wrapped my bra around me and threw on a T-shirt.

"What should we do?" I asked. "Do you want medicine? Should you see a doctor?" He was still trying to get his underwear on himself. He could barely move. Not wanting to see him struggle, I grabbed the waistband of his underwear. I shimmied the back up under his butt as subtly as I could. Then I pulled the front up to his waist. I pulled the blanket from the foot of the bed and I laid it on top of him.

"Do we have any ibuprofen?" he asked me.

There it was. "We." The best kind of "we." Do "we" have ibuprofen?

"I don't myself, I don't think," I said. "Any in the boxes?"

"Yeah, in a box marked 'Bathroom.' I think I saw it in the living room on the floor."

"Okay," I said. "I'll be right back." I kissed his forehead and went into the living room.

I scanned the boxes across the room and finally saw one labeled "Bathroom." It was under plenty of other heavy boxes. I was sure it was one of the first ones we'd unloaded. I moved box after box until I got to it, and then I opened it to find another labyrinth inside. After way too long, I found some ibuprofen and brought it to him with a glass of water.

He lifted his head slightly, eyes scrunched from the pain. He thanked me.

"You're welcome," I said.

"Elsie?" he moaned.

"Yeah?"

"You're gonna have to return the moving truck."

"Totally fine," I said, even though having to drive that huge truck through Los Angeles traffic was not my idea of a good time.

"You actually, uh . . ." he started. "You have to leave now. It's due back in twenty minutes. I'm sorry! I didn't think about how long it would take you to find the ibuprofen."

I jumped up and threw on a pair of pants.

"Where are the keys?" I asked.

"On the front seat."

"Where am I going?"

"Lankershim and Riverside."

"It's in the *valley*?"

"That was the cheapest one I could find! I picked it up on my way home from work."

"Okay, okay. I'm out of here." I kissed his cheek. "Are you going to be okay here alone?"

"I'll be fine. Can you bring me my cell phone just in case?"

I put his phone by the bed and started to take off. "Hey," he called. "Will you pick up dinner too?"

"Of course I will," I called out. "You pain in the ass."

SEPTEMBER

Susan shows up at my door bright and early on Saturday morning. She has in her hands a bag of bagels and cream cheese, and a carton of orange juice. Under her arm is a package of flattened boxes.

"I thought we could use refreshments," she says as she steps in.

"Awesome," I say and put them in the kitchen. "Do you want one now?" I call out to her.

"Sure." She appears in my kitchen. Her voice is next to me and quiet, instead of far away and shouting like I expected.

I put two bagels into the toaster oven, and Susan and I step into the living room. She scans the space. I can tell she is assessing what is Ben's. My guess is she is doing this both because these objects indicate the job in store for us and because they belong to her dead son.

The toaster dings. I pull the bagels out, and when I do, they burn the pads of my fingers. I put the bagels on plates and shake my hands wildly, hoping to mitigate the pain. I've never been sure what the logic is in this gesture, but it's an instinct, so maybe it works. Susan looks at me and asks if I'm all right, and for a moment I think that this is my shot to get out of this. I can say they really hurt. I can say I'm in no position to be using my hands. They do still hurt. Maybe I should see a doctor. But then I realize when I get home from the doctor, Ben's stuff will still be right here in front of me.

"Nothing I can't handle," I say. We pour large glasses of orange juice and sit down at the table. Susan asks where we are going to begin, and I say, "The living room. I need to work my way up to the bedroom." She tries to make small talk as we eat, asking about my job and my friends, but all either of us can think about is the task ahead. It's almost a relief when our bagels are gone. Now, we have to start.

Susan plops herself down in the living room and starts folding boxes. I still have all of the boxes from when he moved in. It wasn't even five months ago. I grab what I have and meet her in there. I take a deep breath, put a box in front of me, and unplug his PlayStation, putting it in the box.

"Annnd done!" I joke, but Susan insists on taking it as a cry for help. She stops folding and speaks to me in a gentle voice.

"Take your time. We are on no one's timetable but yours, you know." I know, I know. She keeps telling me.

"Have you thought about whether you're going to keep all this stuff or try to sell some of it? Give any of it away?"

It hadn't occurred to me to do anything other than store it, honestly. I just figured I'd put it in boxes and shove it in the closet. The thought of giving the things away, of not owning them anymore, it's too much for me.

"Oh," I say. Maybe I should aim toward that. I should hope that one day I can give it away or sell it. One day I will. "Maybe we should divide things into categories as we pack," I say. "Some boxes for keeping, some for giving away, and maybe another for trash. Not trash, I mean. Just like . . . things that are of no use to anyone. It's not trash. If it was Ben's it's not trash."

"Hey," Susan says. "Don't be so hard on yourself. Ben can't hear you call his stuff trash, and even if he could, it wouldn't matter."

I don't know why it is so jarring to hear, because I don't be-

lieve that Ben can hear me. I just thought Susan believed Ben
is here; Ben is with us.

"You don't believe that Ben is . . ."

"All around us?" she says in a half-mocking way. She shakes
her head. "No, I don't. I wish I did. It would make things a lot
easier for me. But no, either he's gone-gone, his soul having disappeared into the ether, or if he's been transported somewhere
else, if his heart and mind are reincarnated or just somewhere
else, I don't think he'd still be here on earth as himself. I don't
see . . . it just seems like something people tell victims' families,
you know? 'Hey, it's okay. Ben is always with you.'"

"You don't think Ben is with you?"

"He's with me because I love him and I loved him and he
lives in my memories. His memory is with me. But no, I don't
see how Ben is here. After Steven died, I thought maybe he
was lying in bed next to me at night, watching me. Or maybe
he was some omnipotent force looking over Ben and I, but it
did no good. Because I just didn't believe it. You know? Do you
believe it? Or maybe what I should say is *Can* you believe it?
I wish I could."

I shake my head. "No, I don't think he can hear me. I don't
think he's watching me. It's a nice idea. When my brain wanders, I sometimes think about what if he's hearing everything
I'm saying, what if he's seeing everything I'm doing. But, it
doesn't really make me feel any better. Whenever I start to
think about where he is now, I ultimately just focus on what
his last moments were. Did he know they were his last moments? What if he'd never left the house? What if I'd never
asked him to . . ."

"To what?"

"He was doing me a favor when he died," I tell her. "He was

buying me Fruity Pebbles." It feels like I've finally put down a barbell. Susan is quiet.

"Was that a confession?" she says.

"Hmm?"

"That doesn't matter. You know that, right?"

No, I don't know that. But I'm not sure how to say that, so I don't say anything.

"You will do yourself a world of good the minute you realize that does not matter. You can play the scenario out a million times, whether he goes to get the cereal or he doesn't," she says. "I'm telling you, he'd still end up dying. It's just the way the world works."

I look at her, trying to figure out if she truly believes that. She can see my skepticism.

"I don't know if that's true," she says. "But that is one thing we *have* to believe. Do you hear me? Learn how to believe that one." She doesn't let me speak. "Get the box," she says. "We're gonna start in the bathroom."

We pack away his toothbrush and his hair gel. We pack his deodorant and his shampoo. It's a small box of things that were only his. We shared so many of the things in here. Susan smells the shampoo and deodorant and then throws them in with the other things.

"When you are ready, this is a throwaway box, right?" Susan asks. "I mean, this is trash."

I laugh. "Yeah, that will be trash."

We move on to the kitchen and desk area, where most of Ben's stuff is also trash. We fill boxes and boxes of crap. I wonder if some of these things are being put right back into the boxes they came here in. We make our way back into the living room, and Susan starts packing his books. She sees a collector's set on one of the shelves.

"May I have this?" she says. "It took me months to convince him to read these books," she said. "He wouldn't believe me that young adult books can be great."

I want them, but I want her to have them more. "Sure," I say. "You should take anything you want. He'd want you to have his things," I say. "He loved those books, by the way. He recommended them to anyone that would listen to him."

She smiles and puts them by the door as she finishes packing the rest of his young adult collection into boxes. "Is this a sell or a keep box, by the way?"

"I'm not sure yet," I answer. She nods. She continues putting books into boxes until she is too exasperated. "Jesus Christ, how many young adult books can one person read?" she says.

I laugh. "He read them a lot. I mean, like one a week sometimes. And he refused to get them from the library. Which was annoying because I work at the library, but he insisted upon going to the bookstore and buying them. I'd bring them home and he'd just let them sit and collect dust until I returned them."

She laughs. "That's my fault," she says. "When he was a kid, my one luxury was buying books. I never wanted to go to the library."

"What?" Sacrilege!

She laughs again, embarrassed. "You're gonna be mad."

"I am?"

"I hate the way they smell, library books."

"You are killing me, Susan. *Killing me.*" I grab my chest and feign a heart attack. The way library books smell is the best smell in the world, other than the smell of the pillow I have trapped in a plastic bag.

"I know! I know! When Ben was a kid, he'd want to go to

the library because they had board games and those chairs with the . . . what are they called? The chairs where they are like this big, soft ball . . . Oh, damn it, what is the word?"

"Beanbag chairs?"

"Yes! He used to love sitting in beanbag chairs, and I would make him go to the bookstore with me instead so I could buy books that didn't smell musty. Totally my fault. I'm sorry."

"You are forgiven," I say, although I'm still hung up on the fact that she doesn't like the smell of library books.

MAY

I got home and Ben was still in bed. He'd been staring at the ceiling for the past hour and a half. It took me forever to get to the rental place in that huge truck, and then I picked up his car that he left there and headed home, only to remember he wanted dinner. I picked up McDonald's and made my way home.

"You okay?" I called out to him as I got into the apartment.

"Yeah, but I still can't move that well," he said.

"Well, you'll be happy to know I almost crashed about four times in the damn truck going up Laurel Canyon. Why do they let normal people drive those things?"

"I wouldn't exactly say you're normal," he said. "But I understand your point."

I put the bag of McDonald's on the bed and helped him to get to a sitting position.

"I really think I should call the doctor," I said.

"I will be fine," he told me and started to eat. I followed suit, and when I was done, my fingers covered in salt, my mouth coated in grease, I took a big sip of my large soda. I lay back, finally resting after the long day. Ben turned on the television and said he wanted to watch something. Then it all got fuzzy and I fell asleep.

I woke up the next morning to an empty bed.

"Ben?" I called out. He answered from the living room. I

walked out there and found that a whole section of boxes had been unloaded.

"How are you feeling? Are you okay?"

"I'm fine," he said. "As long as I stay upright and don't twist, I feel fine."

"I really think you should see a doctor. That doesn't sound good."

"Quit nagging me, wife," he said and smiled. "Can I remove some of your dumb books? I want a place to put all of these," he said. He gestured awkwardly to stacks and stacks of paperback books.

"Maybe we should just buy a new bookshelf," I said.

"Or maybe you should donate some of these lame classics to the library. Do we really need two copies of *Anna Karenina*?"

"Hey! It's two different translations!" I said. "You can't just come in here and throw my stuff out because you need room, you jerk!"

"I'm not saying we should throw it out," he said. "Just . . . donate it." He opened the book up and smelled it and then thrust his head away. "*Owow!*" he exclaimed and rubbed his back. "These books smell all old and gross, Elsie. Let's at least get you some new books."

I grab *Anna Karenina* out of his hand and put it back on my shelf. "I doubt your books smell all that great," I said. "Any book you have for a long time starts to smell of must. That's how it works."

"Yeah, but I don't buy my books at used bookstores and flea markets," he said. "I get 'em hot off the presses so they stay fresh."

"Oh for heaven's sake! Books aren't bagels. They don't go stale," I said as I pulled one from the stack. It had a teenage girl standing in front of what appeared to be an oversize falcon. "Seriously?" I said.

"Let's do a little experiment," Ben said. "What's *Anna Karenina* about?"

"It's about a married aristocratic woman who falls in love with a count but she can't—"

"I am falling asleep just listening to you. Do you know what this book is about?" he asked me, grabbing the falcon-cover book from my hand. "This book is about a group of kids who are part human, part bird." He said it plainly, as if the facts spoke for themselves. "This is a better book."

"You haven't even tried to read *Anna Karenina*. It's an incredibly moving story."

"I'm sure it is," he said. "But I like my books to take place 'in a world where . . .' "

"In a world where what?"

"Just in a world where . . . anything. In a world where love is classified as a disease. In a world where the government chooses your family for you. In a world where society has eliminated all pain and suffering. I love that kind of stuff."

"That last one was *The Giver*," I said. "Right? You're talking about *The Giver*?"

"If you tell me you don't like *The Giver*, this relationship is over," he said to me. "I have a zero tolerance policy on not appreciating *The Giver*."

I smiled and grabbed his copy of *The Giver*. I opened it up and smelled the pages. "I don't know . . ." I teased. "Smells a little musty."

"Hey!" he yelled, trying to pull the book away from me. But the pain was too excruciating. He was wincing and crying out. I took my keys off the table.

"Stand up," I said. "We're going to the goddamn doctor."

"Not until you admit you loved *The Giver*," he muttered.

I knelt down to help him up, and I told him softly, "I loved *The Giver*."

He smiled and groaned as he got up. "I knew it," he said, unfazed. "You want to know a secret though?"

I nodded.

"I would have adjusted the policy for you." Then he kissed me on the cheek and let me help him out to the car.

SEPTEMBER

We have packed up most of his things by the afternoon, saving the bedroom and closet for last. We grab the rest of the boxes and head in there.

I throw the boxes onto the bed and look at the room. I can do this. I can do this. If I can't, Susan will. So at least it will get done.

"Come on!" she says. "Let's go." She opens a dresser and starts throwing clothes into boxes. I watch as striped shirts and dirty jeans are pulled out of their rightful home. I start taking clothes out of the closet with their hangers. You don't realize how dead clothes look on their hangers until the person who owned them is . . . Anyway, I don't even bother to take them off the hangers. I simply throw them in the box with the rest of his clothes. I have made my way through the closet and through his nightstand before Susan is done with the dresser. She has a look on her face like she's fine, but I spot her smelling a shirt before she puts it in the box. She sees me catch her.

"I've just been trying to see if anything still smells like him, you know? It's hard to remember anymore, what he smelled like."

"Oh," I say. "Sorry, I think I smelled all the smell off that stuff."

"Oh." She laughs. "That explains it then."

I think about whether I have it in me to share what I have left of Ben. I know that I do. "Hold on," I say.

I grab his pillow in the trash bag. I untie the top of the bag and hand it to her.

"Smell it," I say, and she looks at me somewhat hesitantly, but then she lowers her face into it, her nose grazing the pillow itself. "That's it," she says. "Oh God. That's him." Her eyes close, and I can see the tears falling down her cheeks. For the first time since the hospital, I see what happens when she lets herself lose it.

MAY

We spent the day at the doctor's office, sitting in cramped chairs with a room full of people with contagious diseases. Ben reminded me multiple times that we did not need to be there. But once we saw the doctor, he seemed very concerned that Ben take it easy. We left with a prescription for Vicodin.

We got home and Ben called to order Chinese. He ordered us the usual, and I overheard him tell the man on the phone that he wanted both white rice and brown rice. I remembered how he told me on our first date that ordering both would be a sign that the romance was gone, but I couldn't help but feel warmed by his doing it now. Ben and I were a team. We knew each other's wants. We knew each other's needs. We knew when to split up and compromise. We weren't each putting our best foot forward. We weren't waiting to see if this was right for us. We dove headfirst into this and here we were, one of those couples that doesn't put up with the other person's stupid shit. I liked brown, he liked white. We ordered both. Nothing fancy anymore. The novelty was gone for us and what we were left with was . . . awesome.

We got into bed that night, and even though we had not unpacked the bedroom, Ben was dead set on finding one thing. Concerned that he not bend or twist, I insisted upon looking for it myself. He directed me through boxes, and eventually, I made my way to a box so light that it felt like it was packed with air. I brought it to him, and he opened the box with joy. It was a dirty pillow.

"What is that?" I asked, horrified that that thing was entering my bed. It was covered in drool spots and orange puddles of . . . something.

"It's my favorite pillow!" he said, putting it down on top of one of my pillows, pillows that I thought were now "ours," but in comparison to his ugly, dirty pillow felt decidedly "mine."

"Please get that thing off my bed," I said.

"Our bed, baby," he said to me. "This is our bed. And our bed should have our pillows. And this is our pillow now."

"No," I said with a laugh. "I don't want that to be our pillow. I want that to be a pillow you used to have when you lived on your own."

"Well, it can't be that. I can't sleep without this pillow."

"You've been sleeping here for months without that pillow!"

"Yeah, but this is my own house now! I pay rent here! I need this pillow in a place where I pay rent."

"Ugh," I relented. "Just put a damn pillowcase on it, would you?"

"Sure." He walked to the linen closet and came back proud as a peacock. He then rolled himself delicately into bed.

"Did you take the Vicodin? It will take the edge off," I said.

"What do I look like? A man that can't handle a little pain?" he asked as he moved toward me slowly and put his head on his pillow. "You wanna try it out? It's *really* comfortable."

I shook my head. "No, thank you."

"Oh, come on. You can lie on it for five seconds. It's a part of us now," he said, teasing me.

"Fine! Fine!" I moved my head to lie on it. "Oh my God, that thing smells awful."

"What? No, it doesn't!"

"I can't believe you thought my books smelled bad. That pillow is terrible!" I laughed.

"No! It smells fine." He smelled it to make sure. "You just have to get used to it, is all."

"Yeah, okay," I said. I turned out the light. He fell asleep within minutes, and I lay there feeling like the luckiest girl in the world that this weirdo next to me was mine; that he lived here; that he had the right to demand his stinky pillow stay in my bed. I smelled it once more as I fell asleep, and I couldn't imagine ever getting used to it, but before long, that was exactly what I had done.

SEPTEMBER

The boxes are mostly packed. Ben's things are almost entirely out of sight. I can see only brown cardboard for miles. I kept his USC sweatshirt and a few of his T-shirts. I left his favorite cup in the cupboard. Susan put some books and photos in her car to take with her. She added a random notebook he'd written in and a few other things that are meaningless to anyone else but mean everything to a mom.

Now that it's all in boxes, there isn't much reason for Susan to stay here.

"Well," she says with a sigh. "I guess that's the last of it."

"I guess so," I say. I feel surprisingly stable.

"All right," she says, nodding. It's the kind of nod that says she doesn't know what to say next; she doesn't know what she's thinking. She gasps for air.

"I guess I'll . . . head home," she says. "It's, uh, this is hard. I don't want to leave but I . . . I mean, it's not like I'm leaving him, you know? I think it's more just . . . I had this to look forward to, if that makes any sense? I'm not making any sense. I'm going to go."

I hug her. "It makes all the sense in the world to me."

"Okay," she says. She breathes out. She breathes with focus. She gathers herself. "Okay, I'll give you a call next weekend."

"Sounds great."

She opens the door and walks out. I turn to see my apartment.

His things are in boxes, but I do not feel that I have lost him. It's a subtle feeling, but it's real. I am now just a little bit ready to realize the beauty of progress, of moving on. I decide to seize the moment. I grab three boxes of clothes and load them in the car. When I'm done with those, I grab two more. I don't go back in for more because I'm afraid I'll lose my nerve. I tell myself this is for the best. This is good!

I pull up in front of Goodwill and park my car. I take the boxes out and walk inside. A large man comes to greet me.

"What do we have here?"

"Some men's clothes," I say. I can't look at him. I'm staring at the boxes. "All good condition."

"Wonderful!" he says, as he takes the boxes from me. "Would you like a receipt?"

"No," I say. "No, thank you."

He opens the boxes and dumps their contents into a bigger pile of clothes, and even though I know that it's time for me to walk away, I can't help but stare. They are no longer Ben's clothes. They are just clothes in a pile of clothes mixed with other clothes.

What have I done?

Like that, they are gone. The man has taken the large pile and shoved it into the back room. I want those clothes back. Why did I give someone else Ben's clothes? What will he wear? I want to jump over the counter and sort through what they have back there. I need to get his clothes back. Instead, I am frozen and in shock over what I have done. How did I do that? Why did I do that? Can Ben see, from where he is, what I have done?

"Ma'am?" the man calls out to me. "Are you okay?"

"Yes," I say. "I'm sorry."

I turn around and get in my car. I can't turn the key in the ignition. I can't shift the car in drive. I just bang my head against the steering wheel. I let the tears fall down on the beige interior. My cheek is blaring the horn and I don't care.

I leave the keys on the front seat of my car and I get out. I just run. I run and run even though it's cold outside, even though my body is starting to heat up faster than it should. Even though I feel like I'm giving myself a fever. And then I stop, instantly and abruptly, because I realize that I cannot outrun myself. I go across the street and walk along the sidewalk until I see a bar. I don't have my wallet, I don't have my keys, but I walk in anyway. It's early enough in the day that they let me right in and then I sit at the bar and I drink beers. I drink beer after beer until I can't feel my nose. When I'm done, I pretend I'm going to the bathroom and then I sneak out the back, not paying, not tipping, not even saying thank you. By the time I get home, knowing full well I've locked myself out, I'm just plain sick.

I puke on my own front lawn. It's barely 8:00 p.m. Neighbors see me and I ignore them. I sit down on the grass when I'm done and I pass out. I wake up around 11:00, and I'm too discombobulated and inebriated to remember where my keys are. I do the only thing that I can do to get back into my house. I call Ana.

"At least you called me," she says as she walks up to the sidewalk to meet me. "That's all I care about."

I don't say anything. She walks up my steps and unlocks my front door. She holds it open for me.

"Are you drunk?" she says, rather shocked. If it were any other time in my life, she'd probably think this was funny, but I can tell she doesn't, even though I kind of do. "That's not like you."

"It's been a rough couple of days," I say and plop myself down on my own sofa.

"Do you want to talk about it?"

"Well, my husband died, so that was hard." I don't want to talk to her about any of this. I don't want to talk to anyone.

"I know," she says, taking my sarcastic remark as something genuine. She can't possibly think that was really my answer. Instead, she is treating me sincerely so that I have no choice but to be sincere. It's crafty, I'll give her that.

"I moved his stuff out," I say, resigning myself to the therapy session that is going to come my way. I don't want to talk to her about our last conversation, about our fight, although I'm sure she's going to force that on me as well. She moves toward me on the sofa and puts her arm around me. "I gave away some of his stuff to Goodwill," I tell her.

Goodwill! That's where my keys are.

"I'm sorry, Elsie," she says. "But I'm proud of you. I'm really, really proud of you for doing it." She rubs my arm. "I don't know if I'd be able to do it if I were you."

"What?" I say. "You were insisting that I needed to start moving on! You said I should do it!"

She nods. "Yeah, because you should. But that doesn't mean I didn't know it was hard."

"Then why did you say it like it was easy?"

"Because you needed to do it and I knew that you could. No one wants to do it."

"Yeah, well, no one else has to."

I want her to leave and I think she knows that.

"I'm sorry about the other night. I was out of line. I'm truly sorry," she says.

"It's fine," I say, and I mean it. It is fine. I should be apologizing too, but I just don't want to talk to anyone right now.

"All right, well, I'm going to go," she says. She gathers herself and leaves.

"I love you," she says.

"Me too," I say back, hoping it passes for an "I love you too." I do love her, but I don't want to say it. I don't want to feel anything. I see her drive away out of my front window, and I think that she is probably going to meet up with Kevin somewhere and she'll tell him all about this little episode of mine and he'll grab her hand and he'll say, "You poor baby, that sounds difficult," as if the world has conspired against her, as if she doesn't deserve this. I hate them both for being able to sigh, make a couple of serious faces about how hard this must be on me, and then go to the movies and laugh at dick jokes.

I walk to the Goodwill the next morning and get my car. My keys are sitting on the front seat where I left them, and yet, no one has stolen anything. It pisses me off, to be honest. It pisses me off that of all times, the world conspires to help me *now*.

At work on Monday, I am scowling at strangers. When they ask me to help them, I do it with a frown on my face, and when I'm done, I curse them under my breath.

When Mr. Callahan makes his way toward me, I have little energy left.

"Hello, my dear," he says as he moves to touch my arm. I instinctively pull away. He doesn't seem to take it personally. "Bad day?" he asks.

"You could say that." I grab the handle on a cart of books to reshelve. It's not technically my job to put them back, but it seems like a good way to graciously end the conversation. Mr. Callahan doesn't get the hint. He walks with me.

"I had a bad day once," he says, grinning. It's a classic cheer-up routine, and it's wasted on me. I don't want to cheer up. I'm honestly not sure I even remember how to smile naturally. What do you do? You pull the corners of your mouth up?

"Bad joke," he says, waving his hand in an attempt to both dismiss the joke and let me off the hook for not laughing at it. "Anything I can do for you?"

"Oh," I say, my eyes focused on the bookshelves above me. I don't even remember what I'm looking for. I have to look at the book in my hand again. The details aren't registering. The call number falls out of my head before my eyes make it back up to the shelf. "No, thanks," I say.

"I've got two ears, you know!" he says.

My face contorts into impatient confusion. "I'm sorry?"

"For listening, I mean. I'm good at listening."

"Oh."

"Anyway," he continues. "You'd rather be alone. I get it. Just know the offer stands. I'm always here to listen." He looks at me a minute, perhaps trying to break through my empty stare. "And I wouldn't say that to just anybody," he says, smiling as he pats my hand gently, and he leaves me to the cart.

I wish I had it in me to tell him he's a good man. I wish I had it in me to say thank you. I just don't. I can't smile at him. I don't even say good-bye. I let him walk away and I turn to the bookshelves as if he was never there. I forget, once more, the number of the book I have in my hand, and instead of checking again, I drop it right there on the cart and I walk away.

I step outside and take a breath. I tell myself to get it together. I tell myself that this situation I'm in is no one's fault. I am by the bike rack, pacing, when I see a young couple with a baby. The man has the baby strapped to his chest, the woman is carrying a diaper bag. She is cooing to the child, the man is looking down. She kisses the man on the lips and laughs as she maneuvers awkwardly around the baby. They play with the baby's hands and feet.

Why me and not them? Why couldn't that guy have died? Why am I not here right now with Ben looking at a sad woman pacing on the street, on the edge of a nervous breakdown? What right do they have to be happy? Why does everyone in the world have to be happy in front of me?

I go back inside and tell Nancy I'll be in the Native American section. I tell her I'm researching the Aztecs for next month's display. I stand in the aisle, running my fingers over the spines, feeling the cellophane crackle as I touch it. I watch as the Dewey decimal numbers escalate higher and higher. I try to focus only on the numbers, only on the spines. It works for a moment, for a moment I don't feel like I want to get a gun. But in that moment, I crash face-first into someone else.

"Oh! I'm so sorry," he says to me, picking up the book he's dropped. He's my age, maybe a bit older. He has black hair and what is probably a permanent five o'clock shadow. He is tall with a firm body and broad shoulders. He is dressed in a faded T-shirt and jeans. I notice his brightly colored Chuck Taylors as he picks up his book. I move to get out of his way, but he seems to want to stop and talk.

"Brett," he says and puts out his hand. I shake it, trying to move on.

"Elsie," I say.

"Sorry to bump into you like that," he says. "I'm not that familiar with this library, and the librarians here aren't very helpful."

"I'm a librarian here," I say. I don't care if he feels awkward.

"Oh." He laughs shyly. "That is embarrassing. I'm so sorry. Again. Wow. This isn't going well for me, huh?"

"No, I guess not," I say.

"Listen, would you let me buy you a coffee, as an apology?" he asks.

"No, that's okay. It's not a big deal."

"No, really. I'd like to. It would be my pleasure," he says, and now he's smiling like he thinks he's cute or something.

"Oh," I say. "No, I really should be getting back to work."

"Some other time then," he says. Maybe he thinks I'm being demure or shy. I don't know.

"I'm married," I say, trying to end it. I don't know if I'm saying that because I think it's true or just to get him off my back, the way I used to say "I don't think my boyfriend would like that" when I was single and hit on by homeless men outside convenience stores.

"Oh," he says. "I'm sorry, I didn't . . . I wasn't expecting that."

"Yeah, well," I say as I lift up my hand and show him.

"Well," he says, laughing. "If it doesn't work out with you and your husband . . ."

That's when I punch him in the face.

I'm surprised at how satisfying it is to make contact: the crack of fist to face, the sight of just the smallest trickle of blood out of a nose.

You are not supposed to punch people in the face. You're especially not supposed to punch people in the face while you are at work. When you work for the city. And when the person you punch in the face is kind of a baby about it and insists that the library call the cops.

When the cops get here, I can't do much to defend myself. He didn't hit me. He didn't threaten me. He didn't use incendiary language. He did nothing to provoke me. I just assaulted him. So, as embarrassing and over the top as it is, I am being arrested. They don't handcuff me. One cop even seems to think this is funny. But apparently, when the cops are called because you punched someone and they show up and you say, "Yes, Officer, I hit that person," they have to at least bring you down to the "precinct." One of the police officers escorts me to the backseat of the squad car, reminding me to duck as I get in. As he shuts the door and heads to the front seat, Mr. Callahan comes outside and catches my eye. I should be ashamed, I'm sure. But I just don't care. I look at him through the backseat window, and I see him crack a smile at me. His smile slowly turns to laughter, a laughter that seems to be equal parts shock and newfound respect, perhaps even pride. The car starts to pull away, and Mr. Callahan gives me a sly thumbs-up. I find myself smiling, finally. I guess I do remember how to do it. You just turn the corners of your mouth up.

When we get to the police station, the cops take my things and book me. They put me in a cell. They tell me to call one person. I call Ana.

"You what?" she says.

"I'm at the police station. I need you to come bail me out."

"You're kidding, right?"

"I'm entirely serious."

"What did you do?"

"I punched someone in the library stacks, somewhere between 972.01 and 973.6."

"Okay, I'm coming," she says.

"Wait. Don't you want to know why I punched him?" I ask.

"Does it matter?" she asks, impatient.

It feels like hours until she's here, but I think she actually gets here pretty quickly. I see her standing in front of my cell and . . . ha-ha-ha, how the fuck did I get here in a jail cell? She's with the officer that arrested me. I am free to go, he says. We'll wait to see if Brett presses charges.

Ana and I exit the building and we are standing outside. Ana hands me my bag of things. I now think this is really funny. But Ana doesn't agree with me.

"In my defense, Mr. Callahan also thought it was funny," I say.

Ana turns to me. "The old guy?"

He's not just an old guy. "Forget it," I say.

"I called Susan," she says. It's almost a confession.

"What?"

"I called Susan."

"Why?"

"Because I think I'm out of my league here. I don't know what to do."

"So you told on me to my mom? Is that it?"

"She's not your mom," Ana says, sternly.

"I know that," I say. "I just mean that's kind of what you've done, right? You don't want to deal with me so you're trying to get me in trouble?"

"I think you've gotten yourself in trouble."

"He was being an asshole, Ana." She just looks at me. "He *was*! How did you even get her number anyway?"

"It's in your phone," she says, like I am stupid.

"Fine. Forget it. I'm sorry I called you."

"Susan will be at your place in about an hour."

"She's coming *over*? I have to work until five," I say.

"Something tells me they won't want you back at work today," Ana says.

We get in her car and she drives me to mine. I get out and thank her again for bailing me out. I tell her I'm sorry to be difficult and that I will pay her back.

"I'm just worried about you, Elsie."

"I know," I say. "Thanks."

I drive myself home and wait for the knock at the door.

Susan knocks, and I open the door. She doesn't say anything. She just looks at me.

"I'm sorry," I say. I don't know why I'm apologizing to her. I don't owe it to her not to get arrested. I don't owe it to anyone.

"You don't need to apologize to me," she says. "I just wanted to make sure you were okay."

"I'm fine."

She comes in and kicks off her shoes. She lies down on my couch.

"What happened?" she asks.

I blow out a hard sigh and sit down.

"This guy asked me out," I say. "And I said no, but he kept at it and I told him I was married—"

"Why did you tell him you were married?" Susan asks.

"Huh?"

"I tell people I'm still married all the time, and I do it for the wrong reason. I do it so I can feel married. So I don't have to say out loud that I am not married. Is that what you're doing?"

"No. Well." I stop and think. "I am married," I say. "I didn't divorce him. We didn't end it."

"But it ended."

"Well, but, not . . . we didn't end it."

"It ended," she says.

Why must everything be a life lesson? Why can't I just act like I'm married and everyone leave me the hell alone?

"Well, if I . . ." I trail off. I'm not sure of my defense.

"Go on," she says. It seems like she knows what I'm going to say, but I don't even know what I am going to say.

"If we stopped being married when he died . . ."

She waits for me to finish my thought.

"Then we were barely married."

Susan nods. "That's what I thought you were going to say."

My lips turn down.

"Who cares?" she says.

"What?"

"Who cares if you were barely married? It doesn't mean you love him any less."

"Well, but . . ."

"Yes?"

"We were only together for six months before we got married."

"So?"

"So, I mean, being married is what separates him from just some guy. It's what proves he's . . . he's the love of my life."

"No, it doesn't," she says. I just stare at her. "That doesn't matter at all. It's a piece of paper. A piece of paper you don't even have, by the way. It means nothing."

"It means everything!" I say.

"Listen to me; it means nothing. You think that some ten minutes you spent with Ben in a room defines what you meant to each other? It doesn't. You define that. What you feel defines that. You loved him. He loved you. You believed in each other. That is what you lost. It doesn't matter whether it's labeled a husband or a boyfriend. You lost the person you love. You lost the future you thought you had."

"Right," I say.

"I was with Steven for thirty-five years before I lost him. Do you think I have more of a right to pain than you do?"

The answer is yes. I do think that. I've been terrified of that. I've been walking about feeling like an amateur, like an impostor, because of it.

"I don't know," I say.

"Well, I don't. Love is love is love. When you lose it, it feels like the shittiest disaster in the world. Just like dog shit."

"Right."

"When I lost Steven, I lost love, but I also lost someone I was attached to."

"Right."

"You didn't have as much time as I did to be attached to the man you loved. But attachment and love are two different things. My heart was broken *and* I didn't remember how to do things without him. I didn't remember who I was. But you, you lived without Ben just last year. You can do it again. You can do it sooner than me. But the love, that's the sharp pain that won't stop. That's the constant ache in your chest. That won't go away easily."

"I just feel like I had him for so little time," I say. It's difficult to talk about. It's difficult because I work so hard to keep the self-pity at bay, and talking like this, talking about all of this, it's like opening the door to my self-pity closet and asking its contents to spill all over the floor. "I didn't have enough time with him," I say, my voice starting to break, my lips starting to quiver. "It wasn't enough time. Six months! That's all I had." I lose my breath. "I only got to be his wife for nine days." I now begin to sob. "Nine days isn't enough. It's not enough."

Susan comes closer to me, and she grabs my hand. She pushes my hair back off my forehead. She catches my eye.

"Sweetheart, I'm telling you, you love someone like that, you love them the right way, and no time would be enough. Doesn't matter if you had thirty years," she tells me. "It wouldn't be enough."

She's right, of course. If I'd had ten more years with Ben, would I be sitting here saying, "It's okay, I had him long enough?" No. It would never have been enough.

"I'm scared," I tell her. "I'm scared that I'll have to move on and meet someone and spend my life with them and it will seem like"—my voice cracks again—"it will seem like Ben was . . . I don't want him to be 'my first husband.'"

Susan nods. "You know, you're in a much different position than I am, and I forget that sometimes. No one begrudges me giving up on my love life. They understand. They know I won't date again. They know I've had my one love and I'm done. But you, you have to meet someone else in this life. I can't imagine how much of a betrayal that would feel to me if I had to do it."

"It *is* a betrayal. All of it feels like betrayal. I had this amazing man—I can't just find another one and forget about him."

"I understand that, Elsie. But you have to find a way to remember him and forget him. You have to find a way to keep him in your heart and in your memories but *do* something *else* with your *life*. Your life cannot be about my son. It can't."

I shake my head. "If my life isn't about him, I don't know what it's about."

"It's about you. Your life has always been about you. That's what makes it your life," she says and smiles at me. "I know nine days is short. I know six months is short. But, trust me when I tell you, if you go on and you marry someone else, and you have kids with them and you love your family and you feel like you would die without them, you won't have lost Ben. Those nine days, those six months, they are a part of your life now, a part of you. They may not have been enough *for* you but they were enough to change you. I lost my son after loving him for twenty-seven years. It's brutal, unending, gutting pain. Do you think I don't deserve to grieve as much as someone who lost their son after forty years? Twenty-seven years is a short time to have a son. Just because it was short, it doesn't mean it didn't happen. It was just short. That's all. Forgive yourself for that, Elsie. It's not your fault your marriage lasted nine days. And it doesn't say a goddamn thing about how much you loved him."

I don't have anything to say back. I want so badly to take all of her words and fit them like the pieces of a puzzle into the hole in my heart. I want to write those words down on little pieces of paper and swallow them, consume them, make them a part of me. Maybe then I could believe them.

I'm quiet for too long; the mood shifts somehow in the silence. I relax and the tears start to dry. Susan moves on, gently. "Did they fire you?"

"No," I say. "But I think they are going to ask me to take some time off."

She looks happy to hear this news, as if it all falls into her master plan.

"Stay with me in Newport then," she says.

"What?"

"Let's get you out of this apartment. Out of Los Angeles. You need a change of scenery for a few weeks."

"Uh . . ."

"I've been thinking about this for a few days, and this is a sign that I'm right. You need time to sit and feel sorry for yourself and get it all out so you can start over. I can help you. Let me help you."

I try to think of a good reason to say no, but . . . I simply don't have one.

MAY

I don't like going home as much as I used to," Ben said to me. We were walking along the streets of Venice Beach. I had wanted to go for a walk in the sand, and Ben always liked to people-watch in Venice. I preferred the quiet, romantic beaches of Malibu, but Ben loved to watch the weirdos along the boardwalk.

"Why?" I asked him. "I thought you said your mom's house was really nice now."

"It is," he said. "But it's too big. It's too empty. It's too . . ."

"What?"

"I don't know. I always feel like I'm going to break something. When my dad was alive, it was not an impressive house. He never cared about that stuff and he hated spending money on, like, crystal vases."

"Your mom has a lot of crystal vases?"

"She could never have them when he was around, so I think she's trying to make the most of the situation."

"Right. She's doing everything she wanted to do when he was around but couldn't."

"Yeah," he said. "But, not really. It's more like she's buying everything she wanted but she's not *doing* anything."

"Well, maybe buying is doing. Maybe for her, that's what's working. Also"—I hesitated to say it and then decided to push it out of my mouth—"maybe it comes from the same place as what you're going through, you know? About how you aren't telling her about us?"

Ben looked at me. "Well, that's because . . ." he started and couldn't seem to find the words to finish. "Maybe," he said, re-signed. "I'm just going to tell her soon. Because it's never going to be the right time, and now, I'm just outright lying. Before it was a gray area, but I live with you now. We live together." His mood took a dive, and I could see the moment when it crashed. He let out a heavy sigh. "I've been lying to her."

Maybe I should have made him call her right then. Maybe I should have told him he was right, he was lying. But I couldn't let him be sad. I couldn't watch as he became disappointed in himself.

"You're not lying," I said. "You're doing this your way and now you can see that you really do need to tell her, and you're gonna do it," I said, as if it was the simplest thing in the world.

"Yeah, no, you're absolutely right." He nodded with pur-pose. "I let this go a bit too far obviously, but it's actually not a big deal. She'll be happy for me. She'll love you." He looked at me with genuine affection. He truly could not understand a world in which people might not like me, or more realistically, a world where people might feel indifferent toward me.

Ben quickly averted his gaze to avoid eye contact with the very thing he wanted to stare at. "Are you seeing this?" he asked me through his teeth. "Are you seeing what I'm seeing?"

"The old guy in the yellow thong skateboarding with a dog?" I asked quietly.

"I promise you, no one is doing that in Malibu," he said, as he put his arm around my shoulders.

I laughed and let him lead me further down the street. He watched the passersby as I disappeared into my own head. I was suddenly nervous about finally meeting his mom. I started to imagine how it would go.

We'd all meet at a formal dinner. I would have to wear a nice outfit and go to a nice restaurant. I'd probably bring a sweater but forget it in the car. I'd be cold the whole time but never say anything. I'd want to go to the bathroom, but I'd be too nervous to even excuse myself. I'd smile so fake and huge that I'd start to feel a little dizzy from all the oxygen. Ben would sit in between the two of us at a round table. We'd face each other head-on. And then I figured out what was really nagging at me. What if the whole time I was sitting across from her, maintaining perfect posture, worrying if there was something in my teeth, she would be thinking, What does he see in her?

OCTOBER

Before I go to Susan's, I discuss taking a leave of absence from my job. Lyle says that he's not comfortable with me coming back right away, and I tell him I understand. But he says when I'm ready my job is here for me. I think Nancy had a lot to do with that, but I just say thank you.

I meet Ana for breakfast and tell her I'm going to stay with Susan.

"What?" she asks. "I just wanted her to talk some sense into you, not take you away." She is clearly unnerved by this. She's throwing food into her mouth quickly. She's barely tasting it before getting more.

"I know," I say. "And thank you for calling her. I think I need to get out of here for a while. I need to find a way to move on. I don't think I can do that here. At least, I can't start it here."

"How long are you leaving for?" She looks like she might cry.

"Not long. A few weeks, tops. I'll be back soon, and you can drive down all the time."

"You really think this is going to help?" she asks me.

"I know that I want it to help," I say. "And I think that's the point."

"Okay," she says. "Do you want me to get your mail and check on the house?"

"Sure," I say.

"Okay." She doesn't say it, but I get the feeling there is a small part of her that is happy to see me go. I have drained her. If I ever stop feeling sorry for myself, it will be time to start feeling sorry for what I've been putting Ana through. I'm not there yet, but I know it's coming. "I like Kevin," I say.

"Okay," she says, not believing me.

"No, really. I was just thrown for a loop is all. I really like him."

"Well, thank you," she says diplomatically. Eventually, I leave and get in my car full of clean clothes and toiletries. I put the address into my phone, pull out of my parking space, and head south.

I ring the doorbell with my bag on my shoulder. I feel like I'm here for a sleepover. Somehow, the house looks so much more inviting this time. It looks less like it will eat me alive when I step into it.

Susan comes to the door with her arms open wide for a hug. She looks genuinely thrilled to see me, which is nice, because I feel like for the past few weeks I simply have not been someone people would be thrilled to see.

"Hi!" she says.

"Hi," I say, a bit more timidly.

"I have a whole evening planned for us," she says before I've even crossed the threshold. "Chinese food, in-home massages, *Steel Magnolias*."

I look at her when I hear *"Steel Magnolias."*

She smiles sheepishly. "I never had a girl to watch it with!"

I laugh and put my things down. "That actually sounds great."

"I'll show you to your room," she says.

"Geez, I feel like I'm at a hotel," I say.

"I decorate when I can't face the day. Which seems to be most days now." The heaviness of her admission startles me. It's always been about me when we talk. I almost don't know what to say to a woman that has lost both her husband and her son.

"Well, I'm here now," I say, brightly. "I can . . ." What? What can I possibly do?

She smiles at me but I can tell her smile can become a frown at any minute. Somehow, it doesn't. She U-turns back to happier thoughts. "Let me show you the guest room!"

"The guest room?" I ask.

She turns to me. "You didn't think I was going to let you sleep in Ben's room, did you?"

"Kind of, I did."

"I've spent far too much time in there, these past couple of weeks, and let me tell you: It only makes it sadder." She doesn't let the emotion deter the moment again. She's dead set on moving through this. She leads me to a gorgeous white room with a white bedspread and white pillows. There are white calla lilies on the desk and Godiva chocolates on the nightstand. I'm not sure if the candles are new, but they haven't been used before. It smells like cotton and soap in here. It smells so good. The whole thing is stunning, really.

"Too much white? I'm sorry. I might be overeager to use the guest room finally."

I laugh. "This is gorgeous, thank you." There is a robe on the bed. She sees me notice it.

"For you, if you want it. I want you to feel pampered here. Comfortable."

"It's great," I say. She's thought of everything. I look behind her to the bathroom and can see Ben's soap message to her.

She sees me looking at that as well. "I couldn't bring myself to wash it away when he was here, I know I won't ever wash it away now."

There it is, finally. I remember trying to find it the last time I was here. I remember why I gave up. And yet, it's right in front of me now. It's like it finally found a way to get me here. His handwriting is so imperfect. He had no idea what he was doing when he did that. He had no idea what it would mean to us.

Susan breaks the silence. "Okay, get settled in, do whatever you wanna do. Masseuse comes in about two hours. I figure we can order Chinese food shortly after that. I'm going to go watch trashy crap television," she says. "And my only rule is that you forget about the real world while you are here and just cry anytime you want to. Get it out, you know? That's my only rule."

"Sounds good," I say, and she takes off. I find myself slightly uncomfortable here, which takes me by surprise because I have been so comfortable around her recently. She has brought me such comfort. But I am now in her house, in her world. I am also in the house that Ben grew up in, and it feels fitting to cry. Yet, I'm not on the verge of tears. In fact, I feel okay. I can't help but think that maybe because it's okay to cry, I can't.

MAY

Marry me," he said.

"*Marry you?*" I was in the driver's seat of his car. I had just picked him up from the doctor's office again. He had bent down to pet a dog that morning and his back had re-spasmed. Apparently, this can happen when you don't take the pain medication the doctor prescribes. Ben got a lecture on how he needed to take the pain medication so he would move normally again and work out the muscles. I had told him that earlier in the week, but he didn't listen to me. So there I was, driving him home from the doctor once again. Only this time, I was being proposed to while he was drugged out on painkillers in the passenger seat.

"Yes! Just marry me. You are perfect," he said. "It's hot in here."

"Okay, okay. I'm taking you home."

"But you will marry me?" he asked, smiling over at me, watching me drive.

"I think that's the painkillers talking," I said.

"Drunk words are sober thoughts," he said, and then he fell asleep.

OCTOBER

I sit out by Susan's pool, reading magazines and getting a tan. Susan and I play gin rummy and drink a lot of iced tea. The days come and go, and I have nothing to show for them. I walk through her herb garden, and sometimes I pick lemons from her fruit trees and then put them in my drinks. I'm finally gaining weight. I haven't stepped on a scale, but I can see the roundness back in my cheeks.

When the days start to cool down and the Santa Ana winds take over the nights, I sometimes sit by the outdoor chimney. I think I'm the first one to light it. But after the first couple of times, it starts to smell like a warm, toasty campfire, and if I close my eyes long enough, I can convince myself I'm on a traditional vacation.

Otherwise, Susan is usually with me, guiding me through her own little version of Widow Rehab. She starts to cry sometimes but always seems to stop herself. I'm pretty sure at night in bed alone is the only time she can really let herself go. Every once in a while when I am trying to fall asleep myself, I can hear her sob from the other side of the house. I never go to her room. I never mention it the next day. She likes to be alone with her pain. She doesn't like to share it. During the day, she wants to be there for me, show me how this is done, and I'm happy to oblige. However imperfect, her system is working for her. She's functional and composed when she needs to be, and she is in tune with her feelings in her own way. I guess I am learning from the best because I do feel a little bit better.

When Susan isn't around, sometimes I sneak into Ben's old bedroom. I imagined it would be here waiting for him, frozen in time from when he left it. I thought maybe I'd find old high school trophies and pictures of prom, maybe one of those felt flags I've seen people pin on their walls. I want to learn more about my husband. I want to consume more information about him. Spend more time with him. But instead, I find a small room that had been cleared out long before Ben died. There's a bed with a blue striped comforter, and in one corner, a half-torn sticker from some skateboard company. Sometimes, I sit on the bed and hear how quiet this house is with just one person in it. It must be so quiet for Susan when I am not here.

I think of a world where I am a mother of three, married to a handsome man. We own an oversize SUV, and he coaches girls' soccer. He is faceless, nameless. To tell the truth, in the scenario, he doesn't matter. I keep trying to think of a way to work Ben into this new life I could have. I could name my son Ben, but that feels too obvious and, quite frankly, too small a gesture. I am beginning to understand why people start funds and charities in other people's names. It would feel good to work at the Benjamin S. Ross Foundation for Not Eating Fruity Pebbles. But I know there isn't actually anything to rally against for him.

To tell the truth, I lack passion for much of anything. Sometimes I wish I had passion for something—which, if you think about it, is a kind of passion in itself. Albeit, somewhat weak.

Susan always plans things for me to do to keep me busy, even if it is just a structured day of lounging and watching television. Sometimes the "camp counselor" shtick she has going on can be a bit grating, but it's not my place to tell her to back off. She wants to help me and she is helping. I'm just that little bit more functional each day.

"My friend Rebecca is in town tonight," she says to me one afternoon. "I was thinking we could all go out to this new Mediterranean place I found."

This is the first time that Susan is inviting me out with any of her friends. It seems odd, somehow, to participate in something together that involves other people. I'm not sure why, though. It feels like this alliance is a private one, one not to be shared. As if she's my mistress mother. But I think I'm really just scared of what to call her. How will she introduce me? "This is my son's widow?" I don't want that.

"Oh, I don't know," I say. I'm fiddling with the pages of a magazine I read days ago. The pages are transparent and curled at the edges from when I left it by the edge of the pool and attempted a cannonball.

"Please?" she says.

"I mean—" I start. She abruptly sits down and puts her hands out, as if she's about to make a great proposition.

"Look, Rebecca isn't the best. She's kind of . . . snobby. Well, she's really snobby. And I could just never stand her snobby little attitude about our kids. When her oldest got into Stanford, it was Stanford this and Stanford that and whoopity-do, isn't Patrick the smartest kid in the world? She always acted like Ben was such a disappointment."

"Wow, okay, now I really don't want to go. And I don't understand why you want to go," I say.

"Well, get this!" Susan says excitedly. "She always, always wanted a daughter. Always. She's got two boys. Neither married yet." Susan catches herself and blushes. "I'm a terrible person, right? I am. I'm trying to use my daughter-in-law to make my friend jealous."

I don't know whether it's that I already hate Rebecca or that I like the idea of indulging Susan, but I agree. "Should we wear matching dresses?" I say. "Maybe tell her we just got back from pottery making together?"

Susan laughs heartily. "Thank you for understanding that I am sometimes a total bitch."

We take naps and then get ready for dinner. I can hear Susan changing her clothes over and over. It's odd to see her so insecure. When we get to the restaurant, we are told that Rebecca has already been seated. We walk through the dining area, Susan just the littlest bit in front of me, and I see her make eye contact. Rebecca stands up to greet us. "Only two minutes late!" Rebecca says, and I see Susan start to roll her eyes. Rebecca turns to me. "So this is the daughter-in-law you won't stop talking about."

And I realize that, more than anything, what made me want to come to dinner was that for the first time, I feel like I am Susan's daughter-in-law, plain and simple. The bizarre circumstances don't matter. I am someone's new, shiny daughter-in-law.

NOVEMBER

Ana is coming down to visit tonight. Susan invited her to stay for the weekend and she accepted. She should be here any minute, and I am excited to show her how nice it can be to just sit by a pool and feel the sun beating down on you. I went to the store this afternoon to get us snacks and wine coolers. I got the wine coolers because I thought they were funny, but then I drank one this afternoon, and you know what? They are actually pretty tasty.

Ana shows up around six, and Susan has a whole dinner planned. I get the impression Susan is deathly bored. I think my being here makes it easier to fill her days, but before Ben died, before she and I became close, she was supremely, soul-suckingly bored. She's in a lot of book clubs, but as far as I can tell, that's about it. So when Ana comes for dinner, it gives Susan an excuse for a seven-course meal.

I walk into the kitchen and find an extra apron. I put it on and splay my hands out. "What can I do?" I ask.

Susan is chopping vegetables so fast I'm sure she's about to lose a digit, but she doesn't. Her cutting board is full of various chopped stuff that she slides easily into a big bowl.

"Can you hand me that jar?" she asks. I do. She sprinkles whatever the hell is in it, possibly Parmesan cheese, onto the salad and puts the salad on the table.

"Salad's ready. The roast beef is cooking. Mashed potatoes

are mashed. Yorkshire pudding is in the oven. I think I'm pretty much done," she tells me. "I hope Ana isn't on a diet. I cooked all the food in Orange County."

The doorbell rings, and I answer. Ana is wearing a white dress and a black cardigan; she's holding a bottle of wine in one hand and her purse with the other. I've spoken to Ana on the phone many times since I got here, but it swells my heart to see her face. She is the life I want back.

She hugs me, and I can smell her perfume. It reminds me of our early twenties, when we went to bars and I stood in the corner nursing a fruity drink while she was in the center of the room. It reminds me of Sunday morning brunches and hangovers. A single life. A single life I loved before I knew anything better.

It's been so long since I've smelled Ben that I have forgotten the scent. I could recognize it in an instant, but I can't describe it, I can't feel it. I knew this would happen. I feared this would happen. Now that it has, it's not so bad. It is. But it isn't.

"You look great!" she says. It brightens my mood immediately.

"Thank you! So do you!" I don't like that our conversation has a somewhat formal quality to it. We are best friends, and best friends don't talk like this.

We walk into the kitchen, and Ana hugs Susan. "What can I do?" Ana asks, and Susan waves her off.

"You girls are so polite," she says. "I'm almost done. Have a seat. Do you want a drink?"

"At least let me get those," Ana says and starts looking for glasses.

"Top cupboard above the dishwasher," Susan says without looking. Ana grabs three glasses and pours us some wine.

It's about five minutes before we sound like ourselves again, and I think how odd it is that I've only been away from Ana for a few weeks, and yet, I already feel estranged. Then it occurs to me that I haven't been away from Ana for a few weeks. I've been away from her since Ben died. I let myself die when he did. I wonder if it was longer than that. I wonder if when I met Ben, part of me lost Ana. If so, I want her back. I want what we had back.

MAY

Ben's back had gotten so bad he couldn't move. He had called in sick to work for three days. I tried to go to work on Monday but left halfway through the day because he was stuck and didn't think he could get out of bed by himself. By Wednesday, I had given up trying to go to work and just stayed with him.

He was pathetic about the pain and acted like a huge baby. He would groan and complain as if he had flesh-eating bacteria every time I asked him how he was doing. But to me, he was adorably ill. I liked being needed by him. I liked making his food for him, running his baths for him, massaging his muscles. I liked caring for him, taking care of him. It made me feel like I had a real purpose. It felt so good to make him feel even the littlest bit better.

It had been a few days since he'd asked me to marry him, but I was having a hard time ignoring it. He was just drugged up. But what if he did mean it? Why was I so affected by it? It was just a silly thing he said when he was on Vicodin. But how much does Vicodin really mess with you? It doesn't make you say things you don't mean.

I think I was just overly excitable about it because I loved him in a way I'd never thought possible. I knew that if I lost him, if I had to live without him, it would crush me. I needed him and I didn't just need him now, I needed him in the future. I needed him always. I wanted him always. I wanted him to be the father of my children. It's such a silly statement now; people say it all the time, they throw it around like it's nothing. And some people treat it like it is nothing, but it wasn't nothing to me. I wanted to have children with him someday. I wanted to be a parent with him. I wanted to have a child that was half him and half me. I wanted to commit to him and sacrifice for him. I wanted to lose part of myself in order to gain some of him. I wanted to marry him. So I wanted him to have meant it. I wanted it to be real.

As he got better and better, he asked me to take one more day off work to spend with him. He said that I had been so great to him, he wanted one day to return the favor. It wasn't difficult to oblige him.

I woke to him standing over me with a tray of breakfast foods.

"Voilà!" he said, grinning as he watched me. I sat up in bed and let him set the tray in front of me. The tray was full of things I would normally consider mutually exclusive: a bagel *and* a croissant; French toast and waffles; cream cheese and butter. He'd even toasted a Pop-Tart.

"I think I went a bit overboard," he said. "But it was all really easy. You can get all of this at your local grocer's freezer."

"Thank you," I said. I smiled and kissed his lips as he bent down toward me. He didn't moan or wail in pain.

"Are you taking the pain medication finally?"

"Nope!" he said proudly. "I just feel better."

"You just feel better?"

"Yes! This is what I mean. You people and your Western medicine," he said with a smile. "I really feel fine. I swear."

He walked around the side of the bed and sat down next to me. He stared at my food as I began to attack it.

"Did you want some?" I offered.

"Took you long enough. Jesus," he said as he grabbed the Pop-Tart. "Were you going to eat this all yourself?"

I kissed his cheek and took the Pop-Tart out of his mouth. I offered him a waffle instead. "I was really looking forward to this. Brown sugar and cinnamon is my favorite flavor." I bit a huge chunk out of it before he could try to wrestle it back from me. He resigned himself to the waffle.

"I think we should get married," he said. "What do you think of that?"

I laughed, completely unsure of how serious he was. "Why do you keep joking like that?" I said. I sounded more exasperated than I wanted to.

"I'm not joking," he said.

"Yes, you are." I finished the Pop-Tart and wiped my hands. "Stop joking about it or you'll end up married," I said.

"Oh, is that so?"

"Yes, that's so."

"So, if I said, 'Let's go get married today,' you'd go get married today?"

"What are you doing? Daring me?"

"I'm just asking a question, is all," he said, but the tone of his voice wasn't one of a hypothetical question. I suddenly became embarrassed and anxious.

"Well, I just . . ." I said. "*You* wouldn't."

"Would *you*? That is my question."

"You can't do that! You can't ask me if I would if you wouldn't!"

He grabbed my hand. "*You* said I wouldn't. I didn't say that."

"Are you asking me to marry you for real?" I asked, finally unsure of how else to figure out what conversation we were actually having.

"I want to be with you for the rest of my life and I know that it is soon, but I would like to marry you. I don't want to ask you to marry me if it freaks you out or you think it's crazy."

"For real?" I was too excited by this idea to trust my own ears.

"Elsie! Jesus! Yes!"

"I don't think it's crazy!" I said. I grabbed him as tears started building in my eyes. I looked at him.

"You don't?" I could see his eyes start to water as well. They were growing red. His face was no longer carefree. It was sincere and moved.

"No!" I could no longer control my voice. I could barely control my limbs.

"You'll marry me?" He grabbed my head on both sides and focused my face on his. I could feel my hair crinkling between his hands and my ears. I knew we both looked silly on our knees in the middle of our crumpled bed, but I could focus on nothing but him.

"Yes," I said softly and stunned, and then it grew louder and louder. "Yes! Yes! Yes!" I said, kissing him. He was holding on to me tightly. I have no doubt that some of our neighbors thought they were overhearing something they shouldn't have.

We fell back onto the bed and proved them right. "I love you," he said to me over and over. He whispered it and he moaned it. He spoke it and he sang it. He loved me. He loved me. He loved me.

And just like that, I was going to be part of a family again.

NOVEMBER

By the time Sunday afternoon rolls around, Ana has been well indoctrinated into this new, luxurious lifestyle.

She, Susan, and I are lying out by the pool. The weather has started to cool during the nights, but the days are still hot enough to lie outside. Given that it's early November, it makes me especially glad to live in Southern California. Winter is upon us, and yet, I can barely feel a chill.

Ana read an entire book this weekend. Susan cooked every meal as if she was a gourmet chef. I mostly lazed around like I have been doing, getting to the point where I am so bored that I yearn for some sort of life again. A couple of times yesterday I pondered whether to pick up a hobby. No final decision has been made.

We are all in a little bit of a food coma from the soufflé Susan made for our "lunch dessert," as she called it. We are all quiet at the moment, but I decide to break the silence.

"So what are you and Kevin doing this week?" I ask.

"Oh, not sure," Ana said. "Although, did I tell you? He asked me to meet his parents."

"He did?" I ask.

"How long have you two been together?" Susan asks.

"Oh, just a few months now. But I really like him. He's . . ."

"He's really sweet," I say to Susan. I mean it, so it comes across like I mean it and I think it touches Ana. I still maintain that he's a bit blah all around, but you don't need spice in the boyfriend of your best friend. You need him to be reliable, kindhearted, and sincere. You need to know he won't hurt her, if he can help it. You need to know he has good intentions. By all of those accounts, I like Kevin. (But he's boring.)

"Are his parents from around here?" I ask.

"He's from San Jose. So it's a few hours' drive, but he said he really wanted them to meet me."

This touches a nerve with Susan. I can see it. Ana probably can't, but I've done nothing but sit around with this woman for five weeks now. I know her like the back of my hand. I also knew her son and I'm learning that they aren't altogether terribly different people.

Susan lightly excuses herself as Ana and I continue to talk. I remember when I was happy like she is, when Ben felt invincible to me like I'm sure Kevin feels to her now. I remember how I felt like nothing in the world could take that feeling away from me. There was nothing I could not do. But instead of hating her for being happy, I can see now that I am feeling melancholy, nostalgic, and a little jealous. It's not perfect, but it's certainly a lot healthier than last month.

Ana gets her things ready, and I walk her out to her car. She's meeting Kevin for dinner tonight in L.A., and I don't begrudge her leaving early for it. I'm also exhausted from the company. I've been alone so many hours lately that talking to two people at once has been a struggle for my attention span.

"Oh!" she says, turning toward her car and digging through it. "I forgot that I brought your mail." She finds it and hands me a big chunk of envelopes. I already know that some of them will have Ben's name on them. Truth be told, I was happy to let the piles accumulate in my mailbox hours away. If my marriage certificate isn't in here, I'm gonna wig out.

"Awesome," I say and give her a hug. "Thank you. For this, and for coming here. It really means a lot to me."

"I miss you, girl," Ana says, as she gets in her car. "But you seem happier. Just a little."

I don't want to seem happier, even if I do feel it a little bit. It feels wrong to be labeled "happier," even if it is incremental. The woman that loved Ben as fiercely as I did would never feel any degree of happy after losing him.

"Drive safe," I say. "Tell Kevin I said hi."

"You got it."

When she's gone, I rifle through the envelopes looking for one from the County Recorder's Office. I come up short. My stomach sinks, and I know that I have to call them tomorrow. I cannot ignore this problem. I cannot pretend it doesn't exist. I need to know what is going on with the legality of my marriage. I have to face it.

At the bottom of the stack is a hand-addressed envelope. The writing is shaky and uneven. I don't have to look at the return address to know who it is from.

Mr. George Callahan.

I put the other envelopes on the sidewalk and sit down on the curb. I tear open the envelope.

Dear Elsie,

I hope you don't mind that I asked the library for your mailing address. They were hesitant to give it to me, but an old man has his ways. First of all, I wanted to tell you that I don't know why you punched that guy but that I hope you won't mind me telling Lorraine about it. It was the most interesting thing to happen in months!

The real reason I am writing is because Lorraine is not well. The doctors have taken her from our home and she is now staying in the hospital. Unfortunately, old age is really starting to catch up to her. I am staying with her here at Cedars-Sinai. Sometimes I take a cab back to our home and get some of her things, but most of the time, I stay right here next to her. She is sleeping most of the time, but that's all right by me. Just being next to her, hearing her breathe, feels like a miracle sometimes.

I wanted to say that I am sorry for telling you to move on. I am now looking at the prospect of living without the love of my life, and I find it daunting and miserable. I do not know how I will live a day after I lose her. I feel like I am standing on the edge of a huge, black hole, waiting to fall.

Maybe there is one person for everyone. If so, Lorraine was mine. Maybe the reason I was able to get over Esther was because she wasn't the right one. Maybe the reason you can't get over Ben is because he was.

I just wanted you to know that even at almost ninety, I'm still learning new things every day, and I think I am learning now that when you lose the thing you love most in the world, things can't be okay again.

I'd like to say I miss you at the library, but truthfully, I don't get down there very much.

As I've reread this now, I realize it's a little bit of a mopey letter, so I hope you'll excuse my rambling.

Thanks for listening.

Best,
George Callahan

I walk inside and ask Susan where her stationery is. She gives me some, and I sit down at her kitchen table. I write until my hand feels like it's going to fall off. My palm feels cramped, my fingers ache. I have been holding the pen too tightly. I have been pressing the pen down too hard. I read over what I have written and see that it makes absolutely no sense. It is barely legible. So I throw it away and I write what my heart is screaming at him.

> *Dear George,*
>
> *I was wrong. You are wrong.*
>
> *We can live again. I'm not sure if we can love again, but we can live again.*
>
> *I believe in you.*
>
> *Love,*
> *Elsie*

MAY

We had filled the day with discussions about how to get married and where to get married and when to get married. I realized I didn't know the first thing about marriage. Logistically, I mean. How does one get married? What does one need to do?

I found out pretty quickly that Ben was thinking of a real wedding. He was thinking of a wedding with bridesmaids and white dresses, flowers in the centers of round tables. Champagne flutes. A dance floor. I wasn't opposed to that; it just hadn't occurred to me. His proposal felt unorthodox; our relationship felt electric and exciting. It seemed strange to seal it with something so conventional. It felt more appropriate to put on some clothes and drive down to city hall. Large weddings with long guest lists and speeches felt like things that people did when they had been together for years. They felt rational and practiced, well thought out and logical—like a business decision. I wanted to do something crazy. Something you'd only do if you were in as much love as we were.

"Okay, so you're thinking a small wedding?" he asked me.

"I mean, it can be as big as you want it to be," I said. "If it were up to me, there wouldn't be anyone there. Just me, you, and the officiant."

"Oh wow, okay, so you're talking about straight-up eloping," he said.

"Aren't you?"

"Well, I was thinking we could do it with our families and really plan something, you know? But now that you say it, eloping does sound much easier. Certainly more exciting," he said as he smiled at me and grabbed my hand.

"Really?" I said.

"Yeah. How does one go about eloping?" he said, and when he did, his eyes were so bright, his face almost maniacally excited, I knew he was on board.

"I have no idea." I laughed. Everything felt funny to me. Everything felt invigorating. I felt light and giddy, like the wind could knock me over.

"*Ah!*" he said, excited. "Okay! Let's do it! Let's get married now. Can we do it today? Can we, like, go somewhere right now and do it?"

"Now?" I said. We hadn't even showered yet.

"No better time than the present," he said, grabbing me into his arms and holding me. I could tell he was smelling my hair. I just lay against his chest and let him.

"Great," I said. "Let's do it today."

"Okay." He ran out of the room and grabbed a suitcase.

"What are you doing?" I asked him.

"Well, we're going to Vegas, right? Isn't that how people elope?"

"Oh!" Honestly, that thought hadn't even occurred to me. But he was exactly right. Vegas was where people went to do those things. "Okay! Let's go."

Ben was throwing clothes into the bag and checking his watch. "If we leave in the next twenty minutes or so, we can be there by 10:00 p.m. I'm sure there are chapels open at ten."

That's when it hit me. This was really happening. I was about to get married.

NOVEMBER

Y ou okay?" Susan asks me from the kitchen. I am addressing the envelope to Mr. Callahan.

"Actually, I am really good. You okay?"

"Mmm-hmm," she said. "I wanted to talk to you about something actually."

"Oh?"

"Well." She sits down next to me at the breakfast nook table. "I closed Ben's bank account."

"Oh," I say. I didn't know she was going to do that. I don't really know if it's her place to do that.

"It really is none of my business," she said. "But I did it because I knew that if you did it, or if I tried to get you to do it, you would not take the money."

"Oh," I say. "I don't feel comfortable—"

"Listen." She grabs my hand. "You were his wife. He would want you to have it. What am I going to do with it? Add it to the pile of money I was left from Steven? It means more in your hands, and Ben would want it that way. It's not some extravagant amount. Ben was a smart guy, but he wasn't brilliant with money. Neither was his father. Actually, if I hadn't taken out the life insurance policy on Steven when we were in our twenties, I'd be in a much different place right now, but that's beside the point. Take the money, okay?"

"Uh . . ."

"Elsie," she says to me. "Take the damn money. I didn't spend forty-five minutes on the phone with the bank convincing them I had the authority to do it for my health. I did it behind your back so I could deceive you enough to get the check in your name." She smiled at me, and I laughed.

"Okay," I say. It doesn't even occur to me to ask how much it is. It seems irrelevant and somehow perverse, like knowing what color underwear your dermatologist is wearing.

"By the way, while we are talking about uncomfortable and depressing things, what did the county say about your marriage certificate? Did you call?"

I am ashamed. I feel like I stayed out past curfew when I knew we had church tomorrow morning. "No."

"What is the matter with you?" she asks me, and her voice is clearly exasperated.

"I know. I need to get it."

"Not just for you, Elsie. For me too. I want to see it. He never told me about it. He never confided in me why he was doing it. I just . . . I want to see the fucking thing, you know? Look it in the face and know it's real."

"Oh," I say.

"Not that your marriage wasn't real. I know you well enough to know that's true. But I just . . . you have a kid and you daydream about him getting married. Getting married was the last big thing he did and I wasn't there. Jesus, was I so terrible that he couldn't tell me what he was doing? That I couldn't have been there?"

I was surprised that this was coming up now because she seemed like it was all behind her, but now I understood that it had never been behind her. It had been right there on the surface the whole time, so large and imposing that it colored everything she saw.

"He wasn't . . ." I say. "You weren't terrible. It wasn't that. It had nothing to do with that."

"Well, what then?" she asks me. "I'm sorry that I sound upset. I'm trying not to sound . . . I just . . . I thought I knew him."

"You did know him!" I say, and this time I am grabbing her hand. "You did know him. And he knew you and cared about you. And maybe the way he did it was misguided, but he loved you. He thought if he told you . . . he thought you couldn't handle it. He worried that you wouldn't feel like you two were a family anymore."

"But he should have told me before you two got married. He should have at least called," she says to me.

And she's right. He should have. He knew that. But I didn't.

MAY

We were two hours outside of Las Vegas when the cold feet set in. Ben was driving. I was in the front seat calling wedding chapels. I also called hotels to see where we could stay the night. My body was thrilled and anxious. The car could barely contain me, but I could see that Ben was starting to tense.

He pulled over into a Burger King and said he wanted a burger. I wasn't hungry, I couldn't possibly eat, but I got one too and let it sit in front of me.

"I'm thinking we should go to the Best Little Chapel," I told him. "They take care of everything there. And then we can stay at either Caesars Palace, which has a pretty good deal on a suite, or interestingly enough, the Hooters hotel has really cheap rooms right now."

Ben was looking at his burger, and when I stopped talking he put it down abruptly. I mean, he basically dropped it.

"I need to tell my mom," he said. "I can't do this without telling my mom."

"Oh," I said. Honestly, I hadn't even thought about his mom, or my own parents. I had briefly thought about inviting Ana to come and be a witness, but I quickly decided I didn't want that either. I just wanted Ben and me, together. And whoever the officiant was.

"Don't you want to invite Ana or something?" he asked. I

did not like the turn the conversation had taken. The turn in the conversation was about to create a turn in the trip, which had the very real consequence of a turn in this marriage.

"Well, no," I said. "I thought we just wanted it to be the two of us."

"I did," he said. "Well, no, you did." He wasn't being combative, but I was still feeling defensive. "I just think that I was being overzealous before. I think I should tell my mom. I think if she found out afterward that she would be heartbroken."

"Why?" I asked.

"Because she wasn't there. That her only child got married and she wasn't there, I don't know."

This was what I had been afraid of. Suddenly, I felt my whole life slipping away from me. I'd only been engaged for four hours, but in those four hours I saw a life for myself that I wanted. Just in the time we had been in the car, I'd thought so much about what our night would be like, what our tomorrow would be like, that I was already attached to it. I had replayed it so many times in my mind that I felt like I'd already lived it. I didn't want to lose what I thought I already had. If Ben called his mother, we weren't going to get back in the car and drive straight to Nevada. We were going to get back in the car and drive straight to Orange County.

"I don't know if that's . . ." I started, but I wasn't sure how to finish. "This is about you and me. Are you saying you don't want to do this?"

"No!" he said. "I'm just . . . maybe we shouldn't be doing this right now."

"I cannot believe you." I thought I was going to leave it at that, but the words kept coming out of my mouth. "I didn't make you propose to me. I wasn't the one who suggested we

get married in the first place. This was all your doing! I have
been telling you for months to tell your mother! So how the
fuck do I end up two hours outside of Las Vegas jilted in a
Burger King, huh? Explain that to me."

"You don't understand!" He was starting to get animated
and upset.

"Why don't I understand? What part of this don't I understand? You asked me to marry you. I said yes. I suggested we
elope. You said yes. We got in the car. We're halfway to Nevada
and you're calling it off while you're eating a fucking Whop-
per."

Ben shook his head. "I can't expect you to understand,
Elsie." Our voices were starting to attract attention, so Ben got
up from the table and I followed him outside.

"What does that mean?" I yelled at him, pushing the door
out of my way like it was the one doing this to me.

"It means you don't have a family!" He turned to face me.
"You don't even try to get along with your parents. You don't
understand how I feel about my mom."

"You're kidding me, right?" I couldn't believe he'd said that.
I wished I could have time-traveled back to five seconds before
so I could have stopped him from saying that and we could
have continued on with our lives without him ever having said
that to me.

"No! I'm not kidding. You don't get it."

"Oh, I get it, Ben. I get it. I get that you're a coward who
hasn't had the balls to tell his mom he's even dating someone
and now, and now I'm getting screwed for it. That's what I get."

"It's not like that," he said, but his voice was resigned. It
wasn't passionate.

"What is it then?"

"Can we just get in the car?"

"I'm not getting in the car with you," I said as I crossed my arms. It was colder outside than I would have liked and my jacket was lying on the front seat, but I didn't want to go near that car, even if I had to suffer for it.

"Please? Don't make a scene out here. I'm not saying we shouldn't get married. I want to marry you. I just . . . want to tell my mom first. There's no need for us to rush this."

"You've had six months to tell your mom! And you always come up with a reason why not. How many times have I heard 'Now I'm really going to tell my mom'? But you know what? She's not a part of this relationship. This is about you and me. It's about what you want and what I want. And what I want is to be with the kind of man that wants to marry me so bad, nothing will stop him. I want to be loved by someone who loves me so much he can't think straight. I want you to love me in a way that makes you stupid and impractical. I *want* to rush into this. Rushing into it is romantic. It makes me feel alive. It makes me feel like I am jumping off a cliff and I know I'll be *fine* because that is how much *I trust you*. And I deserve you jumping off a cliff for me because I am prepared to do it for you. You think I don't know anything about family because I don't get along with my parents? Ana is my family. I love her more than I could possibly love another person, other than you. And I thought about her and I thought, No, I don't need her here for this. I just need Ben. So fuck you, I don't know family. That's not what's happening here at all. What's happening here is that I am ready to risk everything for you. And you are not ready to do it for me."

Ben was quiet for a long time. He had started to cry. I thought that it was a manly cry and couldn't help wanting to hold him despite my furor.

"How do things get fucked up so quickly?" he said. His voice was quiet. It wasn't a whisper. It was just sad. It lacked the confidence I was used to hearing in him.

"What?" I said. My tone was curt and pissed.

"I just don't understand how things can go from great to shitty so quickly. I don't know how I got us here. I love you so much, and I should have told my mom earlier, and I didn't and . . . All of those things you just talked about, I want those. I want that with you. I want to give that to you. I love you the way you want to be loved. I'm telling you that. I am the man to do that for you. I just don't know how I derailed so quickly from showing you that."

He turned to me, his eyes drying up but still pleading. "I want to marry you," he said.

"No, Ben," I said and I started to turn away from him, but he grabbed my arm. He grabbed it hard. "I don't want you to—"

"You are right," he said. "You are right. I want that. I want you. I want what you said. I want to risk everything for you. I want to be stupid with you and reckless with you. I will figure out a way to tell my mom. We'll tell her together and she'll love you. And . . . I want you."

"No, it's not . . . it shouldn't be . . ." I said, trying to find the words that meant "I don't want to do this now because it's all ruined." I settled on "You don't have to do this. I'll calm down and we can wait until we tell your mom." The minute I said it, I believed it. It softened me to see that I needed to be there for him as much as I needed him to be there for me.

Ben listened to me, but he was unmoved. "No! I was wrong! I got scared. But I want you. Please." He got down on one knee. "Marry me."

I was silent and unsure. Was this good for him? Was it what

he wanted? He seemed so genuine now. His eyes were pleading with me to listen to him, to marry him. But I didn't want to have forced his hand. I didn't want this to be something he did because I made him do it. And yet, Ben looked so in love with me, truthfully. He looked like all he wanted in the world was me. It looked so real. It was real. Ben yelled from the base of his throat. *"Marry me, Elsie Porter! Marry me!"*

I pulled him up from the pavement and held him. "I don't want you to do anything that—" I stopped myself and asked what I felt. "Are you sure?"

"I'm sure. I'm so sorry. I'm sure."

A smile crept onto my face faster than I could stop it. "Okay!" I exclaimed.

"Really?" he asked as he spun me around. I nodded. "Oh my God," he said. He buried his head in my shoulder. "I love you so much. I love you so much."

"I love you too. I'm sorry," I said. "I shouldn't have said those things. I just . . . I didn't realize how much I wanted to marry you until . . . It doesn't matter," I said. "I'm sorry. We can take all the time you need."

"No," he said. "I don't need any time at all. Get in the car. We're going to Vegas."

He opened my car door and then got into his side. Before he started the engine, he grabbed my face and kissed me, hard.

"Okay," he said, breathing in deeply. "Nevada, here we come."

NOVEMBER

It was my fault," I say to her. "He wanted to tell you before we got married. He was ready to call it off, actually, until he had time to tell you. But I convinced him not to."

"Oh," Susan says. She is quiet and thoughtful. "When was this?"

"We were on our way to Las Vegas. He wanted to turn around and drive home. He wanted to wait until you knew. Give you the chance to be there."

"Oh," she says. "I didn't realize you were married in Las Vegas." The tone in her voice isn't judgmental necessarily, but it certainly brings out any insecurity I might have over having been married in the tackiest place on earth.

"But I didn't want to. He said I didn't understand family, and at the time I told him that was a terrible thing to say to me, but I think he might have had a point."

"Hmm," she says.

"Anyway, I'm sorry. He wanted to tell you. He didn't feel comfortable doing something so big without you. He loved you. He cared about you a lot and I didn't understand. I was being selfish and I just . . . I really, really wanted to marry him. I think on some level Ben made me feel like I wasn't alone anymore and I thought . . ." I start to cry. "I think I was afraid that you'd tell him how ridiculous we were being and he would listen to you. I knew that if he talked to you, he would listen to you. I was afraid I'd lose him."

"But why would you break up because of that? You wouldn't. At the very most, he'd just decide to wait longer to get married."

"You're right." I shake my head, disappointed in myself. "You're absolutely right. But it didn't feel that way at the time. It felt so scary. We were standing at a rest stop and it was the difference between turning right out of the lot and turning left. It felt so *real*. It felt so . . . I wanted to belong to something, belong to someone, you know?"

"Mmm," she says. I don't even know what I'm about to say next until it comes out of my mouth.

"I think I wanted to meet you after we were married, because I thought . . ." Ugggggh, the lump in my throat is so huge, the tears waiting to drop are so heavy. "My own parents don't seem to think very much of me, and I thought, if you met me before . . . I thought you wouldn't like me. You'd want someone better for your son. I was afraid to give you that chance."

"Wow," she says. "Okay." She pats my hand and gets up from the table. "I just need a little while to gather my thoughts. There is a lot of stuff going through my mind right now and I know that not all of it is rational."

"Okay," I say. "I just wanted you to—"

"Stop talking," she snaps at me. She breathes in deeply and breathes out sharply. "God dammit, Elsie."

I stare at her, she stares back, trying to bite her tongue.

"You don't make it easy," she says. "I try so hard! I try so hard."

"I know you do, I just—"

She shakes her head. "It's not your fault. It's not your fault." She isn't speaking to me, I don't think. "It just . . . *ah*. You couldn't have waited? You couldn't have given me a chance? You didn't even give me a chance."

"I know, Susan, I just . . . I was scared!"

"With everything that I've gone through? You couldn't have just said all of this from the beginning?"

"I didn't know how to say it . . ." I tell her. If I'm being honest with myself, I have to admit I'm not sure I knew it was relevant until I put the pieces together, until I really thought about it.

"I have been thinking for months that my son never even wanted me at his wedding, and now you're telling me he did and you stopped him."

I am quiet. What can I say?

"Elsie!" she yells. She is shrill and teary. I don't want the old Susan back. I want her to stay new Susan.

"I'm sorry!" I say. My eyes start to blur, my lips quivering. "I just . . . Susan, I want you and me to be okay. Are we okay?"

"I'm going to go. I'm going to leave this room. I . . ." She turns and puts her head in her hands and then she breathes in.

She leaves the room, and it suddenly feels so big and hollow.

It is the next morning before Susan feels composed enough to talk to me. I can only imagine what thoughts ran through her mind all night. I have a feeling she spent a great deal of the previous evening hating me and calling me names in her head.

"Thank you for telling me that last night," she says, as she sits down next to me in the living room. I had been fast-forwarding through the contents of her TiVo and eating one of her Danishes from the kitchen. I'll tell you, it feels weird to be a guest in someone's house when they are rip-shit pissed at you.

I nod to her.

"I can't imagine that was easy to tell me, but truthfully, it is good news to me. It makes me feel better to know that Ben had the inclination to tell me. Even if he didn't actually do it."

I nod again. It's her time to talk. I'm just keeping quiet.

"Anyway, it's in the past. I didn't know you then, you didn't know me then. It does neither of us any good to hold grudges. Ben made his own decisions, regardless of how we may have tried to influence them. He is responsible for what he did. You are not. I am not. He loved you enough to marry you the way he did. What mother doesn't want that for her son? You know, you have a boy and you raise him right and you hope that you've raised the kind of son that knows how to love and does it well. Especially as a mother, you hope that your son is sensitive and passionate; you hope that he knows how to treat women well. I did my job. He was all of those things. And he loved. He spent his short time on this earth loving. He loved you."

"Thank you," I say. "I'm still sorry I didn't tell you that earlier."

"Put it out of your head." She waves her hand at me. "The other thing that I want to tell you is . . . I would have liked you," she says. "I don't pretend to understand your relationship with your parents. That is between you and them. But I would have liked you. I would have wanted you to marry my son."

Hearing her say that, I get the feeling that I have done all of these things out of order. I should have met her, then married him; if I did, maybe this wouldn't have happened. Maybe Ben would be here next to me, eating peanuts and throwing the shells in an ashtray.

"Thank you," I say to her.

"I've thought a lot about you and I recently. I think I haven't truly begun to cope with Ben's death. I think that I am still mourning for my husband, and the loss of my son is . . . it's too huge to bear. It's too large to even begin to deal with. I think having you as a part of my life, helping you to deal with this, I think it's helping me to avoid dealing with it. I think I thought that if I could help you to get to a place where you could live again, that I would be able to live again. But I don't think that's the case.

"When Ben was little, he used to get in bed with Steven and I and watch *Jeopardy!* every night. He didn't understand any of the questions, but I think he liked hearing the blooping noises. Anyway, I remember one night I was lying there, Ben between us, and I thought, This is my family. This is my life. And I was so happy in that moment. I had my two guys. And they loved me and I belonged to them. And now, I lie in that same bed and they are both gone. I don't think I have even begun to scratch the surface of what that has done to me."

She doesn't break down. She's calm but sincere. She's lost. I don't think I could see it before because I was so lost. I'm still lost. But I can see that Susan needs . . . something. She needs something to hold on to. For me, she was that something. She was the rock in the middle of the storm. I'm still in the middle of the storm but . . . I need to be a rock too. I realize it's time I was supportive as well as supported. I think the time for "This Is All About Me" actually ended quite some time ago.

"What do you need?" I ask. Susan seems to always know what I need, or at least thinks she does with enough confidence that she convinces me too.

"I don't know," she says, wistfully, as if there is an answer out there somewhere and she just doesn't know where to start looking. "I don't know. I think I need to come to terms with a lot of things. I need to look them in the eye." She is quiet for a minute. "I don't believe in heaven, Elsie." This is where she cracks. Her eyes tighten into little stars, her mouth turns down, and her breathing becomes desperate. "I want to believe so bad," she says. Her face is now wet. Her nose is running. I know what it feels like to cry like that. I know that she's probably feeling light-headed, that soon her eyes will feel dry as if they have nothing left to give. "I want to think of him happy, in a better place. People say to me that he's in a better place, but . . . I don't believe in a better place." She heaves again and rests her head in her hands. I rub her back. "I feel like such a terrible mother that I don't believe in a better place for him."

"Neither do I," I say to her. "But sometimes I pretend I do," I say. "To make it hurt just a little less. I think it's okay to pretend you do." She rests her weight on me and I can feel that I am holding her up. It's empowering to be the one holding someone else up. It makes you feel strong, maybe even stronger than you are. "We could talk to him if you want," I say. "What does it hurt, right? It doesn't hurt anything to try, and who knows? Maybe it will feel good. Maybe it will . . . maybe he will hear us."

Susan nods and tries to gain her composure again. She sighs and breathes deep. She wipes her face and opens her eyes. "Okay," she says. "Yeah."

MAY

"We're in Nevada!" Ben screamed as we drove over the state line. He was emphatic and exhilarated.

"Wooo!" I yelled after him. I put both fists up into the air. I rolled down my window and I could feel the desert air rushing in. The air was warm but the wind had a chill. It was nighttime, and I could see the city lights in the distance. They were cheesy and ugly, overwrought and overdone. I knew I was looking at a city of casinos and whores, a city where people were losing money and getting drunk; but none of that mattered. The city lights looked like they were made just for us.

"Which exit did you say?" Ben asked me, a rare moment of logistics in an otherwise very emotional car ride.

"Thirty-eight," I said and grabbed his hand.

It felt like the whole world belonged to us. It felt like everything was just beginning.

NOVEMBER

It's evening by the time we muster the strength to try to talk to him. It's a warm November night even by Southern California standards. We have the sliding glass doors open around the house. I try to direct my voice to the wind. Speaking into the wind seems just metaphorical enough that it might work.

"Ben?" I call out. I had planned to follow it up with some sort of statement, but my mind is a blank. I haven't spoken to Ben since he said he'd be right back. The first thing I say should be important. It should be beautiful.

"If you can hear us, Ben, we just want you to know that we miss you," Susan says, directing her voice toward the ceiling. She points her head upward as if that's where he is, which tells me there has to be some small part of her that believes in heaven after all. "I miss you so much, baby. I don't know what to do without you. I don't know how to . . . I know how to live my life thinking that you're there in L.A., but I don't know how to live my life knowing that you aren't on this earth," she says, and then turns to me abruptly. "I feel stupid."

"Me too," I say. I am now thinking it matters significantly whether you actually believe the dead can hear you. You can't just talk to the wall and convince yourself you aren't talking to a wall unless you believe.

"I want to go to his grave," she says. "Maybe it will be easier there."

"Okay." I nod. "It's too late to go today but we can go up first thing tomorrow morning."

"Okay," she says. "That will give me time to think about what I want to say."

"Okay, good."

Susan pats me on the hand and gets up. "I'm going to go to bed early then. My mind needs a rest from this." Maybe she really does need a rest, but I know she's going in there to cry in peace.

"Okay," I say. When she's gone, I look around the room and walk aimlessly around the house. I go into Ben's bedroom and I throw myself on his bed. I breathe in the air. I stare at the walls until I can no longer see them. I know that I am done here. I may not be ready for my life back, but it is time to stop avoiding it. I lie in Ben's room for as long as I can stand it and then I get up and rush out.

I walk over to my room to start to gather my clothes. I want to do it quickly, before I lose my nerve. There is a part of me that wants to stay in this purgatory for as long as I can, that wants to lie out by the pool all day and watch TV all night and never live my days. But if Ben could hear me, if Ben could see me, that isn't what Ben would want. Also, I don't think I'd want that for myself.

I get up in the morning and collect the rest of my things. I walk out into the kitchen and Susan is there, dressed and ready to go, drinking a cup of coffee, sitting at the kitchen counter. She sees that my things are packed behind me and she puts down her coffee. She doesn't say anything. She just smiles knowingly. It's a sad smile, but a proud smile. A bittersweet and melancholy smile. I feel like I'm going away to college.

"We should take two cars," she says. She says it as a realization to herself but also, I think, to spare me from having to say it. From having to spell out that after this, I'm going home.

Susan gets there a bit before I do, and as I drive up, I see her standing at the entrance to the cemetery. I thought perhaps that she would have started without me. That she might want time alone with him, but it looks like she needs a partner in this. I don't blame her. I certainly wouldn't be doing this alone. I park the car and catch up to her.

"Ready?" I say.

"Ready," she says. We start the long walk to his gravestone. When we get there, the headstone looks so brand-new, it's almost tragic, like when you see grave markers so close together you know it was a child. Susan kneels on the ground in front of Ben's grave and faces his headstone. I sit down next to her.

She breathes in deeply and seriously. It is not a casual breath. She pulls a piece of paper out of her back pocket and looks at me, shyly. I nod my head at her, urging her, and she starts to read. Her voice is without much emotion at first; she truly is reading the words on the page rather than speaking.

"I just want to know you're okay. I want to know that you didn't suffer. I want to believe that you are in a better place, that you are happy and have all the things in life that you loved, with you. I want to believe that you and your father are together. Maybe at a barbecue in heaven, eating hot dogs. I know that's not the case. I know that you are gone. But I don't know how to live with that knowledge. A mother is not supposed to outlive her son. It's just not supposed to happen."

Now she starts to lose her public speaking voice, and her

eyes drift from the page onto the grass beneath her. "I know that you believed it was your job to protect me and take care of me. If I had one last thing to say to you, Ben, I think I would want to tell you this: I will be okay. You don't need to worry. I will find a way to be okay. I always do. Don't worry about me. Thank you for being such a wonderful son. For being the son that you were. I couldn't have asked for anything more from you other than just more time. I want more time. Thank you for loving Elsie. Through her, I can see that you grew into exactly the type of man I hoped you would. And the two of us . . . will be okay. We will make it through. So go and have fun where you are and forget about us. We will be okay."

That is what true love is. True love is saying to someone "Forget about us. We will be okay," when it might not even be true, when the last thing you want is to be forgotten.

When Susan is done, she folds the piece of paper back up and wipes her eyes, and then she looks at me. It's my turn and I have no idea what I'm even doing here, but I close my eyes to breathe in deeply, and for a second, I can see his face as clear as if he were right in front of me. I open my eyes and . . . here goes.

"There's a huge hole in my heart where you used to be. When you were alive, I used to sometimes lie awake at night and listen to you snore and I couldn't believe how lucky I was to have found you. I haven't wanted to be whole again without you. I thought that if I were okay, it meant that I had truly lost you but . . . I think if you heard that logic you'd think I was an idiot. I really do think you'd want me to be happy again someday. You'd probably even be a little mad at me for all the wallowing I've done. Maybe not mad. Frustrated. You'd be frustrated. Anyway, I'm going to do better. I could never forget you,

Ben. Whether we were married right before I lost you or not, in the short time I knew you, you worked your way right into the soul of me. I am who I am because of you. If I ever feel one tenth as alive as I felt with you . . ." I wipe a tear from my eye and try to gain control of my wavering voice. "You made my life worth living. I promise you I am going to do something with it."

Susan puts her arm around me and rubs my shoulder. We both sit there for a moment and stare at the grave, at the gravestone. As I let my eyes lose their focus on what's right in front of me, I realize that I am in a sea of gravestones. I am surrounded by other people's loss. It has never been so clear to me that I am not alone in this. People die every day and other people move on. If everyone that loved all of these people has picked themselves up and moved on, I can do it too. I will one day wake up and see the sun shining and think, What a nice day.

"Ready?" Susan asks, and I nod my head. We pull ourselves up off the ground. The grass has made our knees wet. We walk in silence.

"Have you ever heard of supernovas?" Susan asks me as we head toward the front gate.

"What?" I almost stop in my tracks.

"Ben was really into space as a kid and he had all of these space books. I used to read them to him when he couldn't sleep, and I always loved the little chapter in this one book he had on supernovas. They shine brighter than anything else in the sky and then fade out really quickly. A supernova is a short burst of extraordinary energy."

"Yeah," I say.

"I like to think that you and Ben were like that," she says to me. "That you ended abruptly, but in that short time, you had more passion than some people have in a lifetime."

I don't say anything. I just take it in.

"Anyway," she says. "You headed home?"

I nod. "I think I'm ready for it."

"All right," she says. "Well . . . I guess this—"

"Do you want to get dinner on Friday?" I ask her. "At the Mexican place?"

She looks surprised but pleased. "I would love that."

"I know you're not my mother. I know that. But I really enjoy your company. Even if the circumstances are a bit strange, I like you."

Susan puts her arm around me and kisses me on the head. "You're one hell of a woman," she says to me. "I'm lucky to know you."

I laugh shyly. I think I am blushing. "Me too," I say, nodding, hoping it's clear just how much I mean it.

She shakes her head to avoid crying. "All right!" she says, slapping me lightly on the back. "Get in the car! Go home. If you need me, call me. But you can do this. You got this."

"Thanks," I say. Our hands lightly touch. I squeeze hers and then I walk away. I'm only a few steps from her when I turn around. "Hey, Susan?" I say. She turns around to see me. "Same goes for me. If you need me, just call."

She smiles and nods. "You got it."

I take the coastal highway instead of the interstate. I look out the window more often than I should. I try to appreciate each moment that I have. At one point, a song comes on the radio that I haven't heard in years, and for four minutes, I let myself forget who I am and what I'm doing. I'm just me, dancing in a car heading north on Pacific Coast Highway and it's not so bad. It's not so bad at all.

When I pull into my driveway, my apartment looks bigger and higher up than I remember. I get the mail and search through it for the marriage certificate. It's not there. However, in the mail is a check from Citibank addressed to me. I go up the steps and I let myself in the house.

It smells familiar. It's a scent I didn't even know I missed until I smell it. Everything is where I left it. It was frozen in time while I was in Orange County. I breathe in deeply and I don't smell Ben here. I just smell myself.

I sit down on my couch and organize the rest of the mail. I clean up some old dishes. I make my bed. I clean out the refrigerator and then take out the trash. As I come back in, I stop and look at the envelope from Citibank. It feels petty to be thinking about how much money I've just inherited, but I have to open the envelope at some point. So here we go.

Fourteen thousand, two hundred sixteen dollars and forty-eight cents, paid to the order of Elsie Porter. Huh. I don't know when I stopped considering myself Elsie Porter Ross, but it seems to have been some time ago.

Here I am, six months after I got married: husbandless and fourteen thousand dollars richer.

MAY

The gazebo ceremony takes place outside in the . . . well, gazebo," she said to me from behind the counter. She was about fifty and appeared to be putting on a fake southern accent. That or she was just from the deep, deep South. Ben was in the bathroom and had left the planning up to me.

"Oh, it's a bit cold, right?" I said. "I think just the simplest thing you have is fine."

"You only get married once, honey. Don't you want to make it special?" How did she not understand that this was special? Pomp and circumstance meant nothing to me as long as I got to be with this man. She must not have understood how lucky I was to have him. She must have thought I was marrying just anybody and I needed a gazebo to make it spectacular.

"I think we are good," I said. "What's this one? The simplicity package? We'll take that one."

"Okay," she said. "How about rings? Do you have an engagement ring that we should match it to?"

"Nope!" I said proudly. "No engagement ring." Honestly, the thought hadn't even occurred to me.

"We'll be getting her one though," Ben said, and he came toward us.

"Oh, stop it," I said.

"Well, do you two want silver or gold?" she asked.

"Gold," I said, but Ben said, "silver," at the same time.

We both quickly swapped our answers to match and missed again.

"Baby, I just want what you want," he said to me.

"But I want what you want!" I said.

"Let's do what you want for this because I want to eat at Hooters after this and I need compromise points."

"You want to eat at Hooters for our first meal as a married couple?"

"If it makes you feel any better, it's because of the wings, not the boobs."

The woman ignored us. "Okay so . . . gold?"

"Gold." She pulled out a tray of gold bands, and Ben and I tried some on until we found ones we liked and ones that fit. Ben paid the bill, and I told him I'd pay for half of it.

"Are you joking? We're not going Dutch on our wedding," he said to me.

"All right, lovebirds. Do you want to order any copies of the certificate?"

Ben turned toward me, his face asking me to answer.

"Yes," I said. "One copy should be fine, I would think."

"Okay, I'll add that to the final charge," the woman said as she put her hand out expectantly. "Do you have the license?"

"Oh, not yet," Ben said. "We need to fill that out, I guess."

The woman put her hands down on the counter, as if to halt everything. "You need to walk down to the Marriage License Bureau. It's about three blocks down. I can't do anything else until you get that filled out."

"How long will it take?" I asked.

"Half hour if there's no line," she said. "But there's often a line."

There was no line. We were seated and filling out paperwork within minutes of walking in the door.

"Oh, I didn't bring my social security card," he said when he got to the question about his social security number.

"Oh, I don't think you need it," I said. "It just asks for the number."

"Well," he said, "I never remember the number."

"Oh." What a remarkably mundane hurdle to find ourselves up against. My excitement started to deflate as I realized this might not happen after all. Maybe we couldn't get this done. He might need to call his mom for it, and then where would we be? "You know what? We can wait until you have it," I said.

"What?" he said, appalled at the idea of waiting. "No, I'm almost positive I know what it is. Here," he said as he wrote it down. "I know it's either 518 or 581, but I'm pretty sure it's 518." He finished writing it and put the pen down triumphantly. He walked right up to the window, handed in the paperwork, and said, "One marriage license, please!" Then he turned toward me. "We're getting married, baby! Are you ready?"

NOVEMBER

I put the check in a drawer where I won't forget it and I look around my apartment. It feels like mine again. It feels like I can live a life here of my own. I know that I envisioned a life for Ben and me here. I imagined we'd move out one day when we had kids. I even imagined that one day, Ben would be moving boxes out of the house by himself while I looked on, eight months pregnant. That life is not going to happen for me. But now I realize that there is a world of possibilities. I don't know what it's going to look like when I move out of this apartment. I don't know when it will be. And that, in its own way, is kind of thrilling. Anything could happen.

My cell phone rings, and it's a number I don't recognize. For some reason, I decide to answer it anyway.

"Hello?"

"Hello, is this Elsie Porter?" a woman asks.

"It is."

"Hi, Ms. Porter. This is Patricia DeVette from the Clark County Recorder's Office in Nevada," she says. I swear my heart stops beating for a moment. "I have a . . . We don't usually call people directly, Ms. Porter, but I have been filing some paperwork here and I wanted to speak with you about your county record."

"Okay . . ." I say. Oh God. I avoided this moment so long that it decided to take matters into its own hands and crash into me.

"It's taken me a while to figure out what exactly went on here, but it appears that Ben Ross put the wrong social security number on your marriage license. I've left a number of messages for Mr. Ross and have not heard back."

"Oh."

"I'm getting in touch with you, Ms. Porter, to let you know that the marriage has not yet been filed with the county."

And here it is. What I have feared all along. Ben and I are not legally married. During Ben's lifetime, we were never recognized as a legal union. My worst nightmare has come true, and as I stand here on the phone, silent, I am surprised to learn that I don't collapse. I don't break down.

"Thanks, Patricia. Thank you for calling," I say. I'm not sure what to say next. It's such an odd predicament to be faced with. All I've wanted since Ben died was proof that we meant something to each other. Now, I realize that no piece of paper can prove any of that.

"Well," I hear myself say. "Ben passed away."

"I'm sorry?"

"Ben died. He's dead. So I'm not sure if you can still file it."

"I'm so sorry, Ms. Porter. I'm so sorry to hear that."

"Thank you."

I get the distinct impression that Ms. DeVette doesn't know what to say. She's quiet for a few breaths before she speaks again. "Well, I can still file it," she says. "Since it's overdue paperwork representing a legal union that did take place. But it's entirely up to you. We don't have to."

"File it," I hear myself say. "It happened. It should be a part of the county record."

"All right, Ms. Ross, will do. Can I get his real social security number?"

"Oh," I say. "What number did he put on the document?"

"518-38-9087."

"Just change the 518 to 581."

"Great, thank you, Ms. Ross," Patricia says to me.

"Thank you for calling," I say.

"And Ms. Ross?" she says as she is getting off the phone.

"Hmm?"

"Congratulations on your marriage. I'm sorry about your husband."

"Thank you for saying that," I say to her. When I put the phone down, I feel a short, sound sense of peace. I was Ben Ross's wife. No one can take that away from me.

MAY

E lsie Porter?" the officiant said to me.
"Yes?"
"Ben Ross?"
"Yes."
"Are you two ready?"
"Yes, sir," Ben said. The officiant laughed and shook our hands. "My name's Dave," he said. "Let's get this show going."
"Okay!" I said, my arms pumped.
"Would you turn to face each other?" he asked, and we did.
"Ben and Elsie, we are gathered here today for you to celebrate one of life's greatest moments and give recognition to the worth and beauty of love, as you join together in vows of marriage."
I couldn't see the officiant; I just kept staring at Ben. He was staring back at me. His face was lit up. I couldn't believe how animated his smile was; I'd never seen anything like it. Dave continued to talk, but I couldn't hear him. I couldn't make out the words. It felt like the world had stopped, like it was paused and muted, like I was frozen in time and space.
"Did you two prepare vows?" Dave asked, as he brought me back to reality.
"Oh," I said, looking at Ben. "No, but we can. Wanna wing it?" I said to Ben.
"Sure." He smiled. "Let's wing it."

"Ben? Would you like to go first?" Dave asked.

"Oh, okay. Sure." Ben was quiet for a minute. "Are vows, like, supposed to be promises you make or just . . . like anything you want to say?" he whispered to Dave.

"Anything you want to say is fine," he said.

"Oh, okay." Ben breathed in sharply. "I love you. I feel like I loved you from the moment I saw you in that pizza place, but I know that doesn't make sense. I can't live my life without you anymore. You are everything I have ever wanted in another person. You are my best friend, my lover, my partner. And I promise that I will spend the rest of my life taking care of you, the way you deserve to be taken care of. My whole life I was never looking for something bigger than myself, and then I met you and I want to dedicate every day of my life to you. You are it for me. You are why I am here. Without you, I am nothing. So thank you, Elsie, for being who you are, and for spending your life with me."

Tears were forming in my eyes, my throat felt like I'd swallowed a brick.

"Elsie?" Dave prompted me.

"I love you," I said and broke down. I couldn't make out words in between my blubbering. As I looked at Ben, I saw he was crying too. "I just love you so much," I said. "I never knew what it was like to love someone so much and to be loved so well," I said. "For the rest of time, I will be by your side, Ben. I will dedicate my life to you."

Ben grabbed me and kissed me. He pulled us together so tight, there was no room to breathe. I kissed him back until I felt an arm between us.

"Not yet, son," Dave said, pulling us apart and laughing. "We still have a small formality to take care of."

"Oh," Ben said, smiling at me. "Right."

Dave smiled and turned to him. "Ben, do you take this woman to be your lawfully wedded wife?"

"I do," he said, looking directly at me.

"And do you, Elsie, take this man to be your lawfully wedded husband?"

"I do," I said and nodded, smiling widely.

"Then by the power vested in me by the State of Nevada, I now pronounce you husband and wife."

It was dead quiet for a minute as we were both frozen. Ben looked at Dave expectantly.

"Now, son!" Dave said. "Now's your chance. Kiss the bride. Give her everything you've got."

Ben grabbed me and spun me. He kissed me hard on the lips. It felt so good, a kiss like that. It just felt so good.

Dave chuckled to himself and started to walk away. "I'll let you kids calm down," he said and, before he made it through the door, "You know, I marry a lot of people, but I have a feeling about you two."

Ben and I looked at each other and smiled. "Do you think he says that to everyone?" Ben asked.

"Probably," I said, and I threw myself onto his body. "Are you ready to go to eat wings?"

"In a minute," he said, running his hands through my hair and then pulling me closer. "I want to spend a few seconds looking at my wife."

NOVEMBER

I pick up the check and I get in the car. I go to Citibank and cash it. I have a purpose and an energy I've lacked for some time, but I know what I want to do and I know I can do it.

The bank teller cashes the check somewhat hesitantly. She has no reason not to cash it, but I imagine she doesn't often have a twenty-six-year-old woman come in and cash a fourteen-thousand-dollar check. I ask for it in hundreds.

It won't fit in my wallet, so I have to take it in a few money envelopes. I get in my car and I drive to the biggest bookstore I can find. I walk into the store feeling like my purse is on fire, and my mind is reeling. I am wandering in circles before an employee asks if she can help. I ask her how to find the young adult section, and the young woman leads me to it. She splays her hand out to show me the shelves—stacks and stacks of books, brightly colored with titles in large display print.

"I'll take it," I say.

"What?" she says back to me.

"Can you help me get it to the register?"

"The whole section?" she asks me, shocked.

It's too many books to fit in my car, too many books to take anywhere by myself, so the store agrees to have them delivered. I take three stacks myself and put them in my car, and then I drive myself to the Fairfax Library.

I see Lyle the minute I walk in, and he comes over to me.

"Hey, Elsie. Are you okay?"

"I'm good," I say. "Can you help me get some stuff out of my car?"

"Sure."

Lyle asks me how I've been and if I feel like coming back to work. He seems eager not to talk about my "episode," and I am thankful for that. I tell him I will be back at work soon and then we make our way to my car.

I open the trunk.

"What's this?" he says.

"This is the beginning of the Ben Ross Young Adult Section," I say.

"What?"

"I'm having another truckload delivered tomorrow and donated to the library in Ben's name."

"Wow," he says. "That's very generous of you."

"There's only one stipulation," I say.

"Okay?"

"When the books start to smell musty, we gotta get rid of them. Donate them to another library."

Lyle laughs. "What?"

I grab a book from the trunk and fan its pages in front of Lyle's face. I smell them myself. "Smell how clean and new that smells?" I say.

"Sure," Lyle says.

"Once they start smelling like library books, we're gonna donate them to another library and replace them with this." I hand Lyle the rest of the cash. It's wrapped in an envelope, and I'm sure it looks like we're dealing drugs.

"What the . . ." Lyle says to me. "Put that away!"

I laugh, finally seeing this from his perspective. "I should probably just write a check . . ."

Lyle laughs. "Probably. But you don't have to do this."

"I want to," I say. "Can we have a plaque made?" I ask.

"Sure," he says. "Absolutely."

"Awesome." I put some books in his arms and grab some myself, and we head into the library.

"You're sure you're okay, Elsie?" he asks me as we head into the building.

"Positive."

Ana comes over for dinner. We eat, just the two of us, on my couch and we drink wine until it's time to stop. I laugh with her and I smile. And when she goes home that night, I still have Ben in my heart and in my mind. I don't lose him just by having a good time without him. I don't lose him by being myself with her.

DECEMBER

I give myself time to adjust, and then one morning when I feel up to it, I go back to work. The air in Los Angeles has officially cooled down and hovers around forty-five degrees. I put on a jacket I haven't worn since last winter and I get in my car. While a part of me feels shaky about this next part, the part where I start my job again for real and I put the past behind me, I walk through the doors. I walk up to the admin offices and I sit down at my desk. There aren't a lot of people in the office yet this morning, but the few that are clap for me as I walk in. I see there's a major donor pin on my desk. They aren't clapping for me because I'm a widow back at work. They are clapping for me because I did something good for the library. I am something to them other than a woman who lost her husband. There is more to me than that.

The day goes by as days at work do. I find myself enjoying the camaraderie of my job for the first time in months. I like being needed here. I like talking to people about books. I like it when kids ask where to find something and I can squeeze in a mini-lesson on the Dewey decimal system.

Around noon, the boxes of books are delivered and brought to my desk. I don't have the shelf set up yet, so they sit on the floor, burying my desk. I recognize some of the titles. Ben used to have some of them before I gave them to Susan. Others look new to me. Some look pretty interesting; others look mind-numbingly stupid. As I take stock, I laugh about the fact that my husband used to love to read children's books. Life never turns out like you think. You don't think you'd end up with a man that likes to read literature aimed at twelve-year-olds; you also don't think you'll lose that man so soon. But if that's the case, I have many more surprises left in my life, and they can't all be bad.

I call Susan and tell her about the books. I can't tell if she's laughing or crying.

"You actually said to them that the books can't get musty?"

"Yep," I say from my desk. "They have to donate them someplace else."

She laughs, even if she's crying. "I might finally take out a library book then," she tells me. I laugh. "Actually," she says, "I want to do it too. I'll add to the fund. I don't want them to ever run out of fresh-smelling books."

"Really?" I ask, excited. "Oh, man! We can make it the Ben and Susan Ross Young Adult Section."

"No, your name should be there too. Oh! And Steven's! It should say The Ross Family Young Adult Section. For the four of us. Cool?"

I try not to acknowledge the tenderness of the moment, but I can't help but be overwhelmed.

"Okay," I say, my voice small and quiet.

"E-mail me later and tell me where to send the check, okay? I'll call you this weekend."

I hang up the phone and try to go back to work, but my mind is fluttering from one thing to another.

Mr. Callahan doesn't come through the doors all day. I ask Nancy when she saw him last.

"Oh, geez," she says. "It's been at least two months."

When five o'clock rolls around, I excuse myself and head to Cedars-Sinai hospital.

I ask the nurse at the front desk where I can find Mrs. Lorraine Callahan. The nurse looks her up in the computer and says there is no Lorraine Callahan currently admitted. I get back in the car and drive down the street from the library. I find the house I think is Mr. Callahan's.

I walk up to the front door and ring the doorbell. It doesn't seem like it's ringing so I knock on the door. It takes a few tries before he comes. When he does, he opens the door and looks at me through the screen.

"Elsie?" he says, disbelieving.

"Hey, George, can I come in?"

He opens the screen and makes room for me at the door. The house looks disheveled and sad. I know that Lorraine is not here.

"How are you, George?"

"I'm fine," he says, not really listening to my question.

"How are you?" I say, this time more sincere, more pointed.

His voice turns to a quiver. "I can't even get out of bed most days," he says. "It's not worth it."

"It is," I say. "It is worth it."

He shakes his head. "You don't know," he says. "No one does."

"No, you're right about that," I say. "You two were together for so long. I can't begin to imagine how lost you must feel. The thing is though, George, you may be old, but you have a lot of fight in you. Lorraine wouldn't want you to go down this easy." I grab his shoulder and focus his eyes on mine. "C'mon," I say. "Let's go get a beer."

And just like that, I am there for someone. I am not the one in pain. I am not suffering. I am helping. My life without

Ben felt like it was nothing, but here I am, doing something with it.

Mr. Callahan nods his head reluctantly and puts on his shoes.

"Think they'll card me?" he says. We both laugh, even though it wasn't that funny. We have to find little ways to smile. No matter how strong you are, no matter how smart you are or tough you can be, the world will find a way to break you. And when it does, the only thing you can do is hold on.

When Mr. Callahan and I get to the bar, he goes straight for the bartender. I hang back for a minute before I meet him. I breathe in and out. I look at what's around me. A guy comes up to me and asks what a gorgeous girl like me is doing here during a happy hour. He asks if he can buy me a drink.

I don't say yes, but I also don't punch him in the face. Mr. Callahan agrees with me that I'm making progress. Plus, New Year's Eve is just around the corner, and who knows what the year will bring.

JUNE

We woke up in the hotel room in Las Vegas. The bed was wide; the sheets were luxurious. There was a Jacuzzi bathtub within four steps of the bed. The bright shining sun was already finding its way through the curtains, peeking around the edges and through the middle. My life had never felt so exciting, so full of possibilities.

Ben was still asleep when I woke up. I just watched him sleep. I put my head on his chest and listened to his heartbeat. I read the news on my cell phone. Even the most ordinary things felt like Christmas morning to me. Everything had this tint of peace to it. I turned on the TV and watched it at a low volume while Ben slept next to me. I waited for him to wake up.

When it got to be 11:00 a.m., I turned to him and lightly shook him awake.

"Wake up, baby," I said. "We have to get up soon."

Ben barely woke from his stupor. He put his arm around me and buried his face in his pillow.

"Come on, Husband," I said to him. "You gotta get up."

He opened his eyes and smiled at me. He lifted his mouth off the pillow and said, "What's the rush, honey? We have all the time in the world."

ACKNOWLEDGMENTS

I owe a great deal of thanks to my agent, Carly Watters, and my editor, Greer Hendricks. You both saw what I was trying to do, you believed in this story, and you made it better, brighter, and more heartbreaking. Thank you. And thank you to Sarah Cantin at Atria for your faith in this book. You are the gatekeeper and it's you who let me through.

I also want to thank the friends who cheered me on along the way: Erin Cox, Julia Furlan, Jesse Hill, Andy Bauch, Jess Reynoso, Colin and Ashley Rodger, Emily Giorgio, Bea Arthur, Caitlin Doyle, Tim Pavlik, Kate Sullivan, Phillip Jordan, Tamara Hunter, and Sara Arrington. Your collective faith in me made me stupid enough to think I could do this.

It's crucial that I acknowledge the bosses and teachers who believed in me: Frank Calore, Andrew Crick, Edith Hill, Sarah Finn, and Randi Hiller. I am so grateful to have had you all as mentors in my life.

Thank you to the Beverly Hills Public Library for giving me a quiet place to write that sells delicious fudge and strong iced tea, and to the community at Polytechnic School for being so supportive.

I cannot let this opportunity go by without mentioning the man who lost the love of his life and posted about it on Craigslist. You, sir, are a far more beautiful writer than I and the tenderness with which you speak brings me to tears every time I read your post. And I've read it a lot.

To the Reid and Hanes families, thank you for embracing me with the warmth you have.

To Martha Steeves, you will always be in my heart.

I have endless gratitude for the Jenkins and Morris families. To my mother, Mindy, my brother, Jake, and my grandmother, Linda: Your belief that I can do anything I set my mind to is why I believe it. I can't think of a greater gift to give a person.

And lastly, to Alex Reid, the man who taught me how a perfectly sane woman can fall madly in love and get married in a matter of months: Thank you for being the inspiration for every love story I find myself writing.

FOREVER, INTERRUPTED

Taylor Jenkins Reid

A Readers Club Guide

QUESTIONS AND TOPICS FOR DISCUSSION

1. The plot of *Forever, Interrupted* isn't strictly linear and, instead, alternates between Ben and Elsie's courtship and Elsie's mourning. How did this affect your reading experience? Why do you think the author made this narrative choice?

2. At various points throughout the novel, Elsie and Ben voice the concern that perhaps their relationship is progressing too quickly. Before reading this, would you have thought that two people could be ready to marry after six months of dating? Did *Forever, Interrupted* affect your opinion one way or another?

3. Romantic love may seem like the driving force behind *Forever, Interrupted*, but in what ways does friendship also shape the novel? In particular, how does seeing Elsie in the role of a friend—and not just as Ben's girlfriend and wife— add to our understanding of her? What do her interactions with Ana, as well as with Mr. Callahan, reveal about her as a character?

4. Elsie is furious with Ana when she tries to give her a copy of *The Year of Magical Thinking*, Joan Didion's memoir about losing her husband, and laments, *"My job is books, information. I based my career on the idea that words on pages bound and packaged help people. That they make people grow, they show people lives they've never seen. They teach people about themselves, and here I am, at my lowest point, rejecting help from the one place I always believed it would be"* (p. 164). Do you share Elsie's perspective about the power of books? Why might this belief system be so painful for her to embrace immediately after Ben's death?

5. Do you understand why Ben never told his mother about his relationship with Elsie? Why do you think Elsie didn't push him harder on this?

6. Why is it important to Elsie that she and Ben were legally married? What do you think about Susan's point of view, that, *"It means nothing. You think that some ten minutes you spent with Ben in a room defines what you meant to each other? It doesn't. You define that. What you feel defines that. You loved him. He loved you . . . It doesn't matter whether it's labeled a husband or a boyfriend. You lost the person you love. You lost the future you thought you had"* (p. 249)?

7. Turn to the scene where Ben and Elsie are driving to Las Vegas and, as a group, read aloud the argument that they get into. Could you see each point of view, or did you side more with Elsie or Ben? Should one of them have handled the conversation differently?

8. When Elsie first arrives at Susan's house, she realizes: *"I can't help but think that maybe because it's okay to cry, I*

can't" (p. 260). Can you find some other concrete examples of the grieving process that are illustrated in the book? Were there particular moments of Elsie's (or Susan's) mourning that especially resonated with you?

9. Ana and Mr. Callahan each try to offer Elsie words of comfort and wisdom after Ben dies. At the time, she mostly rejects what they have to say. How has Elsie's point of view changed by the end of the novel—and have Ana's and Mr. Callahan's perspectives shifted as well?

10. Elsie has a very distant relationship with her parents. How do you think their absence from her life affects first her courtship with Ben—and then later, her experience of mourning? Do Elsie's views on family change over the course of the narrative? Do you think the novel distinguishes between what constitutes friendship and what constitutes family?

11. Ben and Elsie's relationship is twice likened to a "supernova." Discuss the two different contexts that this comparison appears in. Ultimately, do you think it is an applicable analogy for their love?

ENHANCE YOUR BOOK CLUB

1. Pretend you are casting the film version of *Forever, Interrupted*. Who would play Elsie and Ben? Susan and Ana? What about Mr. Callahan?

2. Revisit Susan's quote in question #6. Do you think this argument could be applied to the institution of marriage more generally? That is to say, if it doesn't matter whether Elsie and Ben were married for nine days or zero, does marriage matter at all?

3. In *The Year of Magical Thinking* (the book Ana buys for Elsie), Joan Didion writes: *"Marriage is memory, marriage is time. Marriage is not only time: it is also, paradoxically, the denial of time."* What do you think she means by this?

4. The evening of their first date, Ben and Elsie prepare to order Chinese food and quickly discover that they do not agree on their rice preferences. When Elsie suggests that they get two different orders of rice, Ben responds, *"Maybe when the romance is gone we can do that, but not tonight"* (p. 68). Can you think of something that has in the past (or would in the future) signify to you that you're past the early stage of a relationship? How does a concept like "romance" in a relationship change or manifest differently over time?

5. If Ben hadn't gone out for Fruity Pebbles that night—if he had lived—what do you think would have been in store for Elsie and Ben's marriage? And do you think Elsie would be as close to Susan?

Read on for a first look at Taylor Jenkins Reid's
compelling new novel

After I Do

Coming Summer 2014 from Washington Square Press

We are in the parking lot of Dodger Stadium, and once again, Ryan has forgotten where we left the car. I keep telling him that it's in Lot C, but he doesn't believe me.

"No," he says, for the tenth time. "I specifically remember turning right when we got here, not left."

It's incredibly dark, the path in front of us lit only by lampposts featuring oversize baseballs. I looked at the sign when we parked.

"You remember wrong," I say, my tone clipped and pissed off. We've already been here too long and I hate the chaos of Dodger Stadium. It's a warm summer night, so I have that to be thankful for, but it's 10:00 p.m. and the rest of the fans are pouring out of the stadium, the two of us fighting through a sea of blue and white jerseys. We've been at this for about twenty minutes.

"I don't remember wrong," he says, walking ahead and not even bothering to look back at me as he speaks. "You're the one with the bad memory."

"Oh, I see," I say, mocking him. "Just because I lost my keys this morning, suddenly I'm an idiot?"

He turns and looks at me; I use the moment to try to catch up to him. The parking lot is hilly and steep. I'm slow.

"Yeah, Lauren, that's exactly what I said. I said you were an idiot."

"I mean, you basically did. You said that you know what you're talking about like I don't."

"Just help me find the goddamn car so we can go home."

I don't respond. I just follow him as he moves further and further away from Lot C. Why he wants to go home is a mystery to me. None of this will be any better at home. It hasn't been for months.

He walks around in a long, wide circle, going up and down the hills of the Dodger Stadium parking lot. I follow close behind, waiting with him at the crosswalks, crossing at his pace. We don't say anything. I think of how much I want to scream at him. I think of how I wanted to scream at him last night too. I think of how much I'll probably want to scream at him tomorrow. I can only imagine he's thinking much the same about me. And yet, the air between us is perfectly still, uninterrupted by any of our thoughts. So often lately our nights and weekends are full of tension, a tension that is only relieved by saying good-bye or good night.

After the initial rush of people leave the parking lot, it becomes a lot easier to see where we are and where we parked.

"There it is," Ryan says, not bothering to point for further edification. I turn my head to follow his gaze. There it is. Our small black Honda.

Right in Lot C.

I smile at him. It's not a kind smile.

He smiles back. His isn't kind either.

Eleven and a Half Years Ago

It was the middle of my sophomore year of college. My freshman year had been a lonely one. UCLA was not as inviting as I'd thought it might be when I applied. It was hard for me to meet people. I went home a lot on weekends to see my family. Well, really, I went home to see my younger sister, Rachel. My mom and my little brother, Charlie, were secondary. Rachel was the person I told everything to. Rachel was the one I missed when I ate alone in the dining hall, and I ate alone in the dining hall more than I cared to admit.

At the age of nineteen, I was much more shy than I'd been

at seventeen, graduating high school toward the top of my class, my hand cramping from signing so many yearbooks. My mom kept asking me all through my freshman year if I wanted to transfer. She kept saying that it was okay to look someplace else, but I didn't want to. I liked my classes. "I just haven't found my stride yet," I said to her every time she asked. "But I will. I'll find it."

I started to find it when I took a job in the mailroom. Most nights it was me and one or two other people, a dynamic in which I thrived. I was good in small groups. I could shine when I didn't have to struggle to be heard. And after a few months of shifts in the mailroom, I was getting to know a lot of people. Some of them I really liked. And some of those people really liked me too. By the time we broke for Christmas that year, I was excited to go back in January. I missed my friends.

When classes began again, I found myself with a new schedule that put me in a few buildings I'd never been in before. I was starting to take psychology classes since I'd fulfilled most of my gen eds. And with this new schedule, I started running into the same guy everywhere I went. The fitness center, the bookstore, the elevators of Franz Hall.

He was tall and broad shouldered. He had strong arms, round around the biceps, barely fitting into the sleeves of his shirts. His hair was light brown, his face often marked with stubble. He was always smiling, always talking to someone. Even when I saw him walking alone he seemed to have the confidence of a person with a mission.

I was in line to get into the dining hall when we finally spoke. I had been wearing the same gray shirt I'd worn the day before and it occurred to me as I spotted him a bit further up in the line that he might notice.

After he swiped his card, he hung back behind his friends

and carried on a conversation with the card-swiper. When I got up to the front of the line, he stopped his conversation and looked at me.

"Are you following me or what?" he said, looking right into my eyes and smiling.

I was immediately embarrassed and I think he could see it.

"Sorry, stupid joke," he said. "I've just been seeing you every-where lately." The swiper gave me my card back. "Can I walk with you?"

"Yeah," I said. I was meeting my mailroom friends but I didn't see them there yet anyway. And he was cute. That was a lot of what swayed me. He was cute.

"Where are we going?" he asked me. "What line?"

"We are going to the grill," I said. "That is, if you're standing in line with me."

"That's actually perfect. I have been dying for a patty melt."

"The grill it is then."

It was quiet as we stood in line together but he was trying hard to keep the conversation going.

"My name is Ryan," he said, putting his hand out. I shook it. His grip was tight. I got the distinct feeling that if he didn't want this handshake to end, there was nothing I could do about it. That's how strong his hand felt.

"Lauren," I said. He let go.

I had pictured him as smooth and confident, poised and charming, and he was those things to a certain degree. But as we talked, he seemed to be stumbling a bit, not sure of the right thing to say. This cute guy who had seemed so much surer of himself than I could ever be turned out to be . . . entirely human. He was just a person who was good-looking and prob-ably funny and just comfortable enough with himself to seem like he understood the world better than the rest of us. But he didn't, really. He was just like me. And suddenly, that made me like him a whole lot more than I realized. And that made me nervous. My stomach started to flutter. My palms started to sweat.

"So, it's okay, you can admit it," I said, trying to be funny. "It's *you* who has actually been stalking *me*."

"I admit it," he said and then quickly reversed his story. "No! Of course not. But you have noticed it, right? It's like suddenly you're everywhere."

"*You're* everywhere," I said, stepping up in line as it moved. "I'm just in my normal places."

"You mean you're in *my* normal places."

"Maybe we're just cosmically linked," I joked. "Or we have similar schedules. The first time I saw you was in the Court of Sciences, I think. And I've been killing time there on Tuesdays and Thursdays between Intro to Psych and Psychology of Gender. So you must have picked up a class around that time on South Campus, right?"

"You've unintentionally revealed two things to me, Lauren," Ryan said, smiling.

"I have?" I said.

"Yep." He nodded. "Less important is that I now know you're a psych major and two of the classes you take. If I was a stalker, that would be a gold mine."

"Okay." I nodded. "Although, if you were any decent stalker, you would have known that already."

"Regardless, a stalker is a stalker."

We were finally at the front of the line, but Ryan seemed more focused on me than the fact that it was time to order. I looked away from him for only a second, long enough to order my dinner. "Can I get a grilled cheese, please?" I asked the cook.

"And you?" the cook asked Ryan.

"Patty melt, extra cheese," Ryan said, leaning forward and accidentally grazing my forearm with his sleeve. I felt just the smallest jolt of electricity.

"And the second thing?" I said.

"Hm?" Ryan said, looking back at me, already having lost his train of thought.

"You said I revealed two things."

"Oh!" Ryan said, smiling and moving his tray closer to mine on the counter. "You said you noticed me in the Court of Sciences."

"Right."

"But I didn't see you then."

"Okay," I said, not clear on what he meant.

"So, technically speaking, you noticed me first."

I smiled at him. "Touché," I said. The cook handed me my grilled cheese. He handed Ryan his patty melt. We took our trays and headed to the soda machine.

"So," Ryan said. "Since you're the pursuer here, I guess I'll just have to wait for you to ask me out."

"What?" I asked, halfway between shocked and mortified.

"Look," Ryan said, ignoring my reaction. "I can be very patient. I know you have to work up the courage, you have to find a way to talk to me, you have to make it seem casual."

"Uh-huh," I said. I reached for a glass and thrust it under the ice machine. The ice machine roared and then produced three measly ice cubes. Ryan stood beside me and thwacked the side of it. An avalanche of ice fell into my glass. I thanked him.

"No problem. So how about this," Ryan suggested. "How about I wait until tomorrow night, six p.m.? We'll meet in the lobby of Hedrick Hall. I'll take you out for a burger and maybe some ice cream. We'll talk. And you can ask me out then."

I smiled at him.

"It's only fair," he said. "You noticed me first."

He was very charming. And he knew it.

"Okay. One question though: In line over there," I said as I pointed to the swiper. "What did you talk to him about?" I was asking because I was pretty sure I knew the answer and I wanted to make him say it.

"The guy swiping the cards?" Ryan asked, smiling, knowing he'd been caught.

"Yeah, I'm just curious what you two had to talk about."

Ryan looked me right in the eye. "I said, 'Act like we're having a conversation. I need to buy time until that girl in the gray shirt gets up here.'"

That jolt of electricity that felt small only a few moments earlier now seared through me. It lit me up. I could feel it in the tips of my fingers and the furthest ends of my toes.

"Hedrick Hall, tomorrow. Six p.m.," I said, confirming that I would be there. But by that point, I think we both knew I was dying to be there. I wanted *then* and *there* to be *here* and *now*.

"And not a minute late," he said, smiling and already walking away.

I put my drink on my tray and walked casually through the dining hall. I sat down at a table by myself, not yet ready to meet my friends. The smile on my face was too wide, too strong, too bright.

I was in the lobby of Hedrick Hall by 5:55 p.m.

I waited around for a couple of minutes, trying to pretend that I wasn't eagerly awaiting the arrival of someone.

This was a date. A real date. This wasn't like the guys who asked you to come with them and their friends to this party they heard about on Friday night. This wasn't like when the guy you liked in high school, the guy you'd known since eighth grade, finally kissed you.

This was a date.

What was I going to say to him? I barely knew him! What were we going to talk about? What if I had bad breath or said something stupid? What if my mascara smudged and I spent the whole night not realizing I looked like a raccoon?

Panicking, I tried to catch a glimpse of my reflection in a window, but as soon as I did, Ryan came through the front doors into the lobby.

"Wow," he said when he saw me. In that instant, I was no longer worried that I might be, somehow, imperfect. I didn't worry about my knobby hands or my thin lips. I thought about the shine of my dark brown hair and the grayish tint to my blue eyes. I thought about my long legs as I saw Ryan's eyes drift toward them. I was happy that I'd decided to show them off with a short black jersey dress and a zip-up sweatshirt. "You look great," he continued. "You must really like me."

I laughed at him as he smiled at me. He was wearing jeans and a T-shirt, with a UCLA fleece over it.

"And you must be trying really hard to not show how much you like *me*," I said.

He smiled at me then and it was a different smile than earlier. He wasn't smiling at me trying to charm me. He was charmed by me.

It felt good. It felt really good.

Over burgers, we asked each other where we were from and what we wanted to do with the rest of our lives. We talked about our classes. We figured out that we both had had the same teacher for a Public Speaking class last year.

"Professor Hunt!" Ryan said, his voice almost nostalgic for the old man.

"Don't tell me you like Professor Hunt!" I said. No one liked Professor Hunt. That man was about as interesting as a cardboard box.

"What's not to like about that guy? He's nice. He's complimentary! That was one of the only classes I got an A in that semester."

Ironically, Public Speaking was the only class I got a B in that semester. But that seemed like an obnoxious thing to say.

"That was my worst class," I said. "Public Speaking is not my forte. I'm better with research, papers, multiple-choice tests. I'm not great with oral stuff."

I looked at him after I said it and I could feel my cheeks burning red. It was such an awkward sentence to say on a date with someone you barely knew! I was terrified he was going to make a joke about it. But he didn't. He pretended not to notice.

"You seem like the kind of girl that gets straight As," he said. I was so relieved. He had somehow managed to take this sort of embarrassing moment I'd had and instead of it resulting in me feeling stupid, he had made me feel smart.

I blushed again. This time for a different reason.

"Well, I do okay," I said. "But I'm impressed you got an A in Public Speaking. It's actually not an easy A, that class."

Ryan shrugged. "I think I'm just one of those people that can do the public speaking thing. Like, large crowds don't scare me. I could speak to a room full of people and not feel the slightest bit out of place. It's the one-on-one stuff that makes me nervous."

I could feel myself cock my head to one side, a physical indication of my curiosity.

"You don't seem the type to be nervous talking in any situation," I said. "Regardless of how many people are there."

He smiled at me as he finished his burger.

"Don't be fooled by this air of nonchalance," he said. "I know I'm devilishly handsome and probably the most charming guy you've met in your life, but there's a reason it took so many times of seeing you before I could find a way to talk to you."

This guy, this guy that seemed so cool, he liked *me*. *I* made him nervous.

I'm not sure there is a feeling quite like finding out that you make the person nervous who makes you nervous.

It makes you bold. It makes you confident. It makes you feel like you could do anything in the world.

I leaned over the table and I kissed him. I kissed him in the middle of a burger place, the arm of my sweatshirt accidentally falling into the container of ketchup. It wasn't perfectly timed, by any means. I didn't hit his mouth straight on. It was sort of to the side a bit. And it was clear I had taken him by surprise because he froze for a minute before he relaxed into it. He tasted like salt.

When I pulled away from him, it really hit me. What I had just done. I'd never kissed someone before. I had always been kissed. I'd always kissed back.

He looked at me, confused.

"I thought I was supposed to do that," he said.

I was now horribly, terribly mortified. This was the sort of thing I'd read about in the embarrassing moments section of *YM* magazine as a girl. "I know," I said. "I'm sorry. I'm so . . . I don't know why I—"

"Sorry?" he said, shocked. "No, don't be sorry. That was perhaps the single greatest moment of my life."

I looked up at him, smiling despite myself.

"All girls should kiss like that," he said. "All girls should be exactly like you."

When we walked home, he kept pulling me into doorways and alcoves to kiss me. The closer we got to my dorm, the longer the kisses became. Until, just outside the front door to my building, we kissed for what felt like hours. It was cold outside by this point, the sun had set hours ago. My bare legs were freezing. But I couldn't feel anything except his hands on me, his lips on mine. I could think of nothing but what we were doing, the way my hands felt on his neck, the way he smelled like fresh laundry and musk.

When it became time to progress or say good-bye, I pulled away from him, leaving my hand still in his. I could see in his eyes that he wanted me to ask him to come back to my room. But I didn't. Instead, I said, "Can I see you tomorrow?"

"Of course."

"Will you come by and take me to breakfast?"

"Of course."

"Good night," I said, kissing his cheek.

I pulled my hand out of his and I turned to leave. I almost stopped right there and asked him to come up with me. I didn't want the date to end. I didn't want to stop touching him, hearing his voice, finding out what he would say next. But I didn't turn around. I kept walking.

I knew then that I was sunk. I was smitten. I knew that I would give myself to him, that I would bare my soul to him, that I would let him break my heart if that's what it came to.

So there wasn't any rush, I told myself as I got in the elevator alone.

When I got to my room, I called Rachel. I had to tell her everything. I had to tell her how cute he was, how sweet he'd been. I had to tell her the things he said, the way he looked at me. I had to relive it with someone who would understand why I was so excited.

And Rachel did understand, she understood completely.

"So when are you going to sleep with him? That's my question," she said. "Because it sounds like things got pretty steamy out there on the sidewalk. Maybe you should put a date on it, you know? Like, don't sleep with him until you've been dating this many weeks or days or months." She started laughing. "Or years, if that's the way you want to play it."

I told her I was just going to see what happened naturally.

"That is a terrible idea," she told me. "You need a plan. What if you sleep with him too soon or too late?"

But I really didn't think there *was* a too soon or too late. I was so confident about Ryan, so confident in myself, that something about it seemed foolproof. As if I could already tell that we were so good together, we couldn't mess it up if we tried.

And that brought me both an intense thrill and a deep calm.

When it did happen, Ryan and I were in his room. His roommate was out of town for the weekend. We hadn't told each other that we loved each other yet, but it was obvious that we did.

He understood my body. I didn't need to tell him what I wanted. He knew. He knew how to kiss me. He knew where to put his hands, what to touch, how to touch it.

I had never understood the concept of making love before. It seemed cheesy and dramatic. But I got it then. It isn't just about the movement. It's about the way your heart swells when they get close. The way their breath feels like a warm fire. It's about the fact that your brain shuts down and your heart takes over.

I cared about nothing but the feel of him, the smell of him, the taste of him. I wanted more of him.

Afterward, we lay next to each other, naked and vulnerable but not feeling like we were either. He grabbed my hand.

He said, "I have something I'm ready to say but I don't want you to think it's because of what we just did."

I knew what it was. We both knew what it was. "So say it later then," I said.

He looked disappointed by my answer, so I made myself clear.

"When you say it," I told him, "I'll say it back."

He smiled and then he was quiet for a minute. I actually thought he might have fallen asleep. But then he said, "This is good, isn't it?"

I turned toward him.

"Yeah," I said. "It is."

"No," he said to me. "This is, like, perfect, what we have. We could get married someday."

I thought of my grandparents, the only married couple I knew. I thought of the way my grandmother cut up my grandfather's food sometimes when he was feeling too weak to do it himself.

"Someday," I said. "Yeah."

We were nineteen.